DEAD HAND

a novel

PRAISE FOR DEAD HAND

Pulse-pounding suspense that can only be conveyed by an author who's lived what he writes. You'll lose sleep reading this one — a justifiably terrifying over-the-horizon glimpse at a covert expansion of the present Ukraine conflict.

Racing from one brilliant twist to the next, Dead Hand's final explosive conclusion proves Stejskal's Snake Eaters are a breed apart. Men who rush into the darkest shadows and live and sometimes die to save the world in the space of brutal quiet he writes so well.

—Michael Frost Beckner, author of the *Spy Game* novels &
Hollywood screenwriter

James Stejskal delivers a page-burner from tomorrow's headlines, bringing his old Cold Warriors back for another outing in the brave new world of present-day. Chock-full of the kind of insider detail fans of Stejskal's work have come to expect, Dead Hand takes readers behind the curtain to confront a frighteningly real threat—a ghost from the past that threatens everyone's future.

—Stephen England, author of the best-selling *Shadow Warrior*
thriller series

James Stejskal delivers another knockout thriller. An enthralling, ripped from the headlines tale that explores a terrifying alternate future in Russia and the borderlands of Eastern Europe, Dead Hand, is a propulsive, action-packed thrill ride that simply does not let up. Highly recommended!

—David McCloskey, author of *Moscow X*

DEAD HAND

a novel

by

James Stejskal

DOUBLE‡DAGGER

Library and Archives Canada Cataloguing in Publication
Stejskal, James, author
Dead Hand / James Stejskal

Issued in print and electronic formats.

ISBN: 978-1-990644-73-3 (soft cover)
ISBN: 978-1-990644-74-0 (e-pub)

Editor: Phil Halton
Cover design: Paul Hewitt
Interior design: Winston A. Prescott

Double Dagger Books Ltd
Toronto, Ontario, Canada
www.doubledagger.ca

PRØLØGUE

After us, silence.

Russian Federation Strategic Rocket Forces motto.

THE TALL FIR TREES SWAYED in the early morning wind—cold air swirling in from Siberia. At these lower altitudes it was mostly a pine forest with a few birch mixed in. The sun wouldn't be up for another couple of hours, but the men were already at work. It was Wednesday, so most of them were sober. Weekends or anytime someone scored a bottle of anything were worse. That was hard in the restricted zone, however, where everything was watched, counted, and controlled—man, beast, equipment, and especially alcohol.

"Hurry up, damn it!" The Russian officer yelled, clearly stressed out by the job at hand.

"We're pushing as fast as we can. This thing is totally jury-rigged. You don't want it to fall off the trailer, do you?"

"No, the general would be pissed off."

While it was true that they didn't have the proper tie-down equipment, they did secure the weapon onto the trailer well. On such short notice, he accepted that things didn't always go right. Nobody listened, so he did the best he could. He wasn't sure his commander understood that. The thing had to be moved now or so someone in the headquarters said. He hadn't heard anything about a move and there wasn't any reason he could see why everyone had gotten so spun up about it. He was certain the package was secure. He had to slow the whole process down so no one would screw up.

"He's not the only one. The entire Politburo would be as well." He added emphasis to his concerns.

"The Politburo has no clue, Nikolaevich. Between you, me, and Saint Barbara, this move is on direct orders from the Security Council. Maybe the boss himself."

"Not from headquarters?"

"General Barakayev received the order directly from Moscow. Only our unit is involved."

The huge, dark-green trailer with its precious cargo moved slowly past them. A prime mover attached to the front of the rig with cables pulled it slowly along the track. Young soldiers walked alongside the RS-28 missile. Their presence was only to make observers feel less nervous, not that there was anyone within twenty miles of the restricted area to watch. If the thing did become unbalanced, they couldn't stop it. There was little to do other than run away or become road rash under a 48,000-kilogram rolling pin.

"When it gets to the main track, we take it straight to the trans-loading station and put it on the proper transporter. Then, and only then, we'll load it on the train. They had to roll one in special for us from somewhere. This time, make sure it's properly rigged."

"Yes, Comrade Major." The young warrant officer started to turn away. "But if I may, where is it going?"

"Somewhere far away from here. That's all I know."

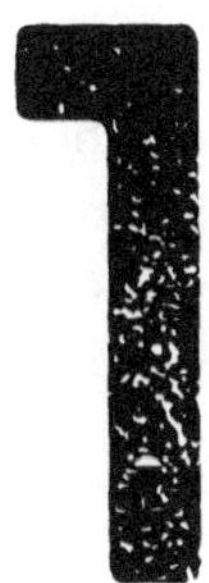

THE CALL CAME LATE—at a time when Joshua usually let them roll over to his voicemail to be answered the next morning. Something told him he should answer this one though he couldn't tell who it was.

"Valhalla calling," said a familiar voice.

"You've got the wrong number, Jamie."

"No, I checked twice before I dialed. It's you alright. Long time, my friend."

"No disrespect, but I was hoping it would be longer."

"Is that any way to greet an old comrade?"

"It's the nature of the game, especially since I retired."

"You know we never retire. Your skills are still in high demand."

"Why? I know I've trained some very good people. Are they all dead?"

"Only a couple. The rest are running around the Middle East. Seems headquarters decided the only languages we needed were Arabic and Pashtu."

"That's our farsighted government. I think we talked about this a while back."

"I know but we were never in position to make anyone listen and now it's too late."

"Too late for what?"

"The problem at hand. Russian President Pynya is out of control, NATO won't budge, and we have few assets capable of doing anything useful."

"There are at least six A-Teams in the Baltics. Most of those guys know at least some of the language. I know of one who speaks several very well."

"I heard your son was deploying. I'm familiar with their mission, but we need something else, and I thought of you."

"I wish you'd stop that. I'm busy. I'm working on my car."

"It'll wait. How's it coming by the way?"

"Just got out of the paint shop. The upholstery comes next."

"That will cost a pretty penny. You must need a cash infusion to finish it."

"Nice try, Jamie, but I'm set."

"We still need to talk. Please."

"For God and Country?"

"Yeah, that too."

There was a pause in the conversation and Jamie knew better than to push. Cajoling never brought about the desired result. It was best to wait.

Joshua, on the other hand, wondered why he should jump back into the fray for a country that could never get things quite right. A country that had no continuity of strategy and a foreign-policy perspective that changed directions every four or eight years depending on who a generally uninformed public elected to power. He settled back in his armchair, enveloped in the warm leather, a short glass of Talisker beckoning him from the side table. He stuck a bookmark in place and shut his newly acquired *Across An Angry Sea* with a thump and breathed deeply.

"Okay, where?" he said.

"Café Nicolo, noon tomorrow. See ya, buddy."

Joshua Devlin, owner of several identities, had spent years second-guessing himself on these things. In the beginning, he had jumped at every opportunity. But his attitude had changed. He wasn't sure if he had become fatalistic or just jaded. It didn't make a difference who called, he felt like there must be someone else available. But there was always some reason, some hook that brought him back into the fold. He was a sucker for sob stories. He had to change his own name because of one, when an operation gone bad put him in the Agency's "agent with a price on his head" protection program. But that was ancient history.

Sort of like the current problem. Maybe if we'd paid more attention to Gorbachev and not pushed east so hard, Pynya might not have become so paranoid. Of course, it would have been better if Pynya had been sent off to Siberia instead of becoming the supreme leader of Mother Russia. But a country always gets the leader it deserves, not the leader it needs. Pynya would have made a great character in one of Pushkin's novels . . . *Boris Gudonov, perhaps.*

Now the Agency called on him again. Why? It might be an opportunity, and a good one at that. It might give him a chance to be close to his son. His wife would have appreciated that, but then she would have already volunteered.

Café Nicolo was one of Jamie's favorites. Not because the food was good, though it was, but because no one he didn't want to see ever dropped by. It was a hole in the wall and one of the few Georgetown restaurants that diplomats, tourists, and spies didn't visit. Which made it perfect.

Jamie was sitting in the back corner, suitably concealed from surprise, watchfully observing all approaches. From the celery stick in the red drink, Joshua surmised it was a Bloody Mary. Almost too early, but, as one of his British comrades liked to say, "It's five o'clock somewhere in the empire."

The decor was typical. Everything was Italian, from the fake ancient Roman statues in the corners and modern paintings on the walls to the red-checked tablecloths—although Joshua knew the owner was Greek. That was just one of those New World quirks, a lot of Old-World restaurants were owned by Greek immigrants. But some would insist that the Italians were just displaced Greeks anyway.

As Joshua approached, Jamie kicked the empty chair out with his foot, the universal signal to sit. Joshua was unaccustomed to having his back to the front door, but Jamie was in charge. At least there was a mirror behind Jamie. He probably made the owner hang it there for his paranoid guests. Like himself.

"You're looking good," said Jamie.

"Feel pretty good, despite the usual aches."

"Thirty-plus years of service will do that to you. Get things sorted with the VA?"

"They finally approved my one hundred percent disability once my senator got involved. Seems there were issues with the official records."

"Imagine that." Jamie smiled. He knew how badly the government could screw up its records, especially when it wanted to. "I saw your packet. Security had to have someone sign off on it and the admin staff didn't want to, so I took it to the Director, the old one."

"He signed it?"

"He did indeed. I explained the problem well."

"I hope you didn't threaten him."

"Not too badly. I mean, he got over it. Too many skeletons."

"I don't want to know."

"No one wants to know what was in his closet. Very ugly, that's why he ended up leaving early. Anyway, enough with the pleasantries and on to saving the Free World."

"It can't be that bad." Joshua knew full well that it could.

Joshua saw Jamie's eyes register the approaching waiter and waited. Jamie sent the young man off in search of Pellegrino before continuing.

"We're sending an officer into Vilnius to meet an asset. A very important one."

"How does that concern me?"

"Our guy's an elderly gentleman. Older than us. He needs a traveling companion."

"You could advertise for an escort."

"Not that kind of companion. He needs someone to watch out for him—cover his six."

"I'm hardly a bodyguard. I haven't qualified with my shooting iron in quite a while."

"That's fairly easy to remedy. I know you can still drive, but, if you want, we can get you a couple of days train-up at the Farm."

Joshua thought he could do better at a different farm, his friend's, where he could shoot a variety of weapons on an improvised range, drive his Defender 110 at high speeds, which invariably included self-induced 180s, practicing skids, and drifting through the narrow lanes. Then the perfect ending to a training day, coming back to an evening on the deck and a twelve-hour smoked BBQ brisket and several Fiddlehead IPA. He thought the Agency's version of "overseas high-threat training" taught by contractors was just too canned to be of any use to him at this point. But he wouldn't mention that to Jamie, he might want to tag along and that would cut into his ammunition and meat allocation. "Tell me, why me?"

"Number one, you don't fit the profile. You know the terrain and you've got a good head on your shoulders."

"That could easily fit you, Jamie."

"I'm in charge. I can't choose me."

"I don't have the language."

"I seem to remember you have German and Russian, among others."

"German, and yes, Russian with a Finnish accent, but more Czech. But no Latvian or Lithuanian."

"Finnish accent? How'd that come about?"

"My teacher was a Finn. She hated Russians so she stuck me with her accent, and I didn't know any better."

"Close enough. You'll be in the background."

"Why not one of the usual gorillas?"

"We don't want a bodyguard. More an adjutant to help with planning and covering the meetings. He needs an experienced case officer but with your additional skills. You've worked both official and non-official, plus it's going to be Moscow Rules out there."

"I suppose you put my social security number into the request?"

"Didn't have to. The other requirements eliminated everyone else."

"What requirements?"

"Your metrics aren't registered anywhere."

Biometrics, the bane of any intelligence agency or terrorist organization. The inventor must have been pissed off at intelligence agencies or a Chinese big wig, because biometrics screwed up everything for spies who wanted to clear foreign customs checks without being hassled. It also made the Chinese government's job of controlling its citizens much easier. The fingerprint, ocular scan, facial recognition, maybe even olfactory tests could sniff out an officer, operative, or tofu-smuggler with near-perfect results. It also prevented people from using fake passports and revolving number plates to cross borders like James Bond or the Jackal used to get away with.

"How do you know?"

"We've got backdoor access into almost every database in the world. You're not in there."

"That's cool, so I can be anyone I want to be then?"

"Yes, once."

Joshua let the deviousness of Jamie's manipulation sink in. Favoritism like this was Jamie's stock-in-trade. If he made up his mind who the best chump for the job was, there was no changing his mind unless the candidate stepped in front of a bus. Or was pushed.

"Assuming I accept the job, what is it?"

"You go with our man to meet a Russian. A well-placed, well-connected guy who may be able to influence things in a way we would appreciate. He leads Moscow's advance team and will be traveling in the neighborhood. Not one of the little green men, he's more than that. A guy who makes things happen."

"Advance team?" Joshua thought he knew but had to ask.

"They're doing pre-invasion preparation of the battlefield. Maintenance on their human networks."

"Grey zone stuff. So, he's a mover and a shaker?"

"He is. Literally. On the tectonic level."

"Can't the locals take him down?"

"For one, they don't know who he is. Second, we don't want them to. We want to know what he has to say."

"Is he ours?"

"He's friendly. He said he might want to leave the motherland someday, so he's collecting our frequent flier miles. He's up to Koh-i-Noor Diamond level."

"But why this case officer? What's his connection?"

"The CO is Gabriel Batkhü, but everyone calls him Batman. He's an old hand in the region, speaks the languages from East to West and knows the terrain. The Russian asked for him by name."

"Backhoe?" Joshua mangled the pronunciation. "What kind of name is that? Where's he from?"

"It's Batkhü, actually. He comes from somewhere out on the steppes of Mongolia."

"Kind of a long commute, isn't it?"

"He lives in Oregon now. Says it reminds him of home. He's

retired cadre; doesn't work at headquarters, never did. He was a NOC his whole career."

A NOC—a true non-official cover officer—was a rare bird. They were the ones who worked with no diplomatic passport to get them out of jail, only a good story and good tradecraft to stay ahead of the opposition. A whole career doing that must have been nerve-wracking, either that or he was a human cucumber… cool as they get.

Joshua had packed for nebulous missions before. Take the basics: documentation, cash, and credit cards. If you forget something you can buy it. Don't take your own cell or a computer; there's too much personal info on them. They'll give you one when you get there anyway. Or…you can buy one.

He sat down in his big leather Morris chair and took a sip of his Talisker. Nebulous indeed, backing up a NOC working a Russian agent in Eastern Europe. Simple. What could possibly go wrong?

JOSHUA LOOKED AT HIS SON with some concern and not a little love.

"They will be coming, you know."

"I know, Dad. That's why we have to go."

"You don't have to."

"Yes, I do. You know that. I go where my team goes."

"I know. The team, the brotherhood. Never the self. Just once, I'd like to be selfish. I'd like you to be selfish."

"Did you ever feel like running away?"

"Many times."

A long silence followed as the older man looked off into the distance, as he often did when searching for answers. The city's lights sparkled in the rippled, slate-colored waters of the Potomac. The mists rising from the river looked like restless spirits emerging from the depths, twisted, tortured, finally disappearing into the night. The Key Bridge stretched across, making its way to Georgetown.

It was one of those movie cigarette moments. He had never smoked, but there were times when it felt right. Standing under the streetlight or on the dock, or next to the piano; waiting for something important to happen, cursing the arrival of an old flame, or just contemplating things.A Dunhill lighter's flame kissing the end of the special Balkan and Turkish blend, like the ones Ian Fleming had Bond order from Morland's with three gold bands. Or Forsyth's own Rothmans.

Smoke curling up into the night. It was almost always night, or inside a bar, or on the airfield in the fog when you declare your friendship to a new comrade before heading off to Brazzaville.

He envisioned several other scenes: a haze of smoke obscuring the contempt on the face of an old-school detective, or maybe a showgirl, her hand held high, pinkie out, head tossed back, her laugh mixed with the smoke, a haughty dismissal.

On the spectrum's opposite end, the cigarette was in the shaking hand of a man, maybe a soldier, sitting in the dirt, fear framing his face as he looked down, never at you. Shamed by something, only the warmth of burning tobacco providing succor.

All of them cigarette moments, Kabuki theater of the senses.

This was another.

But he still didn't smoke.

"I have always wondered why it was up to we few instead of everyone."

"And?"

"That's why people like Pynya do this. If the everyman stood up to them, they wouldn't try."

"That's why we're going," Matt said, balling up the wrapper from his half-smoke and tossing it into the trash bin like he thought Stephen Curry would have made a three-pointer while he chewed up the last of the sausage and onions.

"Matthew Jason Devlin, maybe I shouldn't have taught you so well."

"Mom wouldn't have thought that."

The senior Devlin sniffed at that. It had been six years and Joshua missed Sarah dearly, but he didn't like to dwell on memories. Life was about the present and moving forward, but one still had to remember the past and this Russian problem had started years before. First in Chechnya, then Georgia, Crimea, and Ukraine. Moldova had rolled over in less than two days. Even though the Ukrainians had initially kicked Russian butt. The Russians stormed back with half-a-million armed conscripts, convicts, and contractors. That was when Kyiv began to falter.

The Ukrainians use of tactical nukes—no one knew where they got them—long before the Russians used theirs, shocked their hypocritical international allies. It could have been Russian *Maskirovka* —a deception operation—but who would nuke one of their own divisions? And conscripts no less? *Well, maybe it was the Russians, but no one could prove it now.*

The second cold winter and fuel shortages had done the rest. It started with Germany, then France, even the UK wavered and quit the game. Once that happened, there was nothing to stop Pynya from rolling over Moldova, a tiny country with hardly enough weapons to arm its police let alone its military. It seemed like only the Finns and the Baltic states would remain steadfast.

Soon, the Russians in Kaliningrad would put the squeeze on Lithuania with the help of Pynya's lackey, Vukashenko, that fat, slimy weasel, and his Belorussian stormtroopers from Minsk. Then it would be Estonia's and Latvia's turn. More likely, it would be all three at once.

"Bastards," Joshua finally said, his voice barely audible.

"Who?"

"The Russians, who else?"

"I don't know. There seem to be so many choices these days, even here at home."

"The world used to be black and white. It was just us against them. That was during the Cold War and then we won, or so we thought. Shortly after that I found out that such clarity doesn't exist." Joshua's days in Berlin were seminal in his life, but things had changed since the Wall fell.

"It would be simpler for us if it did. The Russians, Chinese, Iranians all seem to think we're the enemy."

Joshua scoffed, "So the pundits would have you believe. We're just their number one enemy, they all have other enemies."

"I'm going to stick with one bad guy at a time. Otherwise, my brain will start to hurt. Will I see you over there?"

"Not sure. I mean, it's supposed to be an easy trip. In, out, minimum of fuss, plus we have to be careful. I'll be using a different name."

"Dad, when have any of your trips been a minimum of fuss?"

"Good point, but I doubt we will need any back-up from you. Maybe we could meet if we have free time, but I think you'll be pretty busy training your SF counterparts."

"The Lithuanians are good. They take their name, *Aitvaras*, from a mythical firebird and have come a long way since 1990. They don't need much teaching and they've earned their stripes in Afghanistan and Africa. Plus, it's always a two-way thing and they end up teaching us a lot. I mean they have long memories, and they have a good legacy behind them. They fought both the Nazi and Soviet occupations. They hate Stalin even more than they hated Ivan the Terrible and now there's Pynya."

"You sound enthusiastic about them. Just watch out that you don't come down with clientitis."

"It's hard not to when you see their commitment. But depending on our ops tempo, we may have some weekends free if the situation remains calm. We could maybe meet then?"

"If it remains calm. I hope so, because unlike Ukraine and Moldova, I doubt NATO will sit this one out if Russia decides to move, Article Five and all."

"They're coming. It's inevitable." Joshua knew how determined the Russians could be and how everyone including their own people would suffer because of it.

"Agreed. We just need to make sure they pay the price this time."

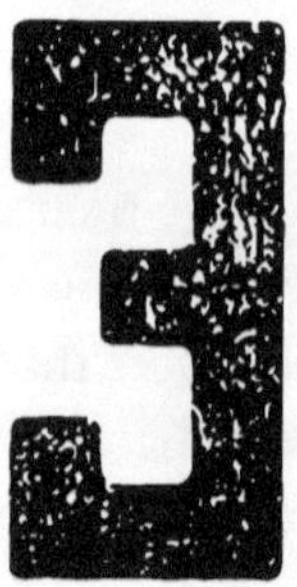

JOSHUA HAD LITTLE TO SHOW for the years of his life except the young man who stood before him. Years of giving of himself not to his family, but to an often ungrateful government. He'd discovered too late that love of family was more important than anything.

He'd lost Sarah too early and watched Matt too often from afar. It was only when he began to slow down in his own career that he began to make up for lost time. That was almost high school when a rambunctious young Matt tried out almost every way to make Joshua's job as a father more difficult. In reality, it was a plea for attention. But Matt got his act together, graduating with decent grades, good enough to get into a university. He learned languages, studied international relations and managed to hang on to get his bachelor's.

By then, Matt knew what his parents were and what they did for a living, even if the details weren't discussed. It was only after Sarah had passed that Matt had asked for specifics of her service, which were many, some *too interesting* to be openly discussed. It was the same with Joshua's career, he even explained why his own name had to be changed and his DD-214 certificate of service locked away.

Joshua and Sarah believed Matt could be almost anything he wanted, but he confounded his parents by joining the army. They had never consciously pushed him in one direction or another, but apparently they had done so unconsciously if only by their example.

Joshua watched as Matt went through training easily. A natural athlete, he graduated basic and his specialty training with ease—

frustrating recruiters by volunteering for infantry instead of a technical job that would have gotten them brownie points—then on to airborne school. It was only a matter of time before he was picked up for officer candidate school. He applied for Special Forces training and Joshua was never prouder than to see his son receive his Green Beret in front of Bronze Bruce, the same statue where he'd won his own beret years before.

Then came the superman phase and, just as Joshua had done, Matt had cavalierly told his family "don't worry" when he went into harm's way. It was at that point where Matt's life could have become just like Joshua's—not enough time for family—but it didn't. And Joshua saw that Matt came to realize he wasn't bullet proof after several tours overseas. Father and son stayed close, spending a lot of off time together. But he still worried about his son. He knew he'd been lucky in a business where there is no luck.

THE TELEVISION IN JOSHUA'S HOTEL ROOM roiled with useless news that morning. CNN International carried reports of storms across the Midwest, a pro quarterback sent to the hospital with a concussion, and congressional candidates exchanging stinging, if baseless, rebukes weeks before the primaries. "News that matters" was the by-line for one cable channel but, as far as he could tell, the only news that mattered was that which garnered audience numbers with sensational but worthless stories and sold advertising.

It wasn't until eight minutes past the hour that Russia was even mentioned and that was only how it successfully evaded sanctions through Iran, North Korea, and half a dozen smaller countries who saw good profit margins in telling the UN where to stick their rules. Long-range camera shots of Russian oligarchs on their yachts surrounded by scantily dressed women accompanied the crawling text on the screen.

Not a whisper on the Baltic countries. Even Ukraine and Moldova had ceased to be news now that they had been annexed back into the empire. The Western nations were tired of conflict, burned out on confrontation, and—more importantly—afraid that another cold winter would catch them without enough fuel. Even the news channels were bored with the war.

A knock on the door brought Joshua back into the room and the moment. He had been caught up watching the images on the screen. He was a bit jet-lagged; he'd arrived late the previous evening. When he first woke, it took him a few moments to remember where he was. Just looking at the decor wasn't enough. It was distressingly like every other hotel room in Europe. It came to him only when he saw the menu card on the table and realized he was in Helsinki. A shower and breakfast had helped, but he still hadn't bothered to look out the window to see the city in the light of day.

The face that peered at him through the spy hole looked like the person he expected, the same face in the photograph Jamie had shown him. Other than that, he knew little of Gabriel Batkhü, only that he was a seasoned intelligence officer who spoke an ever-increasing number of languages—he picked them up as fast as he heard them—last count was twenty-two in addition to his mother tongue. Jamie had told Joshua that Gabriel tried not to listen to foreign language broadcasts in any language he didn't know because his brain was getting cramped with too much babble.

Gabriel pulled his right ear down with his left hand to show he wasn't under duress before Devlin opened the door. It was a signal Joshua had never heard of or seen before he read the contact plan. Joshua suspected that there were other things Gabriel would show him before long.

A compact man of about five foot five, he stepped in without a word and took in everything, poking around the room. He turned the television up loud before turning to Devlin.

"I'm Gabriel."

"I was assuming that."

"Who are you?" Gabriel said.

"I thought you knew. I'm Joshua Devlin."

"I did know, but it's good to hear it from the horse's mouth. Now, the more important question: what are you?"

Joshua thought for a moment. Gabriel Batkhü looked like he had at least five decades of experience at the game. He knew Gabriel was an operations officer—he would have been called a case officer in the hallways of headquarters if he'd ever darkened them—a man adept at getting other people to spy on their own country through some sort of motivation: money, love, status, or revenge.

But Gabriel was also a spy.

The agent who penetrates the hard target to grab the crown jewels and bring them back or, failing that, he's the guy against the wall who doesn't come home. Jamie mentioned that Gabriel had worked all the hard targets, the Soviet Union back in the day, now Russia, China, and North Korea, not places to sneeze at. Especially North Korea, the hardest target among hard targets. Further, he stood in front of Joshua as alive as could be. That meant he probably knew what he was doing.

The things I've been doing are small potatoes in comparison. "I think you're asking what it is that I bring to this operation?"

Gabriel smiled the enigmatic smile of someone who got the answer he sought.

Joshua plowed on, "Well, actually, I'm not sure. The fact I have experience getting out of the difficult places I end up in was mentioned and maybe that I don't come up on anyone's radar was another thing. Beyond that, I'm supposed to be your traveling companion, whatever that means."

"You were a door kicker?"

"I dabbled in that sort of thing for a while, but it was a very long time ago. I've changed jobs, so to speak, and become a kind of a troubleshooter in civilian clothes."

"Like Bond?"

"More like Agent Eighty-six. No casinos, no Aston Martin. Just living on government per diem and being boxed every couple of years. Then I got picked up by the Agency."

He'd already told Gabriel more about himself than a handful of people knew after five years, but Jamie's endorsement and Gabriel's demeanor sucked the information—and any reluctance to share it—out of him. Now Gabriel assessed Joshua with a pair of eyes more effective than a lie detector.

After a moment, Gabriel spoke. "Good. You work any hard places with us?"

"Denied areas? A couple. I passed the course."

"Good, that may come in handy. Now what were you told this was about?"

"Only that you've been asked for by name to meet someone in Lithuania. A Russian."

"Hammer."

"What's a hammer?" said Joshua.

"Not a what, a who. Hammer is the guy I'm going to meet. That's his crypt, his code name. Come sit down." Gabriel gestured toward the seating area.

They sat across from each other, separated by a glass-topped table. The tea that Joshua had ordered on the instructions from Jamie along with some biscotti went untouched.

"You have anything else to drink?"

Joshua went to the mini bar and pulled a couple of tiny 20€ bottles out of the fridge. "Scotch? It's blended, but all I have."

Gabriel made a face but nodded.

At least the glasses weren't plastic.

Suitably fortified, Gabriel continued, "Hammer is a senior Russian officer. We're not sure where he works or who for. He could be SVR, GRU, or a member of the Security Council. All we know is he has access to the crown jewels of Russia. At least, when he feels like telling us about them."

"When he feels like it? What kind of an agent is he?"

"One that doesn't take direction. We made an exception in his case because he produces."

"How do you know his stuff is good?"

"He gave us some easily confirmable information at first, then threw us something we didn't believe."

"So, you thought he was a dangle?"

"Not me, I wasn't involved yet. But headquarters did, at least until the event came to pass."

"Is he validated?"

"Validation is a continuous process, but everything he's given us thus far has panned out."

"What do you think he wants now?"

"Good question. We'll only find that out when we make contact. And when we meet him, don't use my name, just follow my lead."

Despite his seniority, Gabriel didn't act like a superior nor was he patronizing. And, unless he was using the royal "we," he was being inclusive, an oddity in the cut-throat world of case officers where no one liked to share the spoils. There were only two things that counted at headquarters: the number of scalps collected and how many gold stars they got from their reporting. That meant how many agent recruitments and how their intel was graded. Nothing else mattered. Life in the Wilderness of Mirrors, as the brilliant but flawed James Jesus Angleton, once called it, was not a team sport. Gabriel didn't seem to care about any of that.

"Why you?" Joshua asked.

Gabriel paused for a moment, his eyes looking deep into Joshua's and for a moment Joshua thought he had broken some sort of non-disclosure agreement.

Gabriel began the briefing with a down-and-dirty backgrounder on Hammer. "I've been Hammer's handler for a long time. The first guy didn't last long, couldn't get Hammer to do anything he wanted and got frustrated. He asked to be relieved. He was, and I got the job. Among my other operations, I met Hammer whenever he gave word that he'd be out. Singapore, Madrid, Addis Ababa, Stockholm, all over. One time in Curaçao. There was never any rhyme or reason. He can travel whenever and wherever he wants, apparently, which spiked all kinds of alarms in Headquarters. I mean who in Russia can do that? A senior official? Hardly. An oligarch? He didn't seem to have business connections. We worried. But he always came up with good information. Then we didn't worry. We still haven't figured him out. That said, this is the first time we've met so close to the motherland. Now, headquarters is even more concerned."

If Joshua were to fall back on an old cliché, he would say Gabriel seemed inscrutable, even a bit mysterious. His expression didn't give away much, and his movements were those of a patient man, unruffled by requirements or time. He talked about the asset but didn't reveal his own opinion and Joshua was sure that anything Gabriel said about himself would reveal nothing. That was the thing about singletons— especially NOCs— they could make up any story they wanted to, and it was gospel unless there were witnesses to challenge their story. Gabriel didn't seem to be the kind that would leave any of those around.

"How do we do this then?" Joshua asked. No operational details had been discussed. He felt like a bodyguard who was supposed to follow his protectee around town without knowing the destination.

Never a good idea. It's better to know what you're getting into before you get there.

"We don't need anyone connecting us just yet, so we travel separately to Vilnius. Get a good hotel near the city center, like the Royal Astorija. Then we do a meet and go from there."

"How do we talk to each other?"

Gabriel pulled a cell from his jacket pocket and handed it to Joshua. "The latest technology." He demonstrated the key combination that put the phone into secure mode. "It's only for officers, not agents. Totally secure."

"Won't someone hear scrambled commo?"

"That's the beauty of the thing. It isn't visible on any network—cellular, wifi, or internet. Don't ask me how, the techies wouldn't tell me."

"F-M," said Joshua.

"F-M?"

"Something my commo sergeant used to say: Fucking Magic."

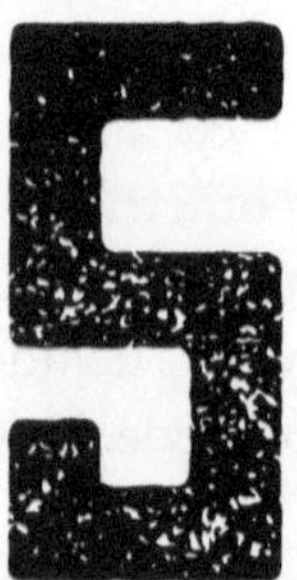

JOSHUA WAS ON TIME as he crossed the street with the flow of people heading their various ways, to work, appointments, or just shopping. He wasn't concerned about surveillance; the Russians didn't know he was in-country, they didn't even know who he was, and his current identity hadn't been used before. He'd done a document swap in Paris, giving up his real life for a counterfeit one produced by the best in the business, the USG. Then, thanks to the Schengen Agreement, he could travel almost anywhere in Europe without ever having to show his passport or worry about modern-day Gestapo at border crossings. Progress came in mysterious ways, though it also made illegal immigration from the Middle East and Africa more of a problem.

He'd arrived in Vilnius two days earlier and used the time as he always did, learning the city. He wasn't sure how long he'd be in town. Gabriel said he had no idea, but thought it best to assume that it could be for a while.

Joshua had met a station officer last night in a small cafe. Perhaps "met" was too strong a word. Encountered. Briefly. The woman dropped a small, cheap shoulder bag in the chair next to him and not a word was exchanged, just a nod. The bag went into the garbage a block away and Joshua shoved the contents under his belt in the small of his back. A leather concealment holster holding a CZ P-10M, plus two spare mags for his pockets. It was a lot smaller than his personal CZ-75 and much easier to hide. He didn't want to show up on police radar as it was, traveling under a false name and passport was a dangerous thing to do in a country on the constant look out for Russians doing the same thing.

Gabriel was on time as well, waiting for him in a coffee shop, his back to the front door, at a table next to the glass wall that looked out on the plaza and the town hall. Only spies, criminals, policemen and people who needed to be paranoid sat with their backs to the wall. Gabriel wasn't.

Joshua placed his newspaper on the table as Gabriel came out from behind his. "May I sit here?"

It was a silly question to ask. The place was empty save one couple in the corner totally engrossed in each other. Gabriel looked around and appeared to sense the same thing before he nodded to the chair. Joshua had thought their contacts would be furtive, a back-alley kind of thing, but Gabriel dismissed the idea. "From our first meeting, we'll be together a lot. Any display of tradecraft would tell them we're up to no good."

He folded his paper. "Please, sit."

Gabriel spoke to the waitress in what Joshua thought to be flawless Lithuanian.

"I ordered you some coffee."

"You speak the language well," Joshua said.

"It's not hard. Similar to Sanskrit."

"You speak Sanskrit?"

"No. Hardly anyone does that I know of. I just mentioned it."

Joshua couldn't tell if that was Gabriel's idea of a joke. It had been decided that German would be the language of choice and Joshua's documentation backed that up. Gabriel's docs were still a mystery to Joshua, but he assumed that would be clarified in due course. The story was he and Gabriel had never met.

"How long have you been in town?"

"Just two days. You?"

"Same."

Their cover stories were already established. Joshua a journalist on the one hand, Gabriel doing commodities export on the other. Not that they planned on doing anything in those fields, it just provided elevator talk. Nothing that would stand up under interrogation because they didn't expect any questions because the locals didn't care about them if they weren't hostile. And neither of them planned on being kidnapped by the Russians.

"Any word from your friend?"

"That's why we're here. Tomorrow, we meet him out of town at a spa resort."

"I didn't bring a swimsuit."

The next morning, they met on the street near a public parking garage. Joshua's mind was still swimming in unanswered questions about Hammer. Mostly he wanted to know what kind of man risked everything to betray his country. That is, if that's what he was doing.

Gabriel had asked one question before they started. "Where's your phone?"

"In an RFID bag. Still turned on, but not trackable."

"Good. I spoofed the rental car's tracker too."

"You can do that?"

"Tech gave me a plug-in. To the rental agency, it will look like the car is parked, but the office will know exactly where we are."

"More FM," said Joshua.

Joshua drove. Gabriel said he couldn't see himself driving a younger man around. Gabriel's rental car was solid and sedate like the man.

At least he didn't sit in the back seat.

Conversation was muted. Neither knew exactly what they were getting into. A meeting with a high-ranking asset who called the shots. Not knowing was never a comfortable feeling and Joshua, for one, had experienced the same tickling unease he had when visiting potentially dangerous places, an uncomfortable feeling of something not quite right that often was later justified. But for now, they glided through a peaceful countryside only fifty kilometers west of the Belorussian frontier.

Joshua checked the rearview mirror as he always did in new terrain and saw nothing but empty road. "What do we know about this spa?"

"Not much except that it was purchased several years ago by a church group. They apparently have retreats there several times a year. Other than that, it sits close to an old Lithuanian army base that's about five clicks away."

"That's a little more than not much. Anything on the church group?"

"A bit. It's Russian Orthodox. They've been doing this across Scandinavia, just like the Chinese buying farms in the States. Setting up safe sites or maybe launch points."

This is getting better by the minute.

"And we're going to drop into this place to see Hammer? Won't that be obvious to the Russians?"

"We're not going as Americans. I'm Maltese, you're my associate."

"I'm from Germany."

"Yes, I know that. But you don't need to mention it. In fact, I'll do all the talking. You're my shadow."

That's all Joshua could think of himself as—a shadow. Yes, he was armed but he doubted his pistol would be much use if they were surrounded by a bunch of heavies.

"Tell me again why I'm here, please."

"Keep your eyes open. I'll be concentrating on Hammer."

"I'll do my best. And, by the way, you don't look Maltese to me."

"Is that a comment on my ethnicity?"

"An observation. You told me to keep my eyes open."

"Good point. I'm not Maltese but it's amazing what a million dollars can buy."

"A Maltese passport?" Joshua said.

"Citizenship, it comes with a passport. Malta's my home base."

"How'd you get Headquarters to shell out for that?"

"Easy, it came out of my net profits." Gabriel closed his eyes. "I need to meditate now."

With that, he went dark.

Outside, close to the road, the pines slid by, deeper behind that, dark green forest all around. Another thirty kilometers to go.

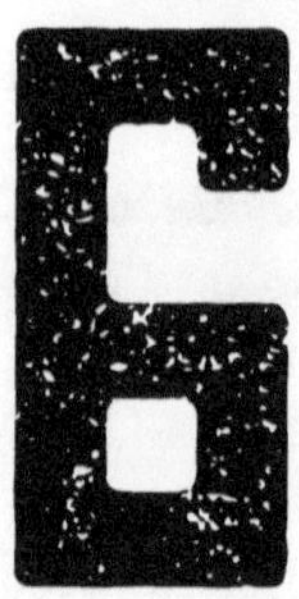

AS RESORT SPAS WENT, the front gate to this one did not suggest anything remotely spa-like or religious. It evoked the feel of a hardened target. A three-meter-high steel fence, pickets topped with arrow-like tips, its base in a rock-faced concrete foundation, a double-strand of razor wire, and closed-circuit television cameras sweeping the expense said nothing about a religious experience on the inside.

Entering the dragon's den.

The two strapping young men on the entry waved them in, apparently unconcerned that two old guys in a rental car might be dangerous terrorists or Lithuanian security officers. They posed no threat.

There were probably guns trained on them from the wood-line.

Gabriel eyes were open, as if his internal sensors had awakened him about five minutes before they reached the property. Head on a swivel, he took in everything while Joshua concentrated on the route ahead. The tarmac gave way to gravel as they turned and crunched their way up a long track to a large, stone and timber lodge with a steep gabled roof. Smoke curled up from the chimney, but with no wind to carry it away, it just climbed until it dissipated into the cool air. Valhalla might look like this to a dead warrior called home.

A tall, gray-haired man waited at the top of the stairs. Wearing a heavy wool cardigan with a shawl collar, with a gray flannel shirt underneath, he was a study in casual elegance. And he waited alone, a cigarette held to his side as either an artful prop or a refusal to bend to the health standards of the spa.

"Is this guy an asset or a warlord?" Joshua asked. His third-world experience slipped out with his incredulity.

Gabriel glanced at him, eyes squinted into a frown. A silent admonishment to shut up.

They almost climbed the stairs together. Joshua lagged one step behind in deference, he was the associate and not equal to the boss. He kept his eyes on the man he assumed to be Hammer, not looking around as a bodyguard would. He knew he was in a place where he had no control, it was up to Gabriel and the Russian. Besides, there was no indication of a threat to either of them.

Flicking away his cigarette, Hammer extended his hand and greeted them in Russian. "Peter, I'm glad you could come! Long journey, no? Come inside where we can talk."

Gabriel shook hands with Hammer. Then Hammer looked Joshua over, a top-to-bottom assessment that took all of two seconds before he turned to walk inside. Joshua thought Hammer's silence was either a dismissal—a comment on his lowly status—or a delay before he decided who he was dealing with. A change in the relationship is always unsettling to the agent and Gabriel had told him they'd always met alone in the past.

The foyer was a soaring, peaked chamber, beamed in heavy timber with stairs to the upper floors at the far end. The floor was rough-finished slate, cut precisely in large squares, covered by a Kazakh rug, which looked old but very fine, very large, and very expensive. The overall effect of the workmanship and decor was stunning, well above anything Joshua had seen before—even Jackson Hole.

Gabriel stopped in his tracks. "Nice place you have here."

"It belongs to friends." Hammer continued walking into a smaller side room. The ceiling was lower here. Bookcases lined two walls. A stone fireplace dominated another, a small fire crackling in its center. There was enough room for two men to stand upright on either side of the blaze and not get burnt. The fourth wall, the one they'd entered through, was paneled from floor to ceiling in dark wood. Another stunning scene, especially with the piece Joshua saw in the corner. An *objet d'art* if he'd ever seen one. Sitting on a table, ovoid, pretty, white and blue with gold filigree metalwork, shimmering enamel and glittering stones—*one of the 69 Fabergé eggs made for the Czar?* he'd wondered.

Hammer reached the center of the room and turned. "Welcome, once again." This time, he had a smile on his face. "And who might you be?" he asked Joshua.

Gabriel said, "This is my associate, Thomas. He's someone I thought you should meet in case anything ever happens to me."

Hammer laughed. "To you? Nothing will ever happen to you, Peter. I think you have the strength of the Khan in you."

"*Temüjin* was mortal, you know." Gabriel's hooded eyes twinkled. His blood line was not invisible.

"Was he? I thought he was still out there riding on the steppes somewhere." Hammer turned to Joshua. "You look like you might come from somewhere farther south, Thomas."

"My parents, sir." Joshua put on his best deferential expression.

"Of course, and I am Andriy Kuznetsov. But Peter has already told you that. Am I right, Peter? All part of the routine, I think."

"Nothing is ever routine with you, Andriy."

And nobody was who they said they were in this business.

"True. Now, we are quite alone here." Kuznetsov swept his hand over the side-table that was set with both coffee and tea. The tea in an old silver samovar, coffee in a thermos. Several plates of savories, blinis, piroshki, and salmon on toast stood between them. Then there was the vodka. "Please, help yourself."

Gabriel led the charge, pouring himself coffee and packing a plate with the small pancakes smothered in glistening, black caviar. He smiled at Joshua with a "when in Rome look" on his face.

"No worries about the locals or your people?" Gabriel asked between bites.

"We're very safe. I have a local friend in the service who looks out for me, and my people think I am busting sanctions with foreigners. You understand me well, Thomas?" He asked the last in English.

"Well enough, sir." Joshua went for the caviar as well as dumplings and coffee.

"Please, I call you Thomas. You call me Andriy."

Remembering Gabriel's warning, Joshua said nothing and shoved a dumpling in his mouth.

With the preliminaries completed, Gabriel jumped into case

officer mode. "What have you got for us, Andriy? Why the urgency?"

"Always straight to the business aren't you, Peter. Never time to relax."

"These days, no one has time to relax. Besides, I get nervous when I'm this close to bear country with no protection." That said, one could be fooled by Gabriel's demeanor. He sat on the divan, calm and cool, with a blini poised halfway between plate and mouth.

"No need to worry, Peter. Like I said, we're safe here."

"I don't wish to belabor the point, but we're never completely safe. You might have an enemy that would like nothing better than to betray you, see you arrested, or dead. You've never told us exactly what it is you do or who you work for. Don't get me wrong, we appreciate all your help, but headquarters has questions, you know that. Always questions. Now, we have a serious security situation in Eastern Europe and things don't seem to be going quite the way we would like. My biggest concern is the assessment that your country could roll into the Baltic countries, occupy them in two days, and completely subdue them in six, maybe less. Exactly how far are we from the border?"

Andriy put down his coffee cup. He paused for a moment as if he needed to put his anger in a box before speaking. "Whose assessment? Yours or ours? After Ukraine, our assessments changed. The nature of warfare has changed. Yes, Russian forces overcame the Ukrainian defenses, but not like we originally expected. Many generals lost their careers over that miscalculation and a number lost much more than that, which I think was well deserved."

"So how do you see it now?"

"As I always did. It was a bad idea then and it is a bad idea now. Volodya wants to recreate something that never existed, a Russian empire that extends all the way to the Elbe, maybe even to the Rhine. He's deranged. I knew him when he was in Dresden. Even then, he was a cruel, little, power-hungry Napoleon. Nothing he says can be trusted. Remember that."

"Volodya? Is that Pynya?"

"Yes, the diminutive."

"You knew him in East Germany? What were you doing there?"

"I have been in this business a long time, Peter. I know many people from the old days, where they served and, more importantly, how they served. He has always been and always will be KGB. All I will say is that Yeltsin made an error when he appointed Volodya."

"You're not going to tell me what you were, how about what you are?"

Andriy picked up his coffee and took a sip before setting the cup down again. "When I made contact with your people—this was before we met—I said I would not discuss my life, what I did, my family, anything like that. But I think you have questions. Questions about where I get my information and how I can survive in Russia. Is that right?"

"That's a good summary."

"Fine, this is all I will say and, write this in your report, Peter, this is the only time I will say it. Understood?"

"Completely."

"Peter, have you read our constitution?"

"No, why?"

"Because it is quite profound. Not unlike yours. Article 2 goes like this: 'Man, his rights and freedoms shall be the supreme value. The recognition, observance and protection of human and civil rights and freedoms shall be an obligation of the State.' Sound familiar?"

"A bit. Why do you tell me this?'

"Because that is what I want for Russia not just on paper, but in daily life. We're not there yet."

"Not by a long shot," said Gabriel.

"In the meantime, I am a member of the Security Council. Not a regular member, understand, you won't find my name anywhere. I'm a special advisor, a kind of privy counselor."

"And what kind of advice do you give?"

"Careful advice. I don't make policy. I say what might happen if a course of action is taken or not. I don't say what should be done."

"What did you advise on Ukraine?"

"That an invasion would be difficult and that the military forces we were using weren't capable."

"And you stayed out of trouble?"

"I did. The generals who promised a picnic didn't. As I said, some of them paid a very heavy price for their foolishness. And I was able to warn you that it was coming. I warned you about Crimea as well."

"You did. What do you wish to warn me about today?"

Andriy stood and motioned for them to follow. He walked to one of the bookcases and put his hand on its edge, stepping aside and looking at Gabriel to make sure he watched. Pulling a section of the wood out, the case moved. Andriy pushed it open revealing a descending stairwell. He motioned them to follow. The stairs, dimly lit with a glowing incandescent strip on the wall, twisted and turned as they dropped steeply into the ground.

Reaching the bottom, Andriy turned on the lights. "Like an Ian Fleming novel, yes?"

A cavernous room, about fifteen by twenty meters square, stood before them. Unlike the rustic design of the building above, this part was modern concrete with LED lighting.

"It's below the frost line, so it never freezes. A good storage facility and no listening devices. There is another access point," he pointed at a set of double doors at the far end, barely visible because the lights were off, "that leads to a tunnel that ends up in a barn in the woods. Equipment can be brought in and out that way."

"I'll ask but I think I know the answer," Gabriel said. "It's a cache site?"

"It is, Russia plans to move on the Baltic nations soon. This place will serve as a launch point for the advance force."

"How soon?"

"Two weeks. At least that's the plan. But it won't happen that way."

"Why not?"

"There will be an uprising in Nagorno-Karabakh that will delay Day Zero, as they call it."

"How do you know?"

"I have sources."

"I know you do. I was hoping for more detail. The analysts always want to know who so they can validate the report."

Joshua watched as Gabriel did his best to pin Hammer down on his access—who he knew, and where he got his information from. Gabriel told him that Hammer had never in his clandestine career provided documentary evidence or sourcing other than his own guarantee, it was all word of mouth. The only thing that kept the relationship going was the fact that his information always turned out to be correct. Nevertheless, Gabriel wasn't a good case officer because he gave up. At least that's what Joshua had heard.

Andriy smiled. "Just say it's from me. You seeing this facility should provide more confirmation."

"So, Day Zero is scheduled for two weeks from today, but you're saying it will be delayed. By how long?"

"One can't know for sure, but Russian forces will first be sent to help the Azeri. Maybe two months, maybe more."

"When will the uprising begin?"

"Five days."

"That's short notice. Is that the reason you wanted to see me?"

"One reason, but not the only one. There is something else."

"And what is that?"

"Perimeter has been reactivated."

It was dark when they started back. In certain open places on the road, Joshua could see a halo of light in the west where the sun had set not long before, but it would soon be pitch black. The Northern Lights might appear. He'd missed them every time he'd been in the upper latitudes, this time would probably be no different. Gabriel sat silent next to him, deep in thought. Possibly assessing what Hammer had told him and writing his report in his head. Gabriel's voice startled him. "Pull over here."

Joshua guided the car to a stop in a small lay by and waited. Gabriel sat for a moment then opened his door. "Let's take a walk."

Joshua stepped out to find Gabriel standing several meters behind the car.

"This is good."

"I thought you said the car was clean."

"It was when we started out this morning, but it sat outside our meet with Hammer. I don't know who might have done something to it." Gabriel's motto was: Don't trust, period.

"Okay then. What's up?"

"Perimeter. Serious stuff. The invasion plans for the Baltics are one thing, Perimeter is another. I will send in a FLASH cable tonight, but just in case something happens, I want you to understand what this means."

"I'm listening."

"Perimeter is a fail-safe system. Not to stop something, but to start it. Pynya has two methods of launching an all-out nuclear strike. The first is what they call *Cheget*, much like our so-called football. But *Cheget* is a triple-key system that requires the separate action of three men, the President, the Defense Minister, and the Chief of the General Staff, to initiate the launch. It's a reasonable system, after all, ours only needs the President to launch a strike. Are you with me?" Joshua nodded. "Good."

Gabriel was on a roll. He'd spent much of his career chasing nukes and disrupting the technology that made them possible. Sometimes, it had been scientists who needed disrupting.

"Perimeter—the second system—is different. It was designed and put in place towards the end of the Cold War, and, from our best information, works the opposite of a dead-man's switch that shuts things down. Perimeter is fully autonomous and if it loses contact with the sensors worn by five senior officials it will launch a full-scale attack. In other words, if there is a coup d'état and the folks wearing the gizmos are taken out, it's curtains for the rest of the world."

"Hammer said there were only two sensors online now."

"Which makes this even worse. It means there are only two men standing between the world and Armageddon."

Joshua and Matt stood on the bank of a different river, over 7,000 kilometers from Washington. Not much had changed in their life. Joshua still worried about his son despite the fact that Matt was much better equipped to look out for himself than his old man had been in the old days. Like the Potomac, the Néris glittered at night in the lights of the old city. The Green Bridge, bathed in light, stretched across the river, with empty plinths at either end where Soviet patriotic statues once stood guard. When the Russians left, the statues had been removed by angry citizens, one last act of defiance against a hated occupier. Now, only the Church of Saint Raphael the Archangel maintained its more peaceful vigil.

Strangers passed the two men by, unconcerned by a father and a son talking. Although the subject of their discussion might have raised eyebrows, they weren't listening. It was just as well, not that many would have understood a word, as the two men were speaking Greek.

The people in the street were very homogeneous compared to the States. Vilnius had once been known as Jerusalem of Lithuania, the spiritual center of the Jewish community in Europe. The Nazis had put an end to that. Now it was mostly filled with Catholics and the spirits of the departed. The majority called themselves Lithuanian, but a large number of Russians filled the void after World War II. Some of them thought of themselves as Lithuanian, while others still identified as Russian. The latter group was a security issue for Lithuania's security service, VSD.

Despite the threat of war that had loomed over Eastern Europe for the past two years, the town was quiet. The populace seemed unconcerned or maybe they were inured to fear.

"Where are you off to now?" Matt asked.

"Germany for meetings," Joshua said.

"Will you be back?"

"Yes, maybe soon. How's training going?"

"We're banging it. You know what that means, right Dad? Our partners have stepped up their game since we were last here, what with Ukraine and all. They've increased their air support capabilities—picked up some new helicopters—-they can move a lot farther, quieter, and faster. The government has been buying them just about anything they want and some stuff they haven't even asked for."

"What are your intel people telling you about Ivan?"

"For the moment, everything's calm. No one has seen much to indicate any build up, so they say nothing will happen in the next three or four months. That gives us some breathing room."

Joshua found himself gazing at the two short steeples across the river. Spotlights illuminated the facade, a red tile roof disappeared into the dark behind them. *Churches were always a comforting sight until the war started. Then they became aiming stakes for the enemy's artillery.* He looked around him as if trying to decide on something before he asked, "Nothing more than that?"

"No. Why? What's up, Dad?" Matt knew a leading question when he heard it.

Joshua's philosophy on classified information had evolved over the years. In the beginning it was don't tell anyone anything. Now it was tell people what they needed to know when they needed it. As long as he trusted that person and he or she had a need … need trumped the bureaucratic B.S. by a long shot. Especially when lives were at stake. Gabriel had filed his report, but it was very restricted intel and the agency would make sure Hammer's information found its way into a cubby hole just like warning the War Department sent Hawai'i just before Pearl Harbor.

Oh, just in case you're interested, Japan declared war twenty minutes ago, but, no worries, it won't affect you.

And there was no better motivator for sharing than having his son in the line of fire.

"What's up is this," Joshua said, "warn your partners they don't have three or four months. More like two. And don't let anything else distract them, like an uprising somewhere south of Russia. Got it?"

"What do I tell them when they ask where that info came from?"

"Nothing. Just tell them they'd better believe it. Tell them to monitor the rail yards in Belarus and the port in Kaliningrad closely."

"Do you believe it?"

"One hundred percent."

"I have to tell my folks something about sourcing."

"The Americans? Are you working any local assets?"

"My warrant officer is running some low-level sources close to the border."

"Is he good? I mean, can you trust him?" Joshua asked.

"He's as good as you were and, yes, I trust him," Matt said with a grin.

"Good as I was? Okay, whatever. What you two need to do is come up with an asset—a close-hold kinda guy, who says he won't deal with anyone but you two. Make up a bio and send that into the registry."

"Make up a fake source? What if the command finds out?"

"They won't. In a while, your agent will disappear forever in the chaos of war. Tragic loss but worth the effort."

"What if they box us?"

"About what? A source that gave you good intel? Besides, even if you spike the box, it isn't admissible evidence. Stick with your story. The only guys that ever get hung out to dry are the ones who are scared and admit wrongdoing. Remember, admit nothing, deny everything, make counter-accusations. Then accuse the examiner of bias."

"Just like that?"

"Just like that."

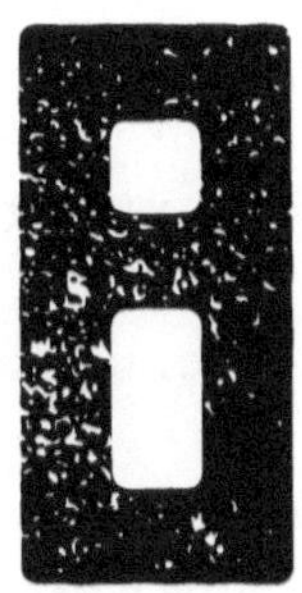

CAPTAIN MATT DEVLIN STOOD in front of a big map of the Balkans, a background to his six-foot, three-inch frame. His face would be hard to categorize. He didn't look Irish, nor did he look Greek or French as his true heritage dictated. He was most appropriately an amalgam, a mix, a mutt, or, in other words, a guy from the United States of America. His Lithuanian audience, the unit commander, Colonel Rimas Bizauskas, Navy Commander Erin Melis, senior intel officer, and Captain Lukas Veržbickas, his team counterpart looked at Matt with disbelief.

Matt tried to deliver the warning to his Lithuanian counterparts without compromising his dad. He wasn't good at lying, but he had practiced this one over and over. At this moment he wasn't sure if he would have bought the story himself, but he knew his hosts needed to hear the information.

Melis wasn't sure if she was buying the American captain's story either. She'd come a long way in this business, she thought, too far to have the wool pulled over her eyes. *I was only seven years old when the Soviets left Lithuania, old enough to know what freedom meant and I didn't earn my bachelor's and master's in international relations and get recruited by Lithuania's naval intelligence corps just to be fooled by anyone.*

"You're telling me that your people recently recruited a Lithuanian source, and he gave you this information?"

"Yes, ma'am. Technically, he's only provisionally recruited. He's not fully on board yet." Matt was nothing if not polite and he carried himself with proper military bearing. He used all the correct ways of addressing his military superiors, sir, ma'am, naming their rank—commander in this case—especially with the senior intelligence officer for the unit. He could even do contrition when needed.

"Why didn't you declare him to us? You know that's the rule. Declare your contact within forty-eight hours. When did this recruitment happen?"

"It was quick. My warrant met the guy and he volunteered. He's a Russian, born here."

"Tell me again what he said."

"He said the Russians will attack in eight weeks and that you need to monitor military movements in Belarus and shipping at the port of Kaliningrad."

"Why? Everything we've seen says it will be at least six months before anything happens. There has been no mobilization or build-up of forces."

"He said it's being done under cover. He didn't know exactly how, but the build-up is starting. It might be the 'little green men' scenario only without them being in uniform," Matt said, thinking he could pass the lie detector test on the information, it was good. If they asked him about the source, that was a different matter.

"Your defense attaché has told us nothing of a build-up. Or your S-2."

"I haven't passed the information to them yet. Only to you. You need it first."

"That is the smartest thing you've said thus far, captain. But I still want details on this source, we need to handle him jointly."

"I understand, commander. That may be difficult though. He is afraid of you." Matt was on a roll, talking the script he'd made up for his source, he was starting to believe his fairytale.

"Me?" said Melis.

"Not you personally, the Lithuanian security service. He's afraid he'll be arrested."

When Melis paused, Colonel Bizauskas spoke, "Convince him. Convince the source that, if he cooperates, he won't be arrested. If he doesn't, it will be a different story."

"I'm to give him an ultimatum, sir?"

"You're giving him an option, captain. There are two sides to every coin."

"I understand. I will instruct my deputy to make it happen."

"Chief Schaffer is your deputy, no?" Bizauskas asked.

"Yes, sir."

"He has a week to do it." Bizauskas turned and left the room.

Matt looked at Commander Melis. There was still irritation in her eyes. She shook her head. "You got lucky, captain. The colonel is more understanding than I am, but don't let this happen again. Get your warrant officer under control. We do these things jointly. Those are the rules of our cooperation."

Then it was Melis's turn to storm out of the room.

Lukas shuffled his feet, head down, staring at his boots. "We had such a beautiful relationship, my friend. I will be very sad to see you go."

"You think I'm out of here?"

"We shall see, Matt. Melis is probably trying to get you thrown out right now. She's a hard one. She plays by the rules, unless she can't win, and then she cheats."

"Fun lady. She's very attractive when she's angry. Too bad she's too old for me."

"I think you would have no chance with her anyway. She eats up guys like us for breakfast. I think we should get back to our team room, comrade."

"Yeah, we better while I still have access…" *What would he say to Schaffer, the man he'd just thrown under the bus?*

Warrant Officer Chief Ron Schaffer, a specialist in unconventional warfare, had grown out of the enlisted ranks. He also had more experience than any other guys on the team including Matt. He was responsible for running the team's intelligence operations. It was nice to have firepower, but nicer still to know what bad guys had planned and Schaffer was always looking for the best way into the enemy's camp.

His specialty was low-level source ops. Schaffer had a talent for finding people who liked to talk about their *Babushka* on the other side of the border. Local stuff, not things like Pynya's diet or bowel movements. He wanted to know what Ivan was doing in his neck of the woods. With enough questions, and a little Holmesian reasoning, he always made a damn good guess about what might happen in his neck of the woods.

He was tinkering with a pile of maps when his boss, Matt Devlin, stuck his head inside the team-room door. "Chief, we need to talk." Ron knew the use of Chief rather than his name indicated that the subject was serious. He followed Matt outside. The team room was generally a fine place to talk if Matt didn't mind sharing the conversation with his Lithuanian colleagues. But with Commander Melis watching and listening, the best place to have a private discussion was the outdoor office. Matt explained to his deputy how their hosts had reacted to the ruse and brought him up to speed on what needed to happen next.

"We're ahead of the game on this. I did up an initial contact report, a naming request, and recruitment proposal. That and an IR on what he gave us, but not too detailed. I didn't want it to look like the reporting anyone else may have received."

"That's good, we don't need this to blow anyone's cover. Anything back yet?"

Ron knew the source, but he was confident they could protect it with a bit of subterfuge.

"They gave us provisional permission for continued assessment and his handle."

"What are we calling him?"

"Something very original, Unicorn34."

"You're kidding? So, they don't have a clue that he's a ghost?"

"As far as headquarters knows, he's as real as any of our other assets," Matt said.

"Good, I need you to make a show of contacting him for our hosts. Then we'll cut his lifespan precipitously."

"Darius and I are due to make a border run to meet Gazelle02. That'll give me the opportunity."

"How soon?"

"We do the first section this evening, if you want. I can plan it out and be gone in an hour."

"Do it," Matt said. "And, Ron, make it real."

With his marching orders established, Schaffer began the routine to make a meet. He hadn't actually set anything up for Unicorn34 yet, because until two days ago he didn't exist. He still didn't, but it was up to Schaffer to make this ghost of an asset come alive. Luckily, he'd visited a suitable village before and was thinking ahead. He'd fill in Darius, his Lithuanian counterpart, on his plan as if they'd really traveled to meet a live asset—live as in actual, not fictional. A Russian-Lithuanian asset who reported tidbits he picked up working as a long-haul driver between Vilnius and Minsk. There were still truckers and freight moving between the two countries, just not as much since sanctions came down on Belarus, which made Gazelle02 a good source of information.

Occasionally, Schaffer could peel off from his team and travel through the countryside. That usually meant traveling with a counterpart so he didn't get in trouble and Darius was his man. He was a good man to have by his side. There had been moments when Ron was able to disappear—either in the field or in the villages. "Exploring," he told Darius.

But today he needed Darius by his side because he was going to walk him through the contact plan for Unicorn34 in preparation for a meeting, a meeting that would never happen, but Darius didn't need to know that. It was all part of the plan to make his and Matt's ghost source/asset appear to be real. He had already plotted out signal sites on a previous visit to the small town of Pagojis, but how they would be implemented and where the meet would take place, not so much.

Time enough to figure out those details.

Darius was cool, Shaffer decided. His playlist of music for the government-issue, civilian registered Škoda Kodiaq SUV was acceptable. Darius's head bobbed up and down and side to side with the beat of the occasional vintage ABBA song as they drove.

"I hate ABBA but tracks were already there," he said.

"I don't believe you. You haven't deleted them," Ron disputed his claim.

Darius's taste in food was good too, he was always hanging around the US team-room hoping there would be a barbecue.

Quite often there was the ritual burning of meat. Part of the team equipment was a custom-built Forward Operating Base grill, an all-stainless steel, wood-burning monster that awed the locals massively (and the Air Force when they rolled it off the C-17). It was Schaffer, after all, who'd contacted the Grillworks company in Michigan directly and he had a hand in its design.

"It has to cook lots of meat that would be eaten by a bunch of very picky and often violent carnivores," he had said, or something to that effect. Yes, shooting together and sleeping in the same foxhole gave the U.S. and Lithuanian troopers a certain camaraderie, but beer and several nice, slow-cooked briskets … that was much better than MRE Turkey Lasagna. And when barbecue wasn't possible, Darius knew all the good, cheap restaurants.

And when it came to weapons, those were second nature to Darius, which Schaffer, having started out as a Light Weapons Sergeant himself, appreciated. Especially, Darius' ability to find enough hollow-point ammunition for their two teams, when all they had been issued was the fully jacketed kind, the kind that was great for punching holes through things, but lousy at stopping enemy soldiers dead in their tracks.

Most importantly, tradecraft and the art of handling assets came naturally to him and that was the business of the day. And the day started early, driving out of their compound on the outskirts of Vilnius with a change of vehicles twenty minutes later at what looked to be a used car sales lot with an attached garage and fenced-in parking around back. On the road again, they used the standard route which took them in several misdirections until both were certain they were not being followed. Populated by a large number of ethnic Russians whose allegiance to Lithuania was always iffy, the eastern half of the country could be a dangerous place.

The next stop was in the village. They parked in a lot near the main market where the car would likely be safe during the on-foot portion of the run. Darius got out and started his run. Ron followed but paused in a small shop to waste time and began again with a long interval along the same route. He was looking for surveillance, but the village was small and a long SDR was not only impractical it looked stupid. Any surveillants needing detection could sit in the middle of the town, watch seventy-five percent of the goings on, and never move, thereby rendering the point of the SDR moot. But Darius needed only the last twenty-five percent to disappear and make his meet. Ron circled the area like a vulture who didn't have an invitation to the feast, but he wasn't staring at the site, he was watching for the hyenas who smelled blood and moved in to ruin the party.

Ten minutes went by before Darius re-appeared on the walkway of the park, this time with a newspaper in his left hand. Ron fell in behind him as they returned to village center. Nearly there, Ron peeled off and walked down another street, until a car pulled up next to him.

"Good meet?" Ron said as he climbed in the car.

"Yeah, how'd it look?" Darius watching the road, confirming there was no one interested in them.

"Clean, no problems. How's your guy doing?"

"He's happy as a clam. I'm paying him almost as much as he earns driving. Gave me some good stuff on the Russians. But now what do we need to do for your Unicorn?"

"Get us to the E28 highway. The truck stop just before the border and I'll show you the plan."

It wasn't a good idea to do two operational acts on the same trip. First, there was always a chance bad timing of one that would screw up the second. The second was surveillance might get drug from one op into the other. Schaffer decided the rules didn't apply this time, since he was putting down a signal for a ghost asset, but Darius had to be convinced that asset was real.

Ron was chatting, maybe too much and too fast for his usual self. He slowed the tempo, didn't want Darius to think he was making stuff up.

"I'm going to place a recontact signal. No one will pick us up placing it and it won't be used again," he said.

At the station, Darius followed Ron into the shop and then the restrooms. The place was big enough to handle twenty or so drivers at once. There were even shower stalls for drivers who wanted to wash off the dust and grime of Belarus after crossing the border.

Fortunately, the place was almost empty and Darius watched as Ron placed a mark on the door frame of the first stall. With that done, they filled the car's tank and headed back toward Vilnius. ABBA's "The Winner Takes It All" played in the background.

Darius was still at the wheel. "Now where?"

"Skaidiškės. The Herkules customs bonded warehouse just off the road. That will be the recontact point. He'll see the signal tonight. He stops at the station every night on the way home from Minsk. Then the recontact will happen tomorrow evening at the warehouse."

"He drives to Minsk every day?"

"Only weekdays, so you wouldn't use the signal on a Friday, Saturday, or Sunday. He wouldn't see it in time or have reason to be at the warehouse."

"So, we're good today."

"We're good. He should be there tomorrow, failing that, the day after. Once we see him, we give him a new contact plan."

The warehouse appeared down the road from them. A large prefab, steel building with a big, open parking area. High up on the side of the building, the word HERKULES appeared in large letters.

"Did you come up with this site?"

"No, Unicorn and I came up with it together when he described his pattern of life. He said he comes here to drop a trailer if it has bonded goods or stops by to look for cargoes that need to be moved onward." Ron tried to keep the story as uncomplicated as he could.

"One more question, when do you tell me his real name?"

"When I introduce you to him." It was easy enough to lie about that because that intro would never come.

"So, we come back tomorrow."

"Yes, tomorrow evening, brother." He hated lying to Darius, but he had to keep the story up and running.

HE WAS WALKING DOWN THE SIDEWALK near the new palace, the *Berliner Stadtschloss,* a replica of the old palace destroyed in World War II, which had in turn been replaced by a communist, monolithic *Volkspalast* recently torn down by the politics of a united Germany. Bombs, politics, and more politics—urban renewal in Germany. The construction was new, but many of the beliefs that built the original remained.

The Spree River ran cold and dark, its waters separated from the walkway by only a simple iron fence and a short drop down the embankment. Long ago, this river was the dividing line between East and West Berlin. He remembered that from the old days when he'd served here during his army time. Then, it was a slash through the city, bordered on one side with a barrier the communists called a protection wall, illuminated with high-powered searchlights on top of eighty-foot concrete towers, and decorated with new razor wire, on top of old rusty barbed wire. In various places along its base in the western zone, there were crosses to memorialize those who tried to escape from the East and never made it. Now, the river was the centerpiece of the new Berlin.

To Joshua, being back in Germany should have been a piece of cake compared to being stuck deep in the forests of Lithuania. Not that being stuck in a chalet worth millions of Euros was a bad thing, but he thought that was where some GRU badasses might kick down the doors and kill everyone before he had a chance to pull out his pistol in a desperate, but ultimately futile, act of defiance.

Luckily that didn't happen—it never happened when you expected it to. Joshua and his partner in crime the inscrutable Gabriel Batkhü, aka the Batman, had escaped with only a case of indigestion from too much caviar and champagne.

He would also remind Jamie never to call Gabriel the Batman to his face. Just a friendly warning.

Their arrangements had gone well enough once Gabriel filed his report and got back an acknowledgement that the FLASH message had been received and understood. Joshua was relieved that he had no further requirement to remember the 'just in case' information Gabriel had entrusted him with. But he could never forget it so long as it put his son in harm's way. He knew he'd never forget the details until the story was finished. He hoped for a happy ending.

He had also hoped he wouldn't see Gabriel again anytime soon. Gabriel was a nice enough guy, but there were other strange things about the case that Joshua couldn't quite pin down that made him uncomfortable. But Jamie told him he wasn't done with Gabriel; the job wasn't finished until someone on high decided it was. Joshua had forgotten about the no quit clause in his contract. Once you're in, you're in. There was no exit in this business.

All those little niggling details ruined his anticipation of a quiet evening. He thought about Gabriel, his son, and Jamie, with whom he was meeting the next morning.

Then there was a rustle of clothing, behind, too close. Before he could move, a strong hand grabbed his shoulder and a steel barrel stuck him hard in the back. His thoughts evaporated and he reacted. A sweeping pivot to the left, his arm knocked the weapon out to the side. A hard jab upward, a strike into the windpipe with knife-edge knuckles, a knee to the solar plexus. Then he grabbed the attacker's wrist, bending it down and under until the pistol fell into his own hand.

A second man was close behind the first, too close, but startled— perhaps that an old man could move so fast. Joshua set the pistol firmly in hand as he brought up his arm and fired a single round. He expected noise, a flash. There was none. Surprised, he pulled the trigger again. He felt the recoil this time. Still no noise. The man, two bullets in the face and minus the back of his head, fell backward, dead. The first man was still bent over, gasping for breath. A third round at the base of his skull stopped that.

Joshua went through their pockets quickly and pocketed two full-moon clips of cartridges. No wallets, no identification, nothing else except a length of nylon cord. He left that, no need to tie up dead men. Looking around, he saw no one. It was time to walk on, quietly, and quickly away. Pain shot up his leg as he moved, his old injury had come back to talk with him again. *The drugs were in the room. Gut it out.*

When he felt he was clear of anyone following, he stepped into a dark spot and placed a call. Instructions received, he headed for the safe space.

The following morning, a car pick-up and a fast trip into the embassy's underground garage provided Joshua some measure of security and cover. He didn't like coming into the chancery, but Jamie had said meeting in public wasn't advisable.

It was colder inside the bubble than outside the building. The embassy's heating system didn't penetrate the roof spaces that looked much smaller on the blueprints than they actually were. Four men sat inside at the table with a ventilation system that seemed to make a lot of noise but didn't actually ventilate and second machine that exclusively made noise. The door was latched down, the thick, insulated acrylic walls and rubber seals kept voices inside and intrusive listening devices out. Of those present, Joshua knew only Jamie. The other was the chief, who said "I am Bob," which was amusing and ironic because the office itself used to be called BOB for Berlin Operating Base. But that was before it became a station. The other man was an analyst who didn't give his name. He wore thick rimmed glasses, befitting his job profile, and had a plastic ID tag with his picture on it and a number. No name. Joshua decided he would be known as Noman.

Joshua was calm this morning, having escaped not only his attackers but also the *Polizei* who should be searching for the unknown perp who killed two unidentified men. Three miniature bottles of scotch from an all-night shop had done their work, muscles which hadn't seen that much violence in years were sore but relatively quiet, his mind was clear, and he had managed to sleep.

He explained to the group what happened and how he escaped the scene.

"There was nothing on the scanner to indicate the police are looking for you," Bob said. "Initial radio chatter pointed to gang violence. The police supposition is that Serb or Croat gangs took it out on each other."

"Were there any security cameras?" Joshua asked Bob. That had concerned him last night, but maybe he got lucky.

"It's one of the few spots on the river walk that's not covered by security cameras," Noman said.

"I don't think they were criminals." Joshua said as he pulled the revolver from his pocket and slid it across the table to Jamie. "Careful, it's still loaded."

"That's some interesting kit… a Stechkin." Jamie picked it up like he might a dead rat.

It looked like a conventional revolver but wasn't. The Stechkin OTs-38 was silent and used special ammunition. The sound was like someone dry firing a pistol, just a click, not even a hiss of escaping gas because it was captured inside the brass cartridge case.

"We had a similar version in Vietnam—a custom Smith & Wesson— the tunnel rats used them to hunt down Viet Cong in their underground hideouts," Jamie said. He had a smile on his face like it was a fond remembrance.

"You want to keep it as a souvenir?" Jamie handed the revolver to the analyst.

"Hell no. Whoever gets caught with that has a big IOU to pay off," said Joshua.

"These things are only for special purpose forces," said Noman. He peered at the cartridges he managed to unload.

"Like SMERSH perhaps?" Joshua asked.

Smert' shpionam or Death to Spies, was the outfit which, in typical Russian fashion, eliminated traitors to the motherland not through the judicial system but by simply killing them. It saved time, money, and accountability, and was good messaging to others contemplating such foolishness.

"SMERSH doesn't exist anymore," said Noman.

"Right. Kinda like the Soviet Union doesn't either. But the spirit lives on," said Joshua.

"Why would Russians be hunting you?" Jamie asked.

"Why indeed? Except maybe something to do with Hammer. And then, why me instead of Gabriel? Where is he?"

"He's safe. When you called in, we picked him up and took him to a safe house," said Jamie.

"That's good, he's starting to grow on me," Joshua said.

"Somehow, I think you're pulling my leg. He said you did good in Vilnius."

Joshua scoffed a bit. "It's easy to be good when you don't do much of anything. I was his back up listener."

"I guess you did that good, then," Jamie said.

"We're avoiding the real question, which is why?" Joshua said. "If the new Russian SMERSH was onto Hammer, why wouldn't they him kill off instead of me? Don't they try to send messages when they kill people?"

"Maybe they did kill him. Maybe he did a flyer out of a window, we don't know yet. We'll have to wait for contact to find out. Maybe they think you know something they don't want us to know and wanted to erase your memory permanently," said Jamie.

"I'm not sure about that. They had rope with them, like they were going to kidnap me."

"Which also means there was probably a back-up team with a vehicle who might now know you took out their Mongos. So much for your journalist cover."

"I think my cover was gone when we showed up at Hammer's spa. And Mongos? Mongo was better than them. He knocked out a horse with one punch. You've been watching too many movies."

"Perhaps, but I may call you Sheriff Bart from here on out. So, another question, did you piss off Hammer?" Jamie asked.

"No." Joshua thought back to their time at the spa. The rumbling ventilation and the noise making machine sent vibrations through his body, while the hot, still air in the box threatened to set off one of his panic attacks.

"So, a Russian wet team tried to take you off the streets for some unknown reason," Bob said.

"I think so, they were well trained. Chose a good spot, where it couldn't be seen," said Joshua.

"Not well trained enough, but then they didn't know who they were dealing with," said Bob. The chief said that like he was soliciting Joshua's approval. Joshua liked him even less.

"It was all reflex. I wasn't ready to die."

"Who is? But all's well that ends well. Anyway, Gabriel might know something. We're bringing him in too," Jamie said.

"I thought he couldn't come in here," Joshua said.

"If you have the right size box, anything can be brought in."

AS HIS CAR RACED BACK to the motherland, Kuznetsov felt he was being watched. It was a strange sensation that he got once in a while. After years of subterfuge, he was attuned to the slightest change in the atmosphere, like when people watched him a touch too long. When a sniper focused on his prey too hard, the prey got spooked.

But no one would mistake him for prey. He was unassuming, quiet, the proverbial gray man. If anyone asked about Andriy Kuznetsov, they answer would be that he was someone, but no one could add anything more to that. He worked the corridors of power. He lived on the edge of the security apparatus—known as the *siloviki*. It was where the oligarchs and the not-so powerful but useful people congregated. He advised them and listened at the same time.

He believed he was safe. His protection was all around him. All of his men had been chosen many years ago for their skills and their loyalty. They were continuously vetted by counterintelligence. Loyalty to the motherland above all. And to him. Skills can be learned.

But still, something felt off. He looked forward to returning to Moscow where he felt safest, among his own.

The two-lane road ahead was straight as an arrow. The first checkpoint was Lithuanian and the diplomatic plates on the car permitted them to fast track through. The second was Belorussian. The car didn't even stop as the swing arm was already up and the border guards at attention.

"To Smorgon Airfield, Evgeny," he said. "Our plane awaits."

"Yes, sir. But I thought Smorgon was no longer active."

"It has been resurrected."

Kuznetsov settled back into the deep leather of the limo. His only dread about Moscow was that there were too many fools around the Kremlin, too many with radical ambitions. If they continued to push Russia forward, too fast, too recklessly, they would only destroy it.

The array of fools there was impressive, especially the official ones. Aleksandr Petrakov, security council, Boris Belyaev, FSB, and Anton Korlov, SVR. All of them hawks, extremists—they would destroy the motherland with their stupidly wild plans and Volodya would let them because deep down he wanted to prove himself worthy and his paranoia would enable the fools to push him too far. Volodya was truly a small man.

Kuznetsov closed his eyes to meditate as he had been taught and briefly the image of his teacher came to mind. The teacher said, "do good in secret without seeking praise, act without any hope of reward." Could he instill restraint in Volodya? He needed to get back and he needed to deliver a message to the boss. In person.

They brought Gabriel into the embassy the next morning. Inside the bubble, he joined the four men who had been there the day before. All seated around the table. Gabriel was not pleased. He didn't care about the noise, he hated having his careful routine upset. He'd worked hard to stay well away from official America and now he was right in the middle of it.

"Why am I here?" He asked.

"We thought you might be in danger," said Bob.

"I'm always in danger," said Gabriel. "I'm a NOC. That's what I get paid for."

"Joshua almost got kidnapped or shot last night," said Bob. "Probably by the Russians."

"He looks healthy enough."

"He handled himself well."

"You seem to have forgotten that I too am fully capable."

Jamie broke into the conversation. "Sorry, Gabriel. I thought it best not to tempt fate. If this has to do with Hammer, I don't want to risk you or Joshua."

"If you're asking, Hammer's okay. He sent me a message. Told me to be careful. I was being careful, then your goons come in and sweep me off the street. It's a good thing they looked like Americans, I might have hurt them."

Gabriel could feel the tension in the room. He had more experience avoiding danger than most people had time in school. He was used to traveling in third and fourth world countries where strangers were labeled spies just because they were strangers. He also had more experience blending into the background than just about anyone. He was like the proverbial ghost. He knew it and so did everyone else at the table.

Lecturing Gabriel on security was like trying to… well, it just didn't make sense.

"You might have told us." Ever the officious chief, Bob appeared a bit miffed that Jamie had shown up without advance notice and taken over his office space. Like any chief, this was his turf, and the chief—even if he was outranked—was always deferred to unless he had really screwed up.

Gabriel had a different opinion.

"I sent Joshua a warning." He glanced at Joshua.

Joshua looked a little sheepish. "I haven't checked the system since we got out Vilnius. I didn't think we were going to be talking through secure comms out here."

Gabriel gave him that look.

"I guess I was wrong," Joshua said.

Mercifully, Gabriel let it drop and changed the subject. "Hammer wants to meet again. This time in Budapest."

"Did he say why?" Bob asked.

"He never says why, besides, this is the wrong place to discuss it."

"Why? These are secure spaces." His pudgy fist swung in an arc indicating his bubble—the high-tech, Faraday cage that kept their every word sacrosanct from outside listeners.

"Perhaps, but Hammer's case is restricted access and neither of you are on the bigot list." Gabriel said, tilting his head towards Bob and Noman.

There was nothing else to say. Bob knew better than to open his mouth to protest in Jamie's presence. The agency equivalent of a four-star general, Jamie wouldn't have said anything, but Bob couldn't take the chance. Careers had been tanked for less. Trying to force access into the restricted files was not taken lightly back at headquarters. All the while, Noman, trying his best to be invisible, stared down his notes.

Jamie gracefully told Bob and Noman to leave them. His eyes told Bob the situation was in hand, and it was best to retreat and stay well away.

Once Bob and Noman left the bubble enclosure, Gabriel was ready to talk.

"Why did Hammer tell us that?" Jamie asked.

"He says he wants to save the motherland from the hawks," Gabriel said.

"An altruistic Russian? Is that possible?"

"Or maybe he's just being practical."

Like he wants to save his own hide from a nuclear Armageddon? Thought Joshua.

"He threw us the tidbit on Nagorno-Karabakh," Gabriel said.

"If it happens, it will validate his access to that one issue, but not Perimeter," Jamie said. "But I think he's telling us that Pynya has a get-out-of-jail-free card. No one can take him out without the threat of launching the missiles. Maybe Pynya wants us to know that."

"They'd also have to take out the other guy with a sensor to initiate the launch," said Gabriel.

"What other guy?" Jamie asked.

"Hammer said there are only two personal sensors now, not five. He didn't say but it would have to be one of the original five. Assuming the president has one, that would mean the secretary of the security council, defense minister, chief of the general staff, and the head of the FSB, the internal security service."

"Assuming Pynya hasn't changed things up. Pick who you think it is."

"The defense minister. He has the most power and is loyal to the boss," said Gabriel.

Jamie nodded. "But you need to find out for sure from Hammer. We need to know who not to take out."

RON AND DARIUS had done a quick dry run at the Herkules warehouse the previous evening to practice the recontact drill. This evening would be real—or as real as it could be with an asset that didn't exist. Ron knew exercise was for show, but he briefed Darius as if it was genuine.

"Unicorn will arrive sometime between nineteen hundred and twenty-one hundred hours. He will drop off his trailer with cargo at the warehouse. Because it's after hours they apparently don't unload, so he leaves it for the next day and deadheads home."

"Deadheads?" Darius asked.

"Drives with just the tractor, no trailer."

"Got it."

"After he comes out of the yard, he'll stop at the lay-by on the road and get out and check all his tires. Then he'll light a cigarette if he thinks he's safe. I'll approach him, do a quick debrief and give him the contact instructions for the next meet."

"And I'm supposed to wait here?"

"Yes."

"What if he sees me?"

"I'll tell him you're one of my teammates, American not Lithuanian. He'll find out who you are at the next meeting."

"When will that be?"

"Tomorrow or the next day, if he can't make it."

"Pretty quick turn around."

"That's what the colonel wanted."

Ron and Darius sat in silence as the dark filled the space around them. The parking lot was filled with cars from the surrounding enterprises, shift workers or others who left their cars overnight. He would let Darius do the talking if anyone questioned their presence. Darius' appearance, standing nearly two meters tall and weighing over one hundred kilos, tended to discourage questions once he got out of the car. Tractor-trailer combinations rolled in and out of the area on a regular basis. The road they watched was the only way in and out of the business hub.

Ron could see small groups of twos and threes, both men and women, hanging out near the entrances to the buildings, smoking and talking on their breaks. Then one person would grind the cigarette under the heel of a boot. Opening the door, a shaft of light fell across the pavement as they all returned to their shift.

No one approached them.

Periodically, Darius climbed out of the car and walked around as much to stretch his legs as to cast a critical eye on their surroundings. For the most part, Ron sat still, knowing nothing would likely transpire, as the meet was a hoax. Except maybe watching out for muggers, but with Darius lurking about, that wouldn't be a problem.

The clock on the dash glowed, showing the numbers 21:15, its blinking colon ticking off the seconds.

Darius said, "I don't think he's coming."

Feigning something between disappointment and disgust, Ron agreed. "Let's try tomorrow night. Maybe he didn't drive today."

It was bad enough to miss an evening at the pub or stay home reading a good book. It was even worse to keep up the charade, no matter how good the cause.

AN EARLY SWIRL OF SNOWFLAKES dusted their overcoats as Joshua stood on the bridge with Gabriel. This time it was the Vltava River that flowed below, the water dark despite Prague's city lights. Tourists and locals passed them, seemingly paying little attention to the two men talking under the crucifix. A boat filled with revelers cruised below them, loud music and laughter floating across the water, some sort of party going on. There was another happening at Klub Lávka, a riverside bar nearby, its music flowing out the windows and doors, mixing with the sounds from the boat to create an annoying cacophony for the people on the bridge.

The terrain was so familiar to Joshua and yet not. Was it because he hadn't been here in so many years or that he'd never actually been here, a cover legend he had once studied in the agency's library but not had time to actually season in-country? He suddenly couldn't remember. *My CRS is kicking in. Can't remember shit. The doctor said this would happen, that it was normal for old people. Still, it was disconcerting.*

"You were lucky, Grasshopper" Gabriel said. "I hope you don't mind being called Grasshopper? I like the name."

"I've been called worse. Does that mean I get to call you Batman?"

"No."

"Too bad. I think it's a cool name."

"It's been used already."

"So? Aren't we saving the world?"

"Yes, but you're not Robin. Anyway, you were lucky."

"I was indeed lucky. I was preoccupied and not paying attention."

"Then your reflexes are still in good shape."

"It's amazing what adrenaline can do." Joshua shivered in the cold as he remembered.

"And a certain amount of training helps. 'Wax on, wax off,' right?" Gabriel said.

Joshua looked around him. "I keep finding myself around bridges and rivers. This is the fourth or fifth in the past weeks, I forget."

"Beats alleys. You can see what's around you and hardly anyone suspects things when they happen out in the open."

It seemed true. Locals and he assumed tourists flowed to and fro across the bridge—mostly they were occupied with being in love or taking in the scenery.

It was true to a certain extent. If a person wasn't under suspicion, bridges were a fine place to meet. Easy to find. These days it seemed like everyone met in expensive restaurants because the office paid for it. Joshua knew that Gabriel, with his businessman cover, could justify meeting in a restaurant. Recruitments made sense in a restaurant, but operationally meeting an established agent in one wasn't always the best idea. And some agents you never met, just impersonal commo for their entire career until they got rolled up and were shot or exfiltrated to the free world, wherever that was. This spot was just fine for them to chat.

"One question though," Joshua said. "You told everyone we were going to Budapest. Do you think we have a security problem?"

"No, but I don't trust anyone."

"What about Hammer? You said he gives us good stuff."

"I don't trust him either. He's Russian, remember. He gives us good information because he wants something. At this point, I think he's trying to keep his country from going down the tubes and the rest of the world with it. At least I hope that's what he's up to."

"When do we meet him?"

"Tomorrow."

"That's day five."

"Indeed. *On verra.*"

"French is another one of your languages?"

"One has to eat," Gabriel said.

The next morning, Joshua put a couple of innocuous query strings into his laptop's search engine and read the news. The opening lines of the first news article were as expected:

"Nagorno-Karabakh rocked by violence. Hundreds displaced by the fighting. Moscow reports their forces are moving to assist in a special humanitarian operation."

Joshua was elated from that buzz a CO gets when his agent produces a good report. He'd never had an asset that produced reports regularly read by the president. At least not before he and Gabriel shared Hammer as a joint asset. But it was just an observation because at this point in his life it certainly wouldn't affect his career. It might, however, give them some breathing room.

Before he left the hotel, Joshua made sure his gear was mostly packed. It would take only a minute if he needed to clear out quickly, assuming he had time to get to the room. He carried everything required for cross-country or cross-continent travel: identification, cash, credit cards, and secure communications. He could always buy more clothes and a toothbrush.

On the street again, he tuned in to his surroundings. Situational awareness it was called, a nebulous title for the perception of environmental elements and events with respect to time or space. Which really meant just paying attention. But then the subject matter experts wouldn't earn their fees without a new name for an old concept and a bunch of PowerPoint slides. Joshua couldn't worry about that now, he had more important things on his mind.

Joshua did a long walking segment through the new city around the Church of Saints Cyril and Methodius to make sure he was clean before he picked up his target. He paused briefly at a bullet-scarred wall, a plaque indicating where two Czech agents had died in the crypt in 1942. They too had chosen a dangerous path when they assassinated the German SS General Heydrich. Joshua breathed deeply and continued on.

Gabriel appeared ahead of him just as planned. They weren't

worried about the cameras that covered Prague like an A-list actor's wedding because the Czechs were friendlies. And the airspace above was empty. They were concerned with any foot or vehicle surveillance the Russians might have slapped together on short notice. Although the short-fused nature of their deployment should keep them at least halfway safe. That said, Hammer might have inadvertently brought along some unwelcome company.

Joshua watched Gabriel's back, who had done his own pre-wash and was in his final walking segment before making the meet with Hammer. Joshua stayed back, watching for any interest in his partner.

So far, so good, no interest in the old man up front and, hopefully, none in the slightly younger guy following him.

In front of them, the corner of an old masonry wall appeared parallel to the sidewalk. Gabriel turned into a passage off the street. A wrought iron gate was open. No one followed as Gabriel entered. It looked like no one noticed. One second, Gabriel was on the street, the next, he wasn't. If Joshua hadn't known where Gabriel was headed, he might have missed it as well.

The Old Jewish Cemetery. Not a place Joshua would usually find himself, but in this case Hammer's choice for a meeting was an interesting one.

Joshua slid inside behind Gabriel. Part of the old town, the neighborhood was quiet. Tall apartment blocks flanked the cemetery. A synagogue took up one corner while a museum took another. The grounds were higher than the street level from centuries of layers of burials.

Eerie.

No one knew exactly how many thousands of souls lay within the grounds, but the place was packed with headstones, many of them hundreds of years old.

Joshua circled the inside of the wall until he found Gabriel near a large crypt under a tree. Hammer stood waiting alone. *Where was his security?* No one else was around.

Gabriel saw Joshua approach and looked his way briefly. A nod to indicate all okay—stay near but not too close.

Hammer moved into his space. "Nice to see you again, Peter."

"And you too," said Gabriel. "I wasn't expecting a meeting so soon."

"I was tidying up a little misunderstanding with the Czechs."

"Let me guess. It was about your Unit 29155 and the munitions bunker sabotage?"

"That's water under the bridge for now. It wasn't my unit but, it won't happen again."

"As long as they don't ship arms to Russia's enemies, right?"

"That was the president's message, yes. Now, you saw the news this morning?"

"Yes, but I hope that's not the reason for this meeting—to celebrate your excellent reporting."

"No, things are beginning to move rapidly, and I have things to tell you, but I'm glad you appreciate my information. I see you brought Thomas."

"As I said, he's my partner now, so he will always be around. What's up? Is everything good with you?"

"Everything's fine. Why do you ask?" said Andriy.

"Because you sent me a message to be careful."

"I'm fine. I hope nothing happened on your end?"

"Nothing worth mentioning," said Gabriel.

"I need to know, Peter."

"Know what? That Thomas got jumped by two men who may have been Russian assassins?"

"That for a start, yes."

"You knew about it?" Gabriel said.

"I suspected." said Andriy.

"How?"

"A new man in my detail reported to a rival of mine that you and I met. That person saw you as a threat to his business dealings. He thinks your sanctions busting will cost him money," said Andriy.

"And he has no idea of what we're really doing?"

"No."

"What has happened to the new man?" said Gabriel.

"What happened to Thomas' attackers?"

Gabriel stared at Andriy for a moment, they both knew that particular exchange would go no further.

Andriy continued. "The man responsible for the attack is someone your service is interested in anyway, Anton Korlov, the SVR chief. He's on your sanctions list and is a business partner with Konstanin Milatovich. Korlov is not a real threat—at least not to me—but Milatovich is ruthless. He was *Spetsnaz* then got into business once the country disintegrated."

"We can't get at Korlov because he never leaves Russia and why should we care about Milatovich?

"First, Milatovich. He deals in sanctioned materials, buying things the *Siloviki* needs. You are a threat to his business, or so he thinks. He is the man who got your information and asked Korlov to take care of you."

"Are you sure?"

"Sure enough. I have ears."

"Byzantine does not go far enough to describe your country, Andriy."

"I am not sure exactly how you mean that, but we do have old and established ways of doing things."

"So this is what you wanted to tell me?"

"Only partly. Korlov will be doing some business in Sofia soon. He's meeting under cover with representatives from Turkey and Iran to buy drones and missiles. I thought your service may want to know."

Andriy shook a cigarette out of a package and absent-mindedly offered one to Gabriel who waved it away. Rebuffed, he lit his own and exhaled the smoke studying the burning tip.

"When will he be there and under what name?"

"He gets in this coming Friday for three days. Try the Sofia Grand Hotel. His passport will be in the name of Rybakov, Viktor Rybakov."

"Next time," Gabriel said, "if you find out there may be a threat, it would be nice if you would let us know."

Andriy shrugged his shoulders and inhaled deeply, exhaling a long stream of smoke. Gabriel thought it might be Andriy's way of deflecting attention from his mannerisms. But it had become its own instead.

"I am sorry, my friend. I only found out how serious it was later. I have patched the leak and I assure you if anything ever comes up, I will send you a message."

Gabriel thought Andriy's smile looked genuine, but so did Pynya's when he talked to POTUS.

"One last question before we break," said Gabriel. "You said only two people carry the Perimeter sensors now. Beside the president, who has the other?"

Andriy's smile faded. "I'm not sure."

"But you know about Perimeter, Nagorno-Karabakh, and the head of the SVR traveling. How is it that you don't know who has the sensor?"

Andriy bristled. "The shuffle only happened recently, and I haven't spent enough time in Moscow. We should go, I'll try to find out and will message you for another meeting."

"When?"

"As soon as I can, but these things take time."

"We don't have much time, Andriy. You told me that."

RON FIDGETED WHILE STANDING in front of the desk, even though it was Matt who was taking the brunt of the vitriol dished out by Colonel Bizauskas. And, while Captain Lukas Veržbickas stood by impassively knowing that by default he was also a target of the colonel's ire, Commander Melis smiled. She always knew the *Amis*—the Americans—were going to cause problems, it was just what they did.

When Bizauskas finished ass chewing of Ron's boss, he ventured out on his own personal limb. "Sir, it was my fault for not establishing a back-up recontact plan. An alternate. Now, the only choice is to re-do the signal and try again."

"And maybe waste three more nights waiting?" Melis said.

"Or the meet will come off," said Ron.

"I'm willing to try." Darius knew he was safe to say that, but he also wanted to help his mate.

"I think your asset might have had second thoughts," the colonel said.

"Or he forgot the instructions." Captain Veržbickas ventured.

"I doubt that," Melis said. "It's too much part of his daily pattern, or at least the one he told you. Maybe he's a fabricator, which means his information isn't worth the trouble. Or maybe he is just scared."

"Sir, I would like to point out that Gazelle gave Darius some interesting information that might back up what Unicorn gave us. Smorgon Airfield seems to have been reactivated," Matt said.

The colonel looked at Matt for an uncomfortable moment, then spoke to Melis. "Commander, do we have any confirmation on that?"

"Not yet, sir. If we could get imagery on it, that might help. But no other ground reporting as of yet."

"Keep on it. Ask our friends for recent commercial or government satellite photos and, yes, that means the Americans." He turned to Matt. "Captain Devlin, while I appreciate your efforts to assist us, you must remember you are in my country. Anything you undertake, you or your men, must be hand-in-glove with Captain Veržbickas and his team. And Captain Veržbickas, you will keep me informed. Am I understood?"

Matt and Lukas spoke in unison, "Understood, sir."

"Good. Now, what's on the training schedule today?"

Matt responded as his demolitions sergeants were the ones presenting the training. "Target Analysis, sir. The CARVER system."

"You Americans have all kinds of systems to work problems out, I hope it's worthwhile."

"It will be, we've been using it successfully since World War II."

"Maybe you should go take a listen, commander," the colonel turned to Melis knowing she wanted as little to do with the Americans as possible. "You can tell me if their system is any good."

"One last thing, gentlemen. Drop Unicorn, I don't think he's worth the effort."

Outside the commander's officer, Ron eyed Matt. "We escaped that by the hair of your chin, chin, chin, boss."

"So far. I just hope they listen to the message."

"They may just blow it off and say Unicorn was full of shit. We can't corroborate that information with anything unless we come up with another source."

Matt stopped in his tracks. "We're not making up any more assets. If anything, I need to find another way to get it to them."

"Like through your original source?" Ron didn't know who, but he knew Matt had something up his sleeve.

"You should pretend you didn't say that. It's best not to know too much sometimes."

THE CEILING IN RESTAURANT FÜNZLE was low but since Germany had an indoor smoking *Verbot*, Joshua wasn't worried about his hair. Their waitress, dressed in a dark green *Dirndl* with a white blouse and a bodice that emphasized her superior cleavage led them to a table. Joshua noted Jamie's interest in the waitress waned as soon as they were seated. His real desire was on the menu the young lady wouldn't give up until she was acknowledged with Jamie's reluctant smile.

"You guys are not going to let me go home to Washington, are you?" Jamie said.

Joshua had no intention of visiting Washington or Berlin anytime soon, so this meeting was in another of his old haunts, Stuttgart, just outside the main city near the Mercedes-Benz factory. Fünzle was a cozy little restaurant in a building that had been around since the thirteenth century. Trying to decide which schnitzel he would eat, Joshua couldn't understand why there was a vegetarian section to the menu, this was Germany after all. Maybe the clientele had changed with the times, but he hadn't. Jamie already said he was going to order the *Haxe*. He didn't seem to be worried about the cholesterol in a pig knuckle.

"It's not my fault that the Russians want to start another blitzkrieg this month. Besides, Hammer gave us some interesting stuff. Korlov will be in Sofia on Friday to do some arms deals. He's on the sanctions list."

"Three days. Pretty short notice. Not sure what we can do," Jamie said.

"Apparently, he plans to be there for a couple of days, so that gives us a little more time. We have an office there, don't we?"

"Yes, but they can't pull off a rendition. Sanctions enforcement isn't our job."

"He's the guy responsible for what happened to me in Berlin."

"Hammer told you that?"

"Yes. One of Korlov's buddies, Konstanin Milatovich, apparently sees Batman and me as a threat to his business and asked Korlov to fix the problem. They tried and, as you can see, failed."

Jamie stared at Joshua. "Just for the record, this isn't about you getting revenge or anything?"

Their beers had arrived. Joshua stuck his thumb in the foamy head as some sort of ancient proofing ritual and then held his mug high. "*Zum Wohl, Kamerad.*" They drank deeply of the cold brew.

"Of course not," Joshua said. "Well, maybe a little, but more importantly, if our security is at risk then it's a good idea to remedy the situation."

"Let me think about it."

"They tried to take me out."

"I heard you, but from what you said, they don't know who you work for," Jamie said.

"Then get the FBI to take him down. It's within their purview."

"You're really hard over on this, aren't you?"

"Yes, I suppose I do hold a grudge."

"So it would seem. What does Gabriel think about this? Where is he now?"

"He's in Sofia trying to find out what Korlov's up to."

"Sounds like advance preparation of the battlefield. I don't remember authorizing that."

"It's easier to ask forgiveness, as they say, besides the early bird gets the worm," said Joshua.

"I need to cable Headquarters and the station. Headquarters will have to get DOJ on board and the chief will need warning if we come into his country. And the Legal Attaché there because it'll be his folks that pick Korlov up."

"So, we're going to do this?"

"If Justice gives the Bureau the green light, yes. But you're not to do anything except be Robin to Gabriel's Batman. You two are just observers."

"I'm just happy to serve, chief."

Their meals came. Jamie snapped off a piece of the pork crackling, dipped it in the horseradish, and crunched on it contentedly. "I told you not to call me chief."

When Joshua met Gabriel in Sofia, they had only one rule to observe. Don't be seen by any Russians. A difficult thing in Bulgaria because it was difficult to tell who was and who wasn't a Russian. Most Russians who ended up there were low-level criminal thugs once employed by the KGB or GRU who made their money ripping off what was left of the old Soviet Union and then disappeared. Some made tons of cash, but the super-rich thugs were all in Monte Carlo or the Seychelles on their yachts. Gabriel seemed to know the ones in Sofia, as if he could smell them, so Joshua followed his lead.

They met in small, off the beaten track restaurants and, in one case, an ice cream parlor under a bridge. It was there that Joshua saw a side of Gabriel he hadn't before, the erudite sage licking a triple scoop cone, attempting to stay untouched by the dripping treat. Which was why Joshua stuck to two scoops. *Risk mitigation.*

Gabriel was doing the leg work—essentially playing detective to find out where Korlov was and what he was up to, while Joshua passed the information he collected to the command center set up in the hotel. Command center was a misnomer in this case. It was Jamie's room and Joshua would go there to dump whatever Gabriel gave him. Then Jamie would go off and brief the Bureau boys at the embassy on Korlov's location and activities and then fire off an immediate message updating Langley on what the Russian spymaster was up to. Or call them if there was a time crunch. The FBI had a real command center with telephones and radios and white boards and maps and television monitors and computers, all the stuff a modern law enforcement agency needs to do their job. There were about twenty special agents, one of whom was in charge and kept the embassy Legal Attaché briefed so he could keep the ambassador informed. They apparently hadn't told the Bulgarians yet but planned to do so imminently. They had given a flimsy cover story that they were an advance team for a VIP visit. They didn't mention which VIP was coming but the Bulgarians still accepted the story because they liked to please their American friends. The Bulgarians would have to do the arrest, assuming they agreed. That was the best idea because the locals would be really hacked off to find Americans arresting people on their turf without permission. Bad form, the British would say.

"He's scheduled to leave tomorrow evening. His pilot filed a flight plan this morning for Moscow, so they seem to be playing by the rules. Korlov met an Iranian last night, and he has a meeting with the Turkish arms dealer tomorrow mid-day, so he'll probably check out, meet the guy, and go to the airport after that," Gabriel said.

"So tonight or tomorrow, our folks need to move in on him."

"That's correct, otherwise he'll be back home safe."

"I'll pass the info to Jamie. What are your plans?"

"I'll hang around until he's hopefully in custody and out of the picture. Then I plan on going to Valletta. Jamie told me to stay in Europe until this is finished and I have a place there. What about you?"

"Maybe the UK. I have friends there. Before I go, I should ask how you found all this information on such short notice."

Batman smiled for once. "I forgot to mention that I worked this country for a while back in the days when it was a Soviet ally. I still have some contacts that are useful."

Joshua thought about Gabriel's answer as he headed back to meet Jamie at a different spot. They'd chosen a restaurant rather than meet in Jamie's hotel room again. Despite all the gadgets the security team had installed to thwart audio and video surveillance, there were still human eyes in the hallways and stairwells that could connect the dots.

Joshua found his boss was already in place nursing a local IPA. Jamie sat facing the door like all good spies do. Joshua joined him with a greeting that made it seem they were two good friends, which was the simplest excuse in a country that was mostly welcoming to Germans and Americans.

Joshua checked out the beer bottle, Faster Bastard, the label said. "Any good?"

"Better than the Amstel. I hate green beer," Jamie said.

"How'd it go with the Bulgarians? They on board?"

"They said no at first and they were a little upset with the Bureau's story about the VIP. But when we told them he's here illegally, meeting arms dealers, and how that might look bad in the press, they rolled over. I think some monetary aid might have been mentioned as well. They plan on moving early tomorrow morning to take him down at his hotel. Surveillance has been set all around the place. His driver, the car, and his airplane are already being watched. Tell Gabriel he did well, but I think he knows that already."

"That's good because Korlov's probably flying out tomorrow. Where will you be when it goes down?"

"With the FBI on the fringes."

"You're not worried about being exposed to the Bulgarians?"

"No, that went out the window when they made me DDO. Besides, the Bulgarian director knows me. We drank *rakia* together in Athens."

"And he remembered you the next morning?"

"It was morning."

Sofia in the morning was dark and cold. Joshua had been on the street for several hours taking nighttime photos of all the usual sights, the Nevsky Cathedral, the Palace of Culture, all before ending up in front of the old Vazov National Theater in the City Garden. It was as good a place as any to watch the show. The Grand Hotel stood next to the park and, as he was taking photos with his telephoto, he could see the Bulgarians massed around entrances and exits. Police cars, marked and unmarked, several vans, even ambulances.

Maybe they're expecting a firefight.

He moved to the south side across the street from the main entrance, that's where they'd bring Korlov out, all the police vehicles were there.

He spotted Jamie with the American contingent, bigger than most of the agents but not the crew-cut ex-football players. There were some women he could see as well, ones he identified by their long hair because the men all had high and tights. The Bureau guys advertised their presence with FBI emblazoned in yellow on the back of their blue windbreakers. They wanted everyone to see that the USA was taking a stand against Russian aggression by arresting the criminals behind it.

At least, they weren't carrying weapons openly.

There were more cultural similarities between Bulgaria and Russia than with the United States, but their president must have accepted he would be called a lackey of the Americans. Joshua wondered how the government would handle the potential backlash from arresting the head of the SVR on their territory. Although he was probably more concerned with remaining a member of the EU and NATO, than worrying about Russian oil. Whatever the political machinations, the take down was about to happen.

A man dashed out of the entrance and ran across the street to where the FBI group stood. An excited exchange took place before the first man and one of the FBI agents ran back across the street. More men in black came out of the hotel, none of them in cuffs, and drove away. Two more came out wheeling a body on a gurney that was quickly shoved into one of the vans and driven off. Other uniformed police officers tightened up the cordon around the entrance.

Making his way to where the American contingent remained staked out,

Joshua moved close to Jamie, standing near, not so close he'd be mistaken for an insider but close enough to hear what was being said.

"What's up?"

Jamie heard Joshua and shifted closer. "You and Batman might want to leave town soon. They found Korlov dead in his room. Shot in the back of the head." Jamie turned back to the group. Joshua had been dismissed.

The back of Joshua's neck tingled and his heart rate increased. He knew he was innocent and hopefully so was Gabriel. But the notion of being brought in for questioning left him cold. How could the local authorities even know he and Gabriel were involved? Jamie wouldn't have told anyone, and Gabriel was too careful, unless one of his recent contacts gave him up as being interested in the deceased. Best to take Jamie's advice.

He keyed up his secure telephone and punched in a pre-arranged message that ended with *See you at Saint Paul's*. He hit send and watched the little green letters disappear off his screen.

MATT DEVLIN WATCHED his team's engineers in full form with their class. He knew they'd rather be blowing stuff up on the range, but instruction was also part of the game and both of them had time behind the podium as well as having their hands deep in plastic explosive. Green Berets had always been known for their abilities as advisors, force multipliers, and general mayhem makers, but also teachers.

Now the two sergeants, Ross and Howell according to their name tapes, did their best to keep two dozen young men awake and show them how to ruin the enemy's day by destroying the things that meant the most to them. It was not unlike teaching back at JFK Center when the day started at zero six hundred and by noon the students were waging close combat with sagging eye lids in the battle against sleep deprivation. The class was straightforward, how to ruin the enemy's day. Find the critical node in his combat systems, any system, the things he needed to make his army function. Find the weakest point, the bottleneck and break it in the simplest, most efficient way possible. That's what target analysis was about, to get the most bang for the buck, so to speak. Destroy the electric generators instead of trying to blow up the whole dam—carry less explosives and get the same effect. A team of three could do the work that might require a squadron of bombers using another plan.

There was a momentary bit of commotion when Commander Melis entered. The door was at the front of the room and every person saw her walk in, a disgusted look on her face. Disgust at being subjected to the Americans' teachings against her will.

Ross wisely carried on with his talk on how to sabotage a hydroelectric plant, conveniently demonstrated with a model, slides, and a documentary film from Norway. A field trip to a local plant later in the week would reinforce their teachings.

After a break, Howell took over to discuss how to destroy the enemy's air assets, an important thing to know when one's own country was considerably outnumbered in almost every way. His first question to the group was, "How do you ground the enemy's air force quickly?"

A hand came up, "Destroy the planes." Another, "Blow up runways." One student jumped up to emphasize his answer, "Cut off the fuel!" Howell took them all in without comment and then silenced the class, "Good answers, but how long does it take to train a pilot?"

No answer. "So, how about we kill all of them in their barracks?"

Critical node 101.

Devlin saw Melis open her mouth as if to say something and then stop, mouth still open.

After the class, Commander Melis complemented Ross and Howell, then took Matt by the arm. For once, Matt thought she looked conflicted.

"Captain," she said when they were alone, "we should we be teaching our soldiers to murder others in their sleep?"

"With all respect, commander, have you seen what those 'others' did to the civilians in Mariupol?"

VALLETTA, LYING AS IT DID smack dab in the middle of the Med, was warm. Joshua appreciated that. Happy to be away from the cold of eastern Europe because in his relatively old age, he was losing his tolerance to winter. Shielded from the sea breeze, he was leaning back letting the sun warm his bones.

"You've been here before," Gabriel said.

"Yes, long ago, under different circumstances. No worries though, I paid all my hotel bills."

Joshua took a sip of his wine and remembered his last trip to the island. His memory was a bit chaotic as was the trip itself. Still fascinated with the history of Malta, the Knights Templar, the castles, and the battles of long ago, but he decided then that he didn't want to live here. It was too far from anything and the lifestyle too monotonous for him. Still, it was a nice place to visit. "Have we heard anything about what happened?"

Gabriel shook his newspaper straight after turning a page. "Only what was in the papers. A Russian businessman was murdered in his hotel room, not much else, not even his name. Even Moscow is quiet."

"The question is who did it and why?"

"It wasn't me."

"I might even believe you. When do we see Hammer again?"

"I told you that already."

"I forgot."

"Your brain is atrophying, Grasshopper."

"I told you that already too."

"We leave tomorrow. Boy, are you cranky."

"Sorry, I was beginning to enjoy myself here and now we have to leave. Where to this time?"

Joshua saw the muscles bulged at Gabriel's temples as he clenched his jaws tight. "I am sorry, Gabriel. I don't like making you feel you're in a remake of The Odd Couple but my brain gets fried sometimes.

"It's a good thing I like you, young man. I can be patient. We're going to Baku."

"If you liked me, you wouldn't take me to Baku. I'd rather go to my ex-girlfriend's engagement party. Aren't they in the middle of a war?"

"That's pretty much isolated to the Nagorno-Karabakh region, which is farther west and north. That's where the Russians are too."

Gabriel didn't seem bothered by travel, no matter how forward or backward the country was. Joshua thought anyone whose nomadic background involved riding horses, taming eagles, eating *curdled milk*, and living in a yurt, was probably open to seeing new places, meeting people, and tasting strange cuisines. Baku was just another weekend jaunt for him.

For Joshua, it was something to keep him from home and his old car that needed work. But then, the money was good, and he had his camera to capture images of far-away places that would reside on his hard-drive until he could assemble them for a show. All he needed was time in his study and a good excuse to explain why he was in those places in the pictures.

"Why don't we have a rewards program to cash in on all these trips?"

"We get to cash in at the end of this with all our happy memories."

"If we survive," said Joshua.

"If we succeed, you mean. If we don't, there might not be any point to surviving."

JOSHUA THOUGHT ANDRIY'S BAKU SAFEHOUSE was a bit of a come down compared to the forest lodge outside Vilnius. For one thing, despite all the money that had been dumped into it, the new place lacked warmth. It must have been built in the quickest method possible, with concrete block and no regard for style. It had been decorated by someone whose idea of good taste involved replica Corinthian columns and urns made of plaster, surrounded by plastic ivy and statues of gold-painted Roman goddesses. Perhaps, the wife of an Azeri oilman who aspired to design an emperor's palace on the shores of the Caspian Sea.

The light filtered in through windows screened by wood panels incised in arabesque scenes, casting patterns on the carpets and walls. Andriy moved in and out of the light and shadows like a hyperactive panther. He lit one cigarette after another and trails of smoke marked his path. "Peter," he said, "why did you kill Korlov?"

"You know I didn't. I think it's more likely you did," said Gabriel.

"And you, Thomas?" Andriy ignored his taunt.

Joshua shook his head. "I wasn't happy with the man, but bygones be bygones, or something like that."

"And your service, didn't they want him dead?"

Gabriel stalked over to the window, his back to Andriy. "You know they didn't. Nor did the FBI. They wanted to put him on trial. Maybe it was the Iranians or the Turks trying to start something. Why was he meeting them?"

"He was negotiating the purchase of drones from Iran and Turkey. Iran has no problem selling them to Russia and Turkey won't do so officially, but with a middleman. We seem to have used up all of our drones in Ukraine. I must say, Peter, you are well informed. To know who he was meeting with must have taken some digging."

"That's what I do, Andriy. You gave me the lead and I followed up on it. It's not hard when you know how. What I want to know is, who got to Korlov before he was arrested? Why am I wrong to think you might have had him taken out?"

"Taken out? That doesn't translate well, Peter. It sounds as if I'm ordering Chinese food. But to answer your question, Korlov didn't have many friends, certainly not me, but his death will cause complications. There was already a power struggle going on, this will just make it worse."

"So, you didn't have him killed?"

"I had nothing to do with it. Korlov was a useful idiot, but some people considered us to be rivals and, therefore, his death makes my position more difficult.

"Maybe a rival in the government?"

"No, for the *Siloviki* shooting is reserved for traitors. Korlov wasn't a traitor. And there are simpler ways to solve rivalries and send a message. Careless men often fall out windows and such, but not outside the Motherland. I don't think this was government, maybe *Bratva*."

Bratva, the mafia, were organized crime groups that controlled a good percentage of the economy in Russia. They started out in black-marketeering and graduated upstairs to controlling industry. And crossing them usually meant bad things.

"Who will replace him?"

"For the moment, Korlov's deputy, Viktor Solovyov, is in charge," said Andriy. "I suspect he'll be replaced by another of the president's friends before long."

"You're a friend of the president," Gabriel said.

"True, but Volodya believes I am more valuable as his privy counsellor."

"Which still confuses us, Andriy. If you're his privy counsellor, why doesn't he listen to your advice?"

"I don't give advice, I counsel. I tell him what might happen if he takes this or that course of action. His ministers give him advice. And all they want is revenge. These men hate that Russia lost its territory to the West without a fight. Now they want it back and, unfortunately, so does he."

"He won't stop?"

"A long time ago, a Polish general said, 'There can be no independent Poland without an independent Ukraine.' He was right. Ukraine is gone. Once a Russian starts a war, he will not stop." Andriy said.

"Then why stay?"

"I'm trying to make a difference."

Gabriel was nothing if not patient, but he had a job to do. A job that became more complicated by the day even if he wasn't sure of its point. If Hammer was trying to make a difference, he was going about it the strangest way, providing counsel to someone who wouldn't accept it. For most, that would be grounds for resignation or at least retirement. But then, maybe that wasn't something a man could do in Russia anymore.

"So, Andriy, why are we here again? Do you think we can help?" Gabriel needed to know what Hammer was thinking, if only to get any idea of Moscow's—Pynya's—intentions.

"My advice to the president is like Cassandra's. He listens but he doesn't believe it. Warning you of his plans might prevent him from succeeding or at least increases its cost. Maybe then he will change his mind, because if his plans go through, they will only destroy Russia. If NATO had done something in Ukraine, we would not be here now."

"We might be dead if they had. Do you think he still plans to occupy the Baltics?" Gabriel said.

"Once the emergency in Nagorno is settled, yes."

"How long do you think that'll take?"

"A while yet. The locals have better backing than last time and the Azeris are low on drones. I will leave in a week. My job is almost done."

"What exactly is your job here?" Gabriel said.

"I'm providing the government some advice and taking notes for ours."

Gabriel was no closer to figuring out Andriy's job description.

"Then, I ask again. What do you have to tell us?"

"I told you about Perimeter, you remember? There is…"

"How could we forget?" Gabriel said. It was a good technique to disturb a contrived story or to irritate the teller, but Andriy was too agitated to notice.

"There is a key component to Perimeter that I just learned about. It is an autonomous command system that consists of three modified RS-28 missiles, which will be launched if Perimeter is activated. They aren't weapons. Each one carries a radio transmitter that sends instructions to all the strategic missile sites across Russia. When their signal is received, the warheads are launched."

"That makes sense. We had a similar system tied to our ICBMs, but it was shut down long ago," said Gabriel. "But ours wouldn't launch an attack based on the orders of a dead man. This Perimeter thing is a completely crazy version of a fail-safe device."

Joshua silently agreed. *Bass-akward, in fact.*

Andriy continued, "I thought I could provide you with the locations of the three missiles and you could devise a way to neutralize them. But there is a small problem."

"What's that?" Gabriel was not pleased with just how many small problems there seemed to be.

"Two of the three missiles are in silos. I know where those silos are located. The problem is that the third missile is unaccounted for."

Gabriel's interest needle went back in the red. "Unaccounted for, as in lost or stolen?"

"Moved."

"And you don't know where it's gone."

"Precisely. Strategic Missile Forces doesn't usually advertise where their toys are situated."

"Well, that's today's not-so-good news. But, while we're on the subject of Perimeter, you promised to find out who had the second sensor."

"That was easier. It's Petrakov, security council secretary."

"Petrakov," Gabriel repeated. "I would have thought it was the defense minister."

"The minister is not so much in favor with Voldya after making a hash of the Ukraine operation," said Andriy.

"So, the Baltic States will be attacked," Gabriel gave Joshua his best I thought I told you to be quiet look which Joshua ignored for once. "And if we eliminate the Russian leadership, we are all going to die."

"Thomas, you're full of happy thoughts today. Andriy, why hasn't anyone announced the existence of Perimeter as a deterrent?"

"Because Perimeter isn't a deterrent, our nuclear arsenal is the deterrent. Perimeter is meant to be retribution if the president is killed." He handed Gabriel a small envelope. Gabriel held it up to the light, flipped it over, and, inspecting it closely. It was sealed. "What is this?"

"A schematic and photos of the missile's operating systems on a disk. They might be useful to you. Also, the coordinates of the two RS-28s, but not the third. Just don't get caught with it. Come, gentlemen. There is something I'd like to show you." Andriy motioned to Gabriel and Joshua to follow him up a wide circular staircase that pierced the ceiling of the living area and into a slightly smaller room at the top of the building, sparsely furnished. All four walls were windows with a small terrace outside them like a moat around a castle. Beyond that was a broad expanse of buildings, looking tiny from their vantage point, and the Caspian Sea beyond.

"Impressive, no?" Andriy indicated the open sky and the city of Baku with a sweep of his hand. "What do you think of Baku, Thomas?"

"It's different. Kind of like a city with ADHD. But at least it has some interesting history."

Andriy laughed, a short, sharp bark and his eyes glistened. He turned serious again. "It's a good place to do business if you have the right connections. Otherwise, the government can be bothersome. Luckily, I have friends here."

"You have friends everywhere, Andriy," Gabriel said.

"And enemies, Peter."

"You've never said anything about enemies, other than Korlov's friend, Milatovich."

"I am a Russian with connections in high places."

"I thought you said you were low profile—that you stayed out of the limelight," said Gabriel.

"Outside Russia that is true. Inside Russia, that is almost impossible at my level. People inside the *Siloviki* know I move in certain circles, especially when Volodya is involved. They don't understand why and that makes me an enemy of jealous people. But we are not here to talk about my enemies. What I want to show you is this…" He pointed at a skyscraper in the distance, three curved towers reaching up into the sky like the antlers of a strange animal. "The Flame Towers. They're illuminated at night. Quite a spectacular sight."

"I saw them when I flew in yesterday," Gabriel said. "How are they important?"

"You're always a step ahead of me, Gabriel."

"I'm beginning to understand a little about you, Andriy."

"Well, let's say I telegraph some things to you very clearly."

"That would suggest I don't know you. Is that it?"

"You know me better than most. Few understand me, I think."

"Perhaps we should leave it at that for the moment. I'm not a psychologist," said Gabriel.

"Indeed." Turning back to the panorama in front of them, Andriy continued, "The Flame Towers are a sign of what Azerbaijan has become. A country that tries to be modern but hasn't bothered with political reform. The skyline has changed, but only for the Azeri elite. For the people, nothing has changed. Russia made that possible. It's the same in Moscow." Andriy paused to light another cigarette off the one he'd been smoking.

Joshua picked up a pair of binoculars from a side table. Russian military issue naturally. He winced as the focus was completely off and hurt his eyes. He spun the knobs quickly to get them roughly into range and then fine-tuned the scene until it turned crisp. Panning the city below him, he saw the difference between new and old, modern and historical. Historical being a matter of perspective—he could have been looking at ancient slums—still it looked better than Dubai, a pristine, modern city built on the backs of immigrants. At the same time, he was doing his best to stay out of the conversation, he could tell Gabriel wasn't happy.

"Why are you telling us this?" Gabriel asked, irritation in his voice.

"I'm sure you know it already. I just wanted you to see it from up here. From my perspective."

"You're right, we do know this. I can read it in the *Herald-Tribune*.

But why did you call us here? Was it only for the information about Perimeter and the missiles? We could have done a brush pass somewhere in Europe."

"There is someone I want you to meet."

"Us? Meet someone we don't know? That's not the best tradecraft, Andriy. How will you explain us this time?"

"It won't be necessary. You will be with me and you're my business associates. That's enough."

"And if someone gets curious or jealous again, what's to keep them from tracking us down like in Berlin?"

"Because he is already too busy avoiding his own government."

"Andriy, can you share with us? It would be nice to know what we're getting into."

"Soon enough, Peter. I want you to watch and listen. Tell me what you think after the meeting."

AFTER THE ROOFTOP, they returned to ground level where the buildings were normal sized, and Gabriel was just as irritated. Black BMWs preceded and followed Andriy's black Mercedes. Two in front, one behind, blue lights blinking in their grills and back windows.

"This is low profile," Joshua said as they emerged from the underground garage.

"We're invisible. No one who sees a black Mercedes with escort vehicles looks at it, unless they want to be stopped by the police. They don't want to know who is in the car," Gabriel said.

"You've done this before?" Joshua asked Gabriel.

"Not often, but enough. But this is a first for us, eh Andriy?" There was a hint of an inscrutable smile on Gabriel's face. Joshua wasn't sure if he was still pissed off or mildly amused with his asset's antics.

Andriy appeared unperturbed, but he did seem intent on the road ahead. "We're going to another of my safe houses on the edge of town. After the meeting, I'll set you free somewhere without your being noticed."

"That's good," Gabriel said. "It's not that I don't like you, it's just that we really don't need to be seen with you too often."

"I understand, but I thought meeting this man would help you better understand my work and motivations."

"We shall see, but I thought some deep one-on-one discussions with you would have sufficed."

Joshua watched the scenery slide by in a blur. From what he could glimpse of the speedo, the Mercedes was doing a little over one hundred kilometers an hour down the broad avenue. Not too fast but faster than anything else on the road, with the exception of their escorts. Most vehicles moved out of the way as soon as they saw the blue lights in their mirrors and the on-coming traffic slowed down on the other side of the road. It was the typical reaction in most third-world countries run by autocrats. Although, he did have to admit, he'd seen similar behavior in Washington with the President's motorcade.

Joshua knew instantly when an orange cloud of flame billowed out to the front right that they had a problem. He'd been in several ambushes and it wasn't a suicide bomb, it was an IED, an unmanned car bomb parked on the street that exploded. Whoever tripped it chose the lead escort BMW as the target. It was enveloped in the blast and Joshua saw it tip to the left just before it was engulfed in the explosion and disappeared in the smoke and fire. The shock wave rolled over them like a thunderclap followed by a chaos of dust, debris, and detritus, which settled down on them like a hard rain.

The second escort was well back. Its taillights came on as it shuddered to a stop. Then the Mercedes pitched nose down as the driver slammed on his brakes. There was no escape in front of them. He threw the car into reverse and twisted his body around to back off the "X" just as the armored glass windshield spalled inward, the large caliber bullet unhampered as it pierced through and hit him in the chest. Driver instantly dead, the car rolled back and stopped when it slammed into something solid. Cubes of glass from the exploded windshield had peppered the interior of the car, while blood from the driver covered the dash. How the bullet was stopped, Joshua had no clue. Anything powerful enough to penetrate Level Four protection should have kept going. Must be armored seat backs.

"We have to get out," Joshua yelled. Andriy looked dazed, Gabriel was transfixed out the left side window. Men ran toward the car, Kalashnikovs in hand.

"Get out!" Joshua pushed open the heavy passenger door on the opposite side. Andriy's lead bodyguard was out, braced against the right side of the car firing his pistol over the roof. Joshua pulled himself out and saw Andriy, get out, then Gabriel. Andriy stumbled and fell to his knees. The bodyguard pushed Andriy down by the rear wheel. Two of the attackers dropped in the street, but more came.

The follow car pulled up next to the Mercedes' rear end on the left. *Partial protection.*

Maybe eight seconds had passed. He pulled his own pistol and followed the bodyguard's example, firing over the roof. The first forty-five caliber slugs were too low. He fired without aiming. The slugs skipped off the roof of the Mercedes and went flying somewhere that did them no good. He calmed himself and fired again, two rounds double tapped, controlling the heavy recoil. The first—or was it the third?—attacker went down. Then another. Rounds flew around them, but from where? Another heavy report and the front of the Mercedes shook with the impact.

Whoever is behind that gun is slow.

"Come on, Joshua!" He turned to see Gabriel kneeling by the third BMW. Gabriel waved Joshua back to where he and Andriy crouched together. The second BMW had done a handbrake turn and spun by and then moved into position behind them providing more cover from small arms fire. At least two more bodyguards returned fire. He sprinted back as best he could, his bad leg slowing him, and knelt next to the others. They were all breathing rapidly, not from exertion, but the adrenaline rush.

Andriy yelled at them. "Go with this car! They'll take you wherever. Contact me when you're safe out of Baku," he said to Gabriel.

They scrambled into the back seat and the door slammed behind them. They kept their heads to the floor as the front door slammed and the car accelerated away. Except for the whine of the engine, it was quiet. Heads came up, like turtles checking the neighborhood before they sat upright and put on seatbelts, feeling exhausted and relieved and still pumped at the same time.

Gabriel said something to the driver and the car slowed and turned off the main road. No blue lights. The driver said something back. Joshua couldn't hear them, couldn't understand them. His ears were ringing.

"We'll go to a spot near my hotel and bail out. They'll leave us. We're on our own now." Gabriel spoke too loudly. "What the hell was that all about?"

"Hijack or kidnap," said Joshua.

"Why do you say that?"

"The heavy gun took out the driver. If they wanted to kill us, all they needed to do was keep shooting with that. They didn't. The attackers wanted to get close … maybe grab Andriy."

Gabriel sat back, looking out again. "I've never been that close to a full-fledged firefight." His eyes sparkled as he spoke, his lips held a slight smile.

"Hopefully, we won't be again."

"I've never seen that many guns all at once. When did you have time to get a pistol?"

"I bought it in the bazaar from an old friend of a friend, before you arrived."

The bodyguard turned to Joshua and in very clear English said, "You shoot well, you know. But perhaps I should take that from you now, please. We wouldn't want the local police to find it and maybe trace it back to this event." He held out his hand with a tight smile on his face.

Joshua had been holding the old Colt down by the side of his seat. He cleared it and handed over the unloaded pistol, magazine, and ejected cartridge along with his spare magazine. The bodyguard began to wipe everything with a cloth, taking the bullets out of the magazine one by one and cleaning them as well. Then, he dumped the pistol and its parts into a small bag. "Can't be too careful."

Gabriel shook his head. "Where did you learn your English?"

"Oxford," the man said. "I got a first in history there." He turned back to the front of the car, silent once again.

JAMIE HAD DECIDED the usual hotel routines were out once Gabriel had told him of the attack. Instead, they were staying in a nice, secluded villa on the edge of Berchtesgaden in the Obersalzberg—the Bavarian Alps. B'gaden as the GIs used to call it had been an American resort during the Cold War. Some say General Patton captured the place in 1945 so his GIs could have a nice place to kick back, relax, and blow off steam. The villa was one of the few buildings that remained in American hands. Most everything else, the hotels and military bases, had been returned to the host government after the Wall fell except for a few properties, this being one.

As it had never officially been on the books, it was relatively easy to keep it off. It was still being used for those occasions when they absolutely needed a place to keep their heads down. The local Germans swore it was owned by a company that used it as a quiet retreat for its executives. The Agency was happy to let them believe that. Any inquiries about the place ended up first with the *Polizei* and then were referred to the BND—the German intelligence service—where each died a long, slow bureaucratic death of silence and inaction.

Jamie took a moment to pour more coffee all around and took a shortbread cookie for himself. Gabriel was standing at the window looking at the mountains to the south. The trams were running, they always ran. During winter for the skiers and summer for the tourists who juts wanted to stand on the peaks and drink wine and schnapps.

Gabriel pivoted back to Jamie and Joshua. "The question is, who were they trying to kill or kidnap. Was it you, me, or Hammer?"

"In Berlin was easier to tell," Joshua said. "I was the only target. This time we get to choose."

"No. You were the only target they found," Gabriel said.

"Maybe it was all three of you?" said Jamie.

"No one knew we were there," said Joshua.

"And yet you were in the middle of it. Just like the time in Berlin, Joshua," said Jamie.

"Hammer sent me a message," Gabriel said. "The locals think it was separatists from Nagorno-Karabakh."

Jamie was shaking his head. "That's convenient for the Azeris, but why would the Armenians want to kill a Russian? They're pretty close to Moscow this week."

"To embarrass the government in Baku?" asked Joshua.

"Not likely. I'll bet it was the Azeris trying to pin something on the Armenians," Gabriel said, "or maybe a Russian with a grievance."

"Which, in all probability, means the attack was directed at Hammer and not you. So, what have we got?" Jamie asked. He knew if anyone had an answer it would be these guys, the asset's handlers, Gabriel and Joshua. Not an analyst in Washington. Analysts could look at the data—reports, intercepts, assessments—conjecture all day long and come up with five solutions, all of them wrong, because what they didn't have was that instinctive feel, *Fingerspitzengefühl*, for a case.

"A mess," said Joshua. *So much for intuition.*

"An asset with enemies. A man who seemingly wants to prevent a disastrous war," Gabriel said.

"A modern-day Penkovsky." Jamie cited the name of the man who helped avert a nuclear confrontation during the Cuban crisis long ago.

"That's one possibility. I just hope he doesn't end up in the basement of Lubyanka with a bullet in his brain," Gabriel said. "At least we know who has the Perimeter sensors and the locations for two of the three missiles along with what he said were the plans for the control missile's operating systems," said Gabriel.

"Who has the sensors?"

"The boss and Nikolai Petrakov, security council secretary."

"So essentially, they have immunity." Jamie shook his head. "We can't touch them as long as Perimeter is operational."

"In theory, we're not supposed to do that anyway. Killing foreign leaders, I mean. At least according to Geneva and Hague."

"Since when did you become a shit-house lawyer, Joshua?" Jamie said.

"It was my feeble attempt to console you, boss."

"Don't call me boss. I know you don't mean it. What do you make of the missile information?"

"It's photos and schematics of something. Looks authentic. It's all in Russian and looks to be for a missile, but I'm not engineer enough to know for sure."

"You looked at the documents on the disk?" Said Jamie.

"Yes, of course. How else would I know?"

"You're not supposed to do that. There might have been some killer virus buried in the data."

"Well, in that case, the entire internet of Switzerland will probably implode."

"You did it in Switzerland?" said Jamie.

"Yes, Geneva Airport, to be exact. Some traveler in the business class lounge who left his computer on while he was sleeping."

"So now he has a copy—"

"No, I wiped his hard drive when I was done. He looked too well-off for me to worry about it."

"Just don't write this into your report. The CI folks would be all over you," said Jamie.

Joshua seemed not to hear or chose to ignore Jamie. He wasn't big on report writing anyway. "But what's interesting, is that the photos show some modules that appear to be of U.S. origin."

"How do you know?"

"They have 'Made in USA' stamped on them."

"That's a pretty good indicator," Gabriel said.

Jamie stared at the small envelope filled with the digital secrets of Russia's most advanced missile and wondered if it was bogus. "What did Hammer tell you about this again?" he asked Gabriel. Joshua could have answered but he knew better than to interrupt his teacher, which was how he saw Gabriel these days.

"He said, quote, 'They might be useful to you' unquote."

THE GULFSTREAM 800 SAT ON THE TARMAC of the military airfield not far from Frankfurt, one of the few operational American air bases left in Germany. Jamie and Joshua had made their way there, leaving Gabriel to return to his hideaway. A place he called, "just a dump in Malta" where he could monitor his agent comms and be ready if anything urgent came up. Besides the storm clouds of an expanded war on the horizon, the only thing that might come up was another meeting with Hammer.

Gabriel and Joshua had spoken before he left the safehouse in his chauffeured, armored G-Wagon. He spoke of seeing bad things in dangerous places, but said he was becoming skeptical about personal meets with Hammer when it seemed entirely too hazardous. He intended to be careful about accepting anymore invitations. He said, "Only when absolutely necessary, otherwise we rely on the technical means."

One thing Joshua noticed as Gabriel talked, was his demeanor. Somewhere between the detachment of Buddha and the cool of a cucumber. There was nothing that indicated he'd almost been killed in the ambush. Gabriel said he'd been in fights—one on one mostly, not urban combat—so it wasn't entirely foreign to him. He said he didn't experience the chaos most first timers do. The Way had taught him to find calm and to accept death as inevitable. He experienced a sort of hyper-awareness. He saw the battle, nothing else, knew where every person was and what needed to be done.

Joshua suddenly realized what happened on the street in Baku. "It was you. You got Andriy to the other car and out of the line of fire."

"Yes," Gabriel said. "He was frozen."

Joshua had grown accustomed to conflict only by repeated exposure. Gabriel seemed to instinctively know what to do. He decided he, as Grasshopper, still had much to learn.

As they sat waiting for the jet to take off, Joshua described Gabriel's actions to Jamie.

Jamie just nodded. "He has studied and practiced from a very young age. Still does. He's a good man to have on your six."

High praise from Jamie, a man also skilled in martial arts.

An hour into the flight, Joshua's stomach pleaded to be fed. They had been forced into a rather precipitous exit from the safehouse by Jamie's secure telephone call to the director which had ended with a demand for their return to Washington. That meant no food before the trip. He got up and spent the first thirty seconds stretching his right calf, still sore from his short sprint to the BMW, still maimed from forty plus years of service in the field.

Jamie watched from his swivel chair. "You look stiff."

"It doesn't take much for me to start hurting."

"Old paratrooper syndrome, know it well. But at least you have VA disability, all that extra money to buy more pain killers."

Joshua stood up and walked back to the galley, past the posh seating and worktables, but before the custom sleeping bays, which each included a small bathroom and shower.

"How much did this thing cost the taxpayers?" Joshua asked, leaning back into the main cabin.

"Like seventy million before the modifications, but those were all done in Nevada, so nobody really knows."

"A bargain at twice the price." Joshua began rooting through all the cabinets and coolers looking for suitable sustenance. It was decently stocked, catered from Langley's kitchen, not airline food, and there was real silverware and china. "Obviously, they're not afraid someone could use these to hijack us," he held up a six-inch Damascus steel steak knife, "or maybe we're supposed to use them to defend ourselves."

"The crew is armed." Jamie joined him in the galley and was rooting through the refrigerator for his own food. He picked up two mini-bottles of Macallan and a glass to go with his food. "I love flying on this thing. I replenish my home bar after every flight." He grinned happily as he looked at all the bottles in the drawer.

"I would still have my own pistol if I hadn't given it to Hammer's thug in Baku." Joshua said as he grabbed a bottle of Talisker.

"Airport security might have had something to say about that."

"I don't know, the screening there wasn't that tight. The woman in front of me got on with her open can of Red Bull. That's seriously dangerous."

While Jamie busied himself picking through a cheese platter, Joshua grabbed a hot Vindaloo curried-something out of the hotbox. There were even fresh chapatti and naan in a custom bread warmer. "Is this kitchen what they added in Nevada? It's worth the price."

They plopped down at the dining table. It was hardwood with a custom world map engraved into the top and accented with blue epoxy oceans. Joshua traced their route to Washington over Greenland and the east coast. "This must be where they plan world domination…"

Jamie wiped his mouth. "I want you to brief the director."

"Me?" Joshua had been in the room with an Agency director twice that he could remember, but he was always in the peanut gallery, the second-tier seating, never in the front. "I'm just a contractor, I can't do that."

"Yes, you can. Since Gabriel is relaxing in the Med, you're the only person at the table who knows Hammer. You're at bat." Jamie took another bite of cheese, clearly enjoying Joshua's discomfort. "You might want to practice in front of the mirror."

Had he not already heard of her, when Joshua first saw the director, he might have been surprised. The director cut an intimidating figure. At well over six feet tall, her brown eyes probed him from behind owlish glasses, while wild, gray hair framed her face. Dressed in a gray flannel pantsuit, the jeweled scorpion brooch on her jacket sent an appropriate warning not to cross her.

Several years ago, she had replaced the previous director, a hapless political appointee who had served in the community for a couple of years before he decided to get elected congressman. Then he tried too hard for spectacular, flew too close to the sun, and got himself relieved. Her appointment was an apolitical compromise between parties who knew someone competent was needed in the job for once. The former head of the Directorate of Analysis, she got the job. A brilliant intelligence officer, she was a real-life Jack Ryan, although she could probably kick Ryan's ass.

As she came into the briefing room, she looked around, Joshua thought she was mentally ticking off each person known to her. Then turning to the one unknown, she approached Joshua and put out her hand. "Clairissa Hall, not related to Virginia Hall despite the resemblance." She smiled at her own joke. There was no resemblance, except their height, and Clairissa Hall wasn't just one of the first female directors, she was the first Black person to have the job.

"Virginia Hall—the only female civilian spy to receive the Distinguished Service Cross in World War II," Joshua said.

"Good, you know some history. What else do you know?"

"I can tell you about the case we're working."

"That's what Jamie said. I've heard that you and Batman have been busy with meetings all over Europe. Someone tried to kill you twice, what else?"

Joshua looked at the others in the room and then at Jamie, who nodded his head to indicate they were all cleared. The director picked up on the exchange and interrupted, "I should introduce everyone. Gentlepeople, this is Joshua Devlin, a long-time officer of ours, who has spent more time overseas doing the Lord's work than most of you have on Earth. Of course, you know Jamie Wheeler, Chief of the Clandestine Service." She introduced the others to Joshua in turn, "This is Gladys Thompson, Russia House, Tom Hopman, Counterproliferation, Mark Phillips, Technical Services, and Andra Billings, Analysis. We're all cleared for this."

"Thank you, ma'am." Joshua picked up with his rehearsed speech. "Batman, as you call him, and I have been meeting with the Russian asset, code-named Hammer since he asked for an emergency meeting. At the first meeting, he gave us the planned date of the Russian incursion into the Baltic States but then stated it would be delayed by an uprising in Nagorno-Karabakh. That uprising came to pass. He also told us about Perimeter, the strategic missile control system, and that it had been reactivated. The important point was that the system now has only two control sensors rather than the previous five. Those sensors are with the president and the secretary of the security council, if they are killed, the system goes to launch mode automatically."

Tom Hopman looked concerned. "Did he tell you how the launch command is given?" Joshua was giving them the only new information on Perimeter since it was rumored to have come into existence.

"Not exactly. Only that when the sensors are activated, a signal is sent to launch three RS-28 missiles each carrying an autonomous command system, which alerts all the missile sites and gives the launch instructions. Once the missiles are launched, there is no recall."

"That's why we call it *Dead Hand*, because it is a Fail-deadly system, the opposite of a Fail-safe system," said Mark Phillips. He turned to the director, "We have no means to stop Perimeter. With their normal launch command system, *Cheget,* they use VLF—Very Low Frequency—radio transmissions between Kuntsevo, Ministry of Defence headquarters, and Kosvinsky, their version of Cheyenne Mountain, and the launch sites. That takes a lot of time and we can interfere with the signal. However, if missiles are used to command the launch, we're toast."

"Okay," the director said, "we have all that technical info, but why did Hammer pass it to us? What's his motivation?"

"He has continually said that he wants to prevent the war from continuing, a war he said that will destroy his country. So, it appears he is being altruistic and patriotic at the same time. But not patriotic to the regime. He doesn't like the hawks who surround Pynya."

"He likes Pynya?"

"He seems to think Pynya is being influenced by the hawks, but also that he is a small, evil man with a Napoleonic complex," said Joshua.

"Which jives with what Psych has written about the man," Director Hall said. She hadn't bothered to sit down. Hall moved around the room one hand supporting her chin. Joshua could almost hear her mind churning through the possibilities and counters that might come into play. "First, we need to inform POTUS and DoD that those two men are categorically off-limits. Not that anyone downtown would ever contemplate assassinating a world leader or his right-hand man, but just in case. Second, how do we find a way to screw with these missiles? Joshua, I think Jamie mentioned you have something else, is that true?"

"Yes, ma'am. Hammer gave us the plans for the RS-28 command operating system."

"Where are they now?" Hall asked.

"We have them, Director," said Tom Hopman. "My rocket scientists are going over them right now. There are at least thirty top-grade IRs in the material. Space Force will be over the moon, so to speak."

Hall stopped dead in her tracks. "To hell with Space Force and intel reports," she said. "As of this moment, this is all compartmented in a new restricted cabinet. No one is to be brought in on it unless they can contribute something besides platitudes to defeating Perimeter. Andra, no FYI reports to anyone. I will personally brief POTUS and SecDef today. The rest of you, figure this out. I want continuous updates. How much time do we have before the invasion? Anyone?"

"Hammer said we have five weeks minimum. Maximum, maybe eight. According to him, it depends on how things in Nagorno go," said Joshua.

She regarded Devlin for a moment, thinking. "You heard the man," she said. "Let's get moving on this."

As everyone began to leave the room, Director Hall spoke again, "Jamie, you and Joshua stay." Once the room was empty, she said, "Joshua, you're doing a good job. This could be getting dicey, not just for you, but all of us. I know you intended to retire, but we need you fully in the game. And our role is let you do your job without interference. So, thank you and be sure to pass that along to Gabriel. Now go get things done."

"Yes, ma'am." Joshua pivoted and walked out.

Once Joshua was gone, Hall turned to Jamie, "We have to figure out how to disable Perimeter soon."

"We're doing our best, but my biggest question is this, what happens if we are able to take out the system?"

"Damn good question. I don't know but at least we'll have

eliminated that wild card."

Hall grabbed Jamie before he could move. "I hope you've put those two in for something," she said.

"I will as soon as this is over, but both of them have most every award the Agency has to offer."

"I know, but the director has certain latitude. Think of something special for them if we win this one," she paused. "If we don't, it probably won't matter." She turned and headed for her office.

Jamie joined Joshua in the hallway. "Let's go get some coffee." He put his hand on Joshua's shoulder. "You did good. She's impressed."

"*She's very impressive*," said Joshua. "That was one the few times I actually felt a superior was listening to what we said."

"Hey! What am I? Chopped liver?"

Joshua stopped dead in the empty hallway. "I never had the feeling you were a superior."

"What then?"

"More a leader, a guide—but one that lets me find my way."

"Thanks, I can accept that. But at the same time, just remember we can't disappoint her. When she's pissed, it's best to be far away from ground zero."

The same cabal, minus the director, agreed to a quick follow-up and met deep inside the so-called new office building at the end of a long corridor, a white maze of a hallway designed to confuse unwanted intruders and stop errant electronic emanations. The director blew out of the underground parking garage riding in her convoy of three Suburbans headed down the GW Parkway for the White House. Joshua supposed she had other things to do and would let her subject matter experts decide on how to save the Free World.

Gladys Thompson, who was well able to dominate any conversation about Russia, its former empire, or military strategy—despite having no practical experience in that subject— took the lead once they settled in. "We have several options and, personally, I think we should consider all of them. The first is diversion. We need to do what we can to keep the uprising in Nagorno-Karabakh going and keep the Russian focus there. Second, we need to be able to degrade *Cheget*, maybe hit their underground command complex with bunker busters. And last, we need to turn off Perimeter." Having demonstrated her grasp of the obvious she sat back in the chair.

Hopman parried. "Easy, no problem, we can have that done by EOD." End of day was in about four hours.

"I feel you're not really committed to this, Tom" she said.

He sighed. "Well, stirring up Nagorno is probably the easiest thing. We can send in some guns and money to assist the rebels fairly quickly. Right, Jamie?" Hopman looked to Jamie for confirmation.

Jamie nodded. "We've begun some preliminary work on that with the regional division." He stood before a map of the eastern hemisphere and waved his hands over the region in question. Not that anyone could follow his meaning, he was in the process of working out which assets would come from where and in what country they would end up. There were no computer-generated images or artificial intelligence to assist, it was all cataloged in his mind to be spelled out in written plans later.

"Think surrogates," he said, "We have troops available and regional stockpiles to draw on that don't point to us."

Hopman said, "That will destabilize things a bit more, keep 'em all occupied. That other stuff? The Air Force's B21 isn't operational yet, so how do we deliver ordnance on top of Kuntsevo or the Kosvinsky Mountain Complex? And since we don't know where all the RS-28s are located, how do we kill them?"

If a rock had dropped no one would have noticed. The room was still as everyone seemed to consider options. The windows of the office looked out over the trees toward the Potomac and Washington D.C.

"We're going through all our holdings for reporting on the Strategic Missile Forces," Andra Billings said, "everything back to 1990 looking for locations and movements. Maybe we can pinpoint where they went."

"Where *it* went," said Jamie. "Singular. We know where two missiles are. We just need the coordinates on the last one."

"Okay. Once you find it, we have to figure out how to take them all out. Can't do it remotely, their circuits are hardened according to the plans," said Hopman.

"I'm not so sure about that, Tom," said Mark Phillips. "We're working on some pretty interesting ideas right now. Joshua, didn't you say it appeared that some American components were used?"

Phillips was the Agency's version of "Q," the gadget man for British SIS, although he didn't look the part. Despite his degrees in aerospace and electrical engineering, he still looked like the former university football player he was. Perhaps because of his force of personality the technical directorate had pioneered many interesting things under his watch. Things he called "toys," were what others called devious instruments of destruction.

"That's what the images show, yes."

"I need all the documentation and photos, Tom," said Phillips.

"You think you can do something, Mark?" Gladys asked.

"The Russians have a tendency to copy our technology verbatim without necessarily understanding why a particular thing is in a certain spot or exactly what it does, if anything. That leaves openings for exploitation."

"So, in technical terms, that's a yes?"

"Technically, it's a maybe."

JOSHUA CHECKED FOR SURVEILLANCE even before he got
into his car. Even though he was back home and had retired several
years before and had few enemies he knew of either in the field or
in the office. Furthermore, he was in the Agency's parking lot, which
probably reduced the chances he'd be followed even more.

But he still checked.

When he got off the compound, all he saw in the mirror was a
police cruiser behind him—never a comfortable sight wherever you
found yourself—and only decided it was safe when the cop passed him.

He ended up on Spout Run and went to a nearby sandwich shop
he knew. Not wanting to wait, he grabbed a pre-made sandwich. In this
shop, that meant it was less than ten minutes old because the turnover
was fast. Its usual Italian simplicity was nearly as good as his other
favorite, which was too far to drive being in Berlin. Jamie had told
him to go kick back and relax for a couple of days. His home wasn't
too far away, but he hadn't quite got used to the silence without Sarah.
He still couldn't think about her without some regret. Regret about
not having enough time with her, with his son. Matt was deployed
and he didn't have any other family to visit. He didn't feel like visiting
any of his few remaining comrades, most of whom had passed over
the bridge to Valhalla, just like his wife. He couldn't visit any of his
liaison friends or the agents he'd recruited. The counterintelligence
folks at headquarters frowned on that. Most weren't the kind of people
he wanted to associate with, anyway. And quite of few of them were

dead as well, victims of age, CI investigations that didn't turn out well, or outright assassination.

Such a wonderful life.

On the way out of the store, he grabbed a bottle of Chianti and a piece of Guanciale for the carbonara he might whip up later, he decided to head back to his studio hotel, watch a movie, and wait for Jamie's next set of instructions.

They weren't long in coming. The next day while browsing through a bookstore in Tyson's Corner, his coat pocket buzzed against his chest. He pulled the phone out to check whether it was a call or a message. A message, and straight to the point: Dulles, General Aviation Terminal, 0800 tomorrow, Ready to Travel. NNNN. That was Jamie, typically he signed off that way. In commo shorthand, NNNN meant end of message.

The next morning, Joshua parked his car on the edge of the lot and walked toward the terminal. It wasn't really a terminal, more a large steel building housing various companies doing livery work in the skies or a place for rich people to sit while they waited for their private jet to tank up. He didn't make it to the front door. A black van with smoked windows pulled up next to him.

Jamie sat in the front, window down. "Hop in."

The side door slid open. Mark Phillips waited for him in the middle seat. Joshua hopped in.

"Give me your keys," Phillips said. Joshua handed them to Mark, who handed them to the driver. "He can find it and dump it off at the rental place. Don't want you to get towed."

"Where we going?" Joshua asked.

"We're going west. There may be some options for us to consider."

"You know the place," Jamie added. "Think Trinity Site."

That narrowed things down significantly. Somewhere in New Mexico.

The van passed through a gate for those rich businesspeople who wanted to arrive at the steps of their corporate plane in style. It was manned by a civilian security guard and the van rolled through with the perfunctory check of a generic Homeland Security pass. Driving around a hangar they arrived at a waiting Gulfstream.

"Same one? Or do you have a fleet?" Joshua asked Jamie.

"I think it's the same. Didn't you memorize the tail number? I thought you did that?"

"Nope, I don't worry so much about friendlies."

"Maybe you should rethink your concept of friendlies, otherwise you wouldn't be involved in this project."

"Encouraging thought, Jamie, but it was you who recruited me for this. What does that mean for you?"

Exhausted, Joshua hadn't noticed on the first flight how quiet the Gulfstream was compared to other aircraft. The quick departure from Baku had drained his energy and even the short stay in Germany hadn't done much to revive him. Now that he was rested, he could better appreciate the expensive accommodations. Mark and Jamie were locked in a discussion about support issues, even at Mach point nine and forty-two thousand feet, there would be no talk of Hammer or Russian missiles until they reached whatever safe haven they were headed for. In the meantime, he contented himself with breakfast out of the gallery. He watched the sky as they flew west trying to outrun the sun and wondered if he could cheat death by flying fast forever. The moment passed and he fell asleep.

Waking just before they landed, Joshua saw the landscape vividly in the morning light. He glimpsed the gypsum dunes before they disappeared behind the low mountains just before they touched down. on the ground, low desert scrub, mesquite, and grasses surrounded the runway, stretching out into an austere vista. As the plane taxied into the apron area, he could see signs of human occupation. A small terminal perched on the edge of the tarmac and beyond that appeared to be a military base with many buildings. The scene, devoid of color, was like a sepia-toned photograph, everything a shade of white, reddish brown, or gray. Even the sky had lost most of its blue.

"Where are we?" Joshua asked.

"South end of White Sands. Not far from Las Cruces. We're going to visit some friends at the test facilities."

Joshua shielded his eyes as he climbed down the stairs to the tarmac. It was late morning, and the sun was already heating up the desert, its slanting rays hitting him full force square in the face. A van, painted white out of deference to the environment and unmarked save for a two-digit motor pool number, waited for them at the bottom of the stairs. Their small suitcases went into the back, and they headed off the airfield toward a complex on the edge of the main base area.

"These are the best folks in the country for figuring out what we're up against and how to defeat it," Tom said before they climbed into the vehicle. "I sent them the plans once the director okayed the idea, and they've been looking at things. They know where we're from, but nothing about you or the project."

"I'll keep my mouth shut."

"Unless you have something to contribute or if you think some idea is crazy," Jamie said. "It's amazing what kind of stupid shit these genius rocket scientists can come up with." He glanced over at Phillips and winked a conspiratorial wink. Phillips just glared back.

"I'm going to take that personally, Mister Wheeler," he said.

If it came down to a wrestling match between the two, Joshua did not want to be caught up in the melee. A quarter ton of beef could do serious damage to your health if you got trampled underneath. Luckily, protocol overcame the issue.

The scientists who met them fit the mental picture Joshua already had. There were five people, three men and two women, met him at the entrance way to the facility. Most of them wore glasses, all of them in regulation white coats with a plastic ID hanging around their neck. Most looked like mild-mannered rocket scientist nerds. None of them appeared to be at all responsible for the ruthless objects they created in their lab deep inside the secure facility.

On their way down into the lab in the elevator, Phillips lectured. "This project is so sensitive, I will personally be responsible for your demise if it's leaked."

"Mark," Jamie said in his even-keel voice that intimated physical violence if necessary, "The security briefing is really unnecessary because Joshua and I both carry tip-top clearances with access to about every secret program that ever existed. We wouldn't be here otherwise. That said, this place wasn't far from where the first set of nuclear secrets were stolen—by one of the rocket scientists that devised them."

Suitably chastised, Phillips shut up.

Phillip's scientists were aware of Perimeter and *Cheget,* as many scientists around the United States in installations like White Sands, Tonapah, Lakehurst, and Eglin had been working on defeating the system since it first came to the government's attention. What they weren't aware of was that the system had been brought out of hibernation. The rocket schematics and images were also new to them, but decidedly interesting, they said. Joshua wondered what they would think if they heard the story of how the plans were acquired. He doubted they would understand what it was like beyond the sterile walls of their lab. The elevator had dumped them on a subterranean level with long hallway led them past doors marked in a mix of letters and numbers. Nothing to indicate what lay beyond. Only the last door had a sign that said conference room which someone decided could be done without giving away secrets. They group filed in and took places around a long table. The room was devoid of any sign of the work being done in the lab or even a photograph, just gray walls.

The conversation focused quickly on ideas they'd come up with, some having been thought of before, some new as of yesterday's look at the schematics.

"The fact that the system is carried on the RS-28 is good news," one said. "If it was on a submarine-launched missile, it would be a different story." Her name tag said only Lee, Joshua wasn't sure if it was her first or last name.

"A submarine missile would make no sense. How would Moscow launch it when the submarine is most likely running silent? VLF radio takes too long, and it would have to be launched back over Russia to command the launch of their ground-based systems." Joshua said, pleased with himself for keeping up with the experts.

The scientists looked at Joshua for a moment. Lee had daggers in her eyes. Jamie hid his smile behind his hand.

"Well, that much is true, I suppose. Anyway, we have options for the RS-28. Jessica, will you outline what we've come up with?" Phillips said.

Jessica stood up and clicked the PowerPoint slides into motion.

Luckily there were only three. "Based on what we know about Perimeter, the system would have to be destroyed in the initial boost phase over Russian territory. This is all Star Wars kinds of stuff but we do have a couple of test systems we might be able to use. A laser intercept is one method to knock them out. But it would require a lot of luck. A laser platform has to be up and ready. A satellite system might work but the airborne version wouldn't. Another possibility is directed energy pulse, but that has the same issues as with the laser. And we need a good idea of the launch window and the missile's flight path, which I don't think you have?"

Phillips shook his head.

"I didn't think so. We don't have them either. We could target the launch sites for attack with over-the-horizon weapons before launch, but that might set off WW3." The scientists all wagged their heads in unison.

"One last question. Do you have any information on the VIP's sensors themselves? If we knew more about them, we might be able to devise a way to disable them," said Phillips.

Joshua shook his head. "No, just that there are only two, but we have no clue how they work. Don't know if they fit in a pocket, are carried, or if they are ankle monitors. Three sensors are apparently offline, but again, we don't know where they are."

"I wonder what power source they use because if the batteries failed on both sensors at the same time…" said Jessica.

"I would hope they've figured that part out." The man identifiable as Ulbricht by his name tag said. His head buried the papers he'd been carrying.

"So essentially you're saying that we don't have any workable options?" Phillips said.

"There is one other possibility." Jessica queued up the last slide. "Manipulation of the guidance system itself."

On the slide was an image of a small module taken from the schematics.

"This is an Electronic Control Unit—an ECU—from the plans and images you provided us. As you can see from its markings, it's American. Someone got them through sanctions. But we looked at its function and we're sure it can be re-programmed."

"To sabotage the control systems?" Phillips asked.

"Yes, all you would have to do is introduce it into the motherboard. It's easy, it's a plug-in," said Jessica.

"All you would have to do…" said Jamie very slowly.

"Yes, but it would work. And it's probably our only option."

"How long would it take you to modify them?" Phillips asked.

"Once we receive the modules, we can program them in a couple of minutes. We're already looking at rewriting the code. If you tell us to order them, we can have them to you in a couple of days."

Phillips glanced at Jamie, who gave him a shrug that said what other choice do we have? "Do it. We need them yesterday."

Leaving the facility in the van, Jamie turned to Joshua. "Now comes the tricky part, introducing the modules into the system, but if Hammer got the plans out, he must have a way to get them in. No matter what, he will have his work cut out for him."

"No shit. It took the Greeks ten years to get that damn wooden horse into Troy."

"It often takes a while to convince someone to swallow a pill."

JAMIE, JOSHUA, AND THE RUSSIA HOUSE CHIEF Gladys Thompson trooped in together across the deep flowing meadow of Clairissa Hall's office carpet. Joshua thought he could sleep better on this floor than his hotel bed it was so thick. With their coffees in hand, everyone found a seat while the director allowed herself a moment of contemplation as she stirred her coffee. She favored Ethiopian with a hint of cardamom, which required personal intervention as her aides were too accustomed to K-cups to know how to brew it properly.

The director hated to sit behind a desk when she chatted with her officers. And she did look on them as hers because just as she brought in her own coffee and furniture, she was responsible for the care, feeding, and upbringing of her employees, her case officers, analysts, support officers—everyone in the Agency. She might not have hired them, but they were hers to have and hold, to protect, and to fire if necessary. She looked at the three in front of her with approval; no executions would be required today. She smiled after a sip from her cup. "Where are we?"

"Sabotage," said Gladys. "The most probable method of disrupting the Russian missiles is to insert bad code into their system. The DART scientists will provide a programmed module that will replace the original."

"What is DART?"

"The Defense Advanced Rocket Technology facility at White Sands."

"Intriguing. How exactly do you plan on getting the Russians to do us the favor of inserting this module in their missiles?"

"Hammer will do it," Joshua said. "He got us the plans. He must have access."

"And you've already confirmed he is willing and capable?"

"No, ma'am. That will be our job at the next meeting to convince him. It's in his interest to help."

"That's a couple of big 'ifs' you're talking about."

"Agreed, ma'am, but I don't think we have any other choice in the matter."

"Jamie? Gladys?"

"It's the only way we can see to move this forward," Jamie said. "All the other options require technology we can't deploy or would risk World War III."

"Which we are on the cusp of, right now." Clairissa set her cup on its saucer and tented her hands in front of her face. "Alright, we do it like that. I briefed POTUS and SecDef. They understand that we can't kill the leadership if we wish to survive. So that's one thing resolved. POTUS signed the finding that gives us authority to take action in Nagorno. You are working on that already, Gladys?"

"Yes, we have a team who are prepared to go in and cause significant disruption."

"Who are they and how many?"

"Peshmerga and less than one hundred. The Armenians will provide us cover."

"Whose handling them?"

"One of our NOC contractors. Has the unfortunate funny name of Rudy Kipling."

"Why unfortunate?"

"He's Parsi from India. Doesn't really care for the Brits."

MATT SAT ON HIS BUNK in his team's very spartan living area. He would have called the building a barracks, but it was more a prefab warehouse that had been built out. This place was furnished with a cross between modern IKEA practical and army-issue green, not unlike the German barracks he'd experienced. A little brighter but not much. As team leader, he had his own room, the presumption being—at least in the Lithuanian military—that officers needed some remove from the enlisted scum that worked for them. Also from his deputy commander, a warrant officer, who was also former enlisted scum. Despite the fact that Ron was working the same job a first lieutenant would do, but with greater skill and for much less money—most armies didn't quite understand that American warrant officers were actual if underpaid officers. They were just super specialized—not like Heinlein meant when he wrote that specialization is for insects—SF Warrants know the art of unconventional warfare backwards and forwards, better than the so-called "real live" officers. That was the job his father had before he went over to the dark side with the Agency. But he didn't worry about the Agency, worrying about the army was quite enough.

He sighed, reflecting on events. Since the ghost asset incident, Matt had played everything low-key. Ron took some of the heat, but ultimately the colonel held him responsible for the infraction, which was right because he had caused it.

Well, actually, Dad caused it.

At least Commander Melis hadn't succeeded in getting him sent home. Matt was knee-deep in self-pity, which he would have preferred to share with someone. *Like Dad.* But he took some comfort in knowing he'd tried to make a difference by giving his hosts the warning. It was just the execution of the plan that didn't work well. It wasn't that big of a deal anyway.

At least to everyone but Melis.

That didn't change the fact that they were or soon would be directly in the line of fire of a Russian offensive. He was not looking forward to that. Any Special Forces trooper would tell you they'd rather be behind the lines pulling the tail of the bear rather than in front of its claws. They were both dangerous places, but in one, the bear couldn't see you.

He put his phone down, the one with the local Lithuanian SIM card. The Americans had been issued generic mobiles because the Russians were pretty good at intercepting cell numbers and geo-locating them off the towers.

He wanted to send a note to Dad just to update him on the basics, something simple like: Hi Dad, I'm OK, miss you. But he had no clue where Dad was at the moment, or even if he could receive a message. When Dad traveled he followed the same rules as Matt. Rules which came into force when the security gurus figured out the weaknesses of modern technology twenty years earlier. It was the same set of weaknesses the Syrian and Egyptian governments had exploited to destroy the rebels of the Arab uprisings. They used the rebels' own social media. Sort of like Murphy's Law: tracers point both ways.

A knock on the door announced someone's presence. It was lighter than the usual loud thump of a team-mate.

"Yes?" When no one answered, he opened the door and took a step back. *The devil herself.*

Commander Melis was dressed casually, no uniform: denim trousers, a dark green sweater. Her auburn hair was still carefully restrained behind her head.

"Good evening, captain. May I?" She took a short, tentative step toward him.

"Of course." He stepped aside, leaving the door open, something required in modern American military etiquette.

"You can close it," Melis said. "We don't worry about that so much here."

"Here, as in Lithuania or here as in your army?"

"Both. Besides, I can handle myself."

"I would not want to find out, ma'am." He left the door open a crack anyway. "For my sake." He smiled. She didn't return the gesture. Chastened, he asked how he could be of assistance.

"I wanted to talk with you about your mission here, captain."

"You can call me Matt. But do you want to talk about my mission or my team's mission."

"I would assume they are the same, captain." Melis wasn't going to take up his offer on the name change. Strictly professional distance, then.

"They are, ma'am." He motioned for her to sit on one of the two chairs in the room he used for meetings or the infrequent counseling sessions necessitated by his position. He took his place on the edge of his bunk a respectful distance away. In the chair, she looked like a lecturer at the university, a business executive, anything but an officer. He chided himself for the thought. All modern militaries had women soldiers, enlisted and officers. He'd met many and worked with some. Even his mother was already working with the Agency by the time he came around.

He never thought of his Mom as military, however, and maybe that was where he and his father differed. He just accepted Mom in whatever role it was that she did. He needed to accept Melis the same way.

"Then tell me why you're here, Captain Devlin."

"Beyond the fact that we were ordered here, this is why we exist. Assisting nations to resist oppression by training their people."

"That's what it says on your insignia, 'from oppression, a free man.'"

"You must have studied Latin because our translation is 'to liberate the oppressed.' Yours is the correct version."

"Yours is close enough. So why do you want to do this? To volunteer to fight in another country's war, another person's war?"

"First, if Ukraine is any example, we'll be pulled out of here as soon as hostilities break out. But, if we stay, it will be because this is our war too."

"Why?"

"Article Five of the North Atlantic Treaty for one. We can't let Russia do what Stalin did after World War Two."

"And you are willing to fight for that?"

"Either we do it now, or someone else will have to do it later. Look at what's happening where the Russians have taken control again."

"Is that the official position or yours?"

"Both. I support my country's commitment."

"But your country doesn't have the best record for what happens afterwards. Look at Vietnam or Afghanistan."

"I can't argue with you there, although that was mostly politics, but maybe you should think of El Salvador or Grenada."

"You're saying you tend to do better in small places then?"

"Like Lithuania."

Finally, a hint of a smile showed. The wind changed directions.

"What do your parents do?"

"My mother passed away ten years ago. My father is a retired consultant."

"Sorry to hear about your mother. What does your father think of your chosen profession?"

"My father served in the army, and he is the reason I volunteered. And as far as my mom goes, I miss her, but they say a parent shouldn't outlive their children. I think she's happy where she is now."

"I guess there is wisdom to that. But I also wanted to compliment you on your team's efforts. Your men speak good Lithuanian and they have prepared their classes and instruction well. The colonel is pleased."

"And you?" Matt asked.

"For the most part, yes."

"You just worry about the team leader."

"I think that episode is behind us, captain. At least I hope it is."

"Don't worry, commander. We'll not go off the reservation again."

"Off the reservation?"

"It essentially means we won't break the rules again. Hopefully."

"Hopefully."

"And if I may say, your English is quite good."

"Thank you, it's not quite as good as my Russian but I did plan for the future."

Melis' eyes sparkled in the light, something he hadn't seen in her before. And for a moment, briefly, he saw a path open that had been closed, one he took as a sign of trust, something he had never experienced from a woman before.

THE MEN AND WOMEN ON BOARD the helicopters were, simply put, mercenaries. The Turks, Iranians, and Azeris would call them terrorists, the Armenians would call them freedom fighters. They called themselves Peshmerga. Their commander was called Sirwan by everyone. Those who truly knew the man would not discuss his family or his origins. Each of the fighters had adopted their own *nom de guerre* to protect their families back in the homeland.

They had come in only hours before after a harrowingly long flight, launching out of Northern Iraq, fueling up at a forward refuel point, before entering unfriendly airspace. The Mi-17 helicopters had flown low and slow over enemy territory, being shepherded by another, a Mi-19 packed with countermeasures gear to confuse and suppress enemy air defense systems, of which there were many, including Turkish, Iranian, and now Azeri. Although the design was old, these were top-of-the-line machines. Purchased from a middleman in Algeria before being diverted to Iraq months ago, they weren't on anyone's register; the tail numbers, already false, had been removed completely before this mission. The aircraft would end their flight empty, the eighty passengers and their kit having left early somewhere on the edge of Nagorno-Karabakh, before the helicopters lifted off, made a turn, and headed for their new base and owners in Armenia.

Sirwan recruited them to fight for the Armenians in the rebellious enclave with promises of a good salary, medical care, and a gratuity paid to the families in the event of death. Some were skeptical, but when half the salary was passed out after the papers were signed, enthusiasm grew. Of course, many suspected others might be involved behind the scenes. A mysterious man known only as KB held many conversations with Sirwan in Erbil before the deployment, but no one could pin down were he came from. Perhaps because he spoke Arabic fluently and had been overheard speaking what someone thought was Hindi on his satellite telephone. Sirwan knew, but he wasn't saying.

Outside it was dark, the whining of the turbines shrill. These weren't stealth helicopters in that regard, they could be seen and heard from the ground, just not picked up on the radars that dotted the landscape below. An infiltration route had been chosen to avoid known concentrations of the enemy and their air defense systems and it appeared to have been well-plotted.

On the second bird, KB pressed his headphones tight against his ears to listen before turning to Sirwan and flashed the fingers on one hand twice to everyone on board as he leaned in to tell the Peshmerga leader, "Lead aircraft says we're ten minutes out." The same message was passed to the three other birds.

The passengers started checking equipment, hoisting rucksacks up, and cradling their weapons as Sirwan stood up and gave them the signal to stand by. The minutes ticked down slowly. Finally, KB gave a thumbs up. They were on final approach into the landing zone.

Trucks waited on the ground. A small reception party was scattered across the open field, while security teams guarded the single road leading into the area. Any hostile approach would be met by fire. As the Mi-19 circled above, the four other helos settled to the ground, their landing gear flexing from the impact and the weight they carried. The fighters poured out and took up four separate defensive perimeters as the helos lifted off in a still swirling maelstrom of loose grass, brush, and dirt that couldn't be seen, but was felt on everyone's face.

The four aircraft clattered off to the west, leaving silence behind. KB spoke with Sirwan in the center of one group as the leader of the ground party approached them. Recognition signal passed, he came into the circle to conference briefly. Runners went out to the other groups and there was a collective sigh as everyone stood and made their way to their load points.

Vestiges of light began to trace the sky in the east as KB, Sirwan, and the leader watched and listened to the fighters loading onto the trucks. Seventy fighters, split into four groups, began heading for their designated destinations.

"Ten days, Sirwan," KB said. "Cause as much damage as you can, then bring your people out. Call me when you're ready for exfil and we'll be here." KB shook Sirwan's hand and saluted the reception party leader once, then followed it up with a slap on his back. The two men left him standing in the center of the LZ. He heard the noises as the trucks drove off and waited a moment before he spoke into his hand-held, "Ready for pick up."

The Mi-19 returned low over the trees on the edge of the field, swooped in, and touched down lightly for just a moment as KB climbed on board. Then it too was gone. Daylight would arrive soon.

JAMIE WALKED INTO ANDRA BILLINGS' OFFICE unannounced but expected. She knew when she messaged the director to let her know they had made progress, it was only a matter of time before Jamie showed up like a shark to blood in the water.

"What have you got?" he asked.

"We've been tracking military movements around the country trying to figure out where the missile went. There's a lot of information and a lot of static…"

"And?" Jamie was squirming a bit which made Andra happy. She loved to torment the big man.

"A lot of static. But then we concentrated on the strategic rocket forces. Less static, but still static. Then the nuclear forces. Same thing. There is just too much movement to discern."

"You're not making my day bright."

"Bear with me, Jamie. Then we decided on looking at the 12th Chief Directorate of the Ministry of Defense. Probably should have started there, but never mind. Anyway, short history. The 12th GU is located in Sokoliniki in an underground facility northeast of Moscow. A very hardened facility. It's commanded by a Lieutenant General Borokov and he is responsible for everything nuclear. All their communications—telephone, cable, whatever—are encrypted, full stop. No way into them, but that's just within the 12th. When they talk to someone outside, the protocol changes. So, I decided to look at their outside commo and what did we find?"

"You're killing me, Andra."

"Communications with the railway service. Not the cargo or anything, but routing and clearances. We found one interesting thing from several months ago. The 12th ordered the railway service to give priority clearance to a military train originating out of Verkhnyaya Salda, which is located north of Yekaterinburg."

"Why was it interesting and where did it go?" Jamie knew full well the Chief of Analysis wanted to—had to—lay out the entire chain of evidence to his evident discomfort.

"Interesting, because there is a strategic missile base near Verkhnyaya Salda and it was a small train, a single carriage and a couple of flatcars. That would probably mean it carried the mobile launch vehicle, support vehicles, and its crew, plus maybe security. Where did it go? West to the border of Belarus then across and to a final rail stop southeast of Minsk at Asipovichy, which is convenient because the town is home to the Belarusian missile brigade."

"Any confirmation of its final location?"

"Not yet. I've tasked satellite coverage of that whole area. If it's above ground, we'll find it."

"And if it's underground?"

"I doubt it will be. Belarus doesn't have suitable silos. Unless they dug a new one that would fit the RS-28 and there's been no reporting on that."

A manmade breeze rustled the leaves of the fake palms of the Congo Café. Made up to resemble an African jungle, it was all deepfake. Even for the non-reality of Tyson's Mall it was outlandish. Colorful digital holograph projections of peacocks and parrots screamed their calls on a computerized schedule, while a artificial waterfall splashed noisily into a plastic pond filled with giant, living goldfish—the only real thing in the place beside the patrons, shoppers who had been drug into the place by overly excited children, or maybe the old spies who wanted to sit in a place where they could talk without being overheard.

Luckily, it was a weekday and there weren't too many squealing kids around.

Jamie was content with his cheeseburger and fries, drinking overpriced, bottled mineral water while Joshua picked around the crust of his toasted ham and cheese sandwich and tasted the tomato soup, all as he wondered about the food sourcing too, finally deciding that most American fast food was of questionable origin. All in all, however, it was better than a headquarters cafeteria that was operated by a big contractor serving food that confirmed it was only interested in the profit margin.

Jamie reached into his jacket pocket and pulled out his phone. Pushed a series of buttons, he looked at the screen and put it back in his pocket, Jamie said, "Kipling says they're in."

"Was that him?" Joshua asked.

"No, that was the office. He relayed the message through a cut-out in Punjab, who called someone in Chicago, who called headquarters, who called me."

"I hope that's not what he does for Flash traffic."

"There are quicker methods. This was just immediate precedence."

"Comforting. And what does he do when he needs emergency extraction?"

"He has his own air force."

Of course, he does. This is an Agency operation.

"Okay, now what happens?"

"Our surrogates, subcontractors actually, will raise some hell in-country and hopefully help get the Russians to commit more troops into the region."

"Thereby delaying moving into the Baltics."

"Hopefully. We're assuming they can't handle two operations at once."

"I haven't heard anything from Gabriel," Joshua said. "I assumed he was talking to you on his regular covcom system."

"He says it's been quiet on the Eastern Front."

"Things are moving too slow."

"Too slow? Things were crazy for a couple of weeks and now it's calmed down a bit. I think we'll have a bit more time now that Operation Honey Bear has kicked off."

"Honey Bear? Sounds too cute."

"It'll confuse anyone listening to us. Even if they understood, no one would believe it."

"Of course, if they did, it has the potential to rile up at least three nations, crossing their borders with mercenaries and all," said Joshua.

"You're such a pessimist sometimes, they all do the same thing. The Russians sent Wagner to Africa, the Turks have the SNA in Libya, the Iranians use Afghans in Lebanon … it's all fair in love and war. Besides, you seem to forget the things you did in your early days."

"Different person, different name. It wasn't me."

"At least you should be happy to hear that the techs finished the modules. They arrived yesterday. Phillips has them and is working up instructions in Russian on how they need to be installed."

"So, all we have to do is get them to Hammer and then convince him to introduce them into the system."

"He needs to make sure they are actually installed in the missiles."

An excited whoop, whoop, whoop—the pant-hoot of a chimpanzee claiming its territorial dominance—distracted Joshua He looked up into the crown of the palm trees for the source then realized there was no chimp, real or stuffed, to see. It was just another recording. "Does this place make you nostalgic for the jungle?" he asked.

"No, it's too fake and too loud. When we were in the jungle, especially when we were moving, the animals were quiet. They sensed danger."

"From you?"

"They were scared about being caught up in the middle of a firefight, which is how most of our missions ended up."

"What was the longest SOG mission you had?"

"My longest was five days. It was the only one we didn't make contact. The shortest was ten minutes. We landed too close to a North Vietnamese regiment coming down the Ho Chi Minh trail. It was like tripping over a hornet's nest. We realized we screwed up and called for an immediate extract. Luckily, our insert helicopters weren't too far away, and they pulled us out with minimal damage to us or the birds."

FROM HIS SEAT IN THE CAB, Sirwan watched the track ahead as the ex-Soviet army truck, a Ural 375, waddled slowly forward, the low brush scratching its sides as it rolled. In the dark with its headlamps off, the driver tried to make their final approach as quiet as he could. Every rut and bump shook the old truck with a collective crash that was the sum of its parts. Sirwan motioned to the driver with his hand. "Slower, slower."

Moments later, Arkady, the reception party leader held up a hand. "Stop. We're here."

Arkady glanced at him in the dark. "This is the spot you requested from the map. The base is over the ridge line about three kilometers ahead."

"We off-load here. We'll continue on foot. When you hear the action, come forward and wait for us where you see yellow tape tied to a tree on the right side. That will be our rally point. Turn the truck around and when we come back, we will load and go to the base camp." Sirwan pulled a length of hi-visibility tape out of his pocket and showed to the leader and driver. "If we are not at the rally point after one hour, disappear. We will make our own way from that moment. Do you understand that?"

The driver nodded. "Yes, we move forward and wait one hour at the rally point for you to return."

Sirwan and his force leaders had planned out their campaign as best they could, using all the information KB and his friends had provided. None of his Peshmerga had set foot in the region before, so they had to rely on the locals for transport and current information on the situation. Beyond that, he and his people were self-sufficient, not to mention that hidden caches had been stashed before their arrival. He knew he could count on locals to support them if they needed to escape and evade. There was a long history of conflict in the region since the Soviets left. Nagorno-Karabakh was an island of Armenians inside Azerbaijan and both sides had struggled to gain control of the land.

Sirwan and his fighters had no particular attachment to this place—they were mercenaries after all. The assistance KB had given him over the years, and would continue to provide to the Kurdish homeland, was what convinced him to support this operation. Before KB, the American's had been fickle and offered things and took them back before he could grab them. It was a back-and-forth relationship much like two alcoholics in love, who get embarrassed and break up for a while. But when the only other choices are Turks, Syrians, Iraqis, or Iranians, there was not much choice. And kicking the Russians in the teeth for all the grief they'd caused in Syria was a plus. He'd stick with his man in spite of the foibles of KB's masters. Besides, it was kind of a crazy plan, audacious even, maybe that was why he liked it.

The men and women he led made up the smallest of the four groups. Each headed to their own target and hopefully would be on time when they executed their raids. KB wanted the attacks to be simultaneous, or as close to it as one could get without radio contact, to make it appear to be a coordinated offensive. Sirwan told his three other team leaders to observe radio silence and go with a set time. But, for the moment, he had to worry about his own part of the mission and the fourteen fighters under his command.

Getting the job done was the only thing he knew. That had been ingrained in him from his first days as a Peshmerga fighter. His family had been suffocated by Saddam in a gas attack on his village of Halabja. He was in the hills training, and wasn't at home. It was only when his chief told him that he had could not return that he knew he would never see his home or family again. That was 1988, so he stayed with the fighters, doing his best to even the score against the Ba'athists. Since then, he had fought at least three other enemies, now he was about to begin on his fourth.

His group, his team was strung out in front of and behind him. It was roughly five hours until nautical dawn, that magic moment when the sky begins to crack open in the east and scatter its light into the sky. Not sunrise, but almost. He wanted to be gone long before that.

Two fighters in front of him, the point man and his mate. The point man navigating and breaking trail—although there was no trail to break just a dirt track. His mate covered the point man as his immediate backup. Then came Sirwan. Then the rest. The point man stopped ten meters ahead and went to one knee, one hand up. The signal to halt repeated itself down the line. Sirwan closed the gap and looked out over the point man's shoulder. They looked down on the Russian peacekeepers encampment. The front gate across the main road was clearly visible, illuminated by two lights on either side, a small gatehouse, and behind, the silhouettes of several barracks. They knew the layout from the aerial photos KB had shown them. He shifted his rifle to his right hand, taking his left off the foregrip, and squeezed the man's shoulder lightly. This would be the line of departure. The rally point was behind them about nine hundred meters back up the road where they would assemble after the attack. He turned to his deputy and whispered for him to bring up the element leaders. Those two, along with Sirwan, would lead the fighters into action.

Waiting, he went back through his plan to reconfirm details—to make sure it was sound. He saw now at ground level what he'd seen from above in the satellite images KB had given him. The track they were on met the main road close to the gate. With the element leaders at his side, he quietly confirmed their instructions and the timing. The third element would break down into two smaller teams to provide security to the right and left of the road. The second would cross the road and approach from the flank, while his own would engage the gate house first. Two rocket-propelled grenades into the gatehouse would signal the beginning of the attack as his command element moved forward. Then the largest element would attack from the flank. A simple plan because rarely do plans survive first contact intact. The security teams moved first, followed by Sirwan and the gate element, while the largest moved last. If they were compromised en route, they could always do a full-frontal assault. Ground cover was sparse and they had to crawl the last fifty meters, the point man started out and as Sirwan crawled forward, the camp's details became clearer. He could see the sign declaring the facility to be RUSSIAN PEACEKEEPER BASE 5 in four languages, although he could read only one. One soldier sat on a chair tilted against the wall of the gatehouse, his cap tilted down over his eyes. Inside the building, he saw at least two heads through the window. They looked engaged in something like playing a card game. The guards were not on high alert. Behind the gate, two buildings stood with a solitary light over each entrance door. The windows were dark. Sirwan hoped the contingent was sleeping. Reportedly, thirty soldiers were based here. Sirwan could see at least two GAZ trucks parked inside the fence. He realized he was holding his breath, in anticipation or excitement, and exhaled long and slow. From the dim light across the road, he saw it steam in front of him and rise up, to disappear into the night.

No movement. He just hoped the three other Russian check points were as quiet as this one.

Two clicks in his headset. The security teams were in position. He sent one click back. Acknowledged. Now wait some more. Ten minutes later, three clicks. Assault force ready across the road. Acknowledged. Sirwan checked his watch. Almost.

Inching closer to the main road, he positioned the men on either side of him. Reflexively, his hand ran over his AK, checking the safety and that the magazine was well seated, before he turned to his two teammates. They both watched him for the signal. He nodded to each, and looked on as their two RPG-18s slid open and locked in firing position. He checked his watch once more. The minute hand clicked, half past the hour.

Show time. The phrase that KB had used.

He raised himself to one knee and tapped the man on his right with his hand. A whoosh followed by a flaming tail, as first one then a second rocket shot across the road. Almost instantaneously, the soldier on the chair was lifted up and thrown somewhere into the explosion. The second rocket pierced the window and exploded. Glass, wood, and a door blew out across the ground and into the road, while smoke and flame billowed-into the air. The attackers closed their eyes against the brightness of the fires.

"Let's go!" Sirwan's element stood and walked forward at a fast clip, their Kalashnikovs held at the ready. A careful peek in the window of the gatehouse. Three bodies, minimal damage, the blast overpressure killed them. They walked through the gate. A splintered plastic chair lay next to a leg, fatigues and a boot still attached. A mangled corpse lay farther on, neither his hat nor head anywhere to be seen. No live targets yet.

Sirwan halted their progress. He could see the assault element cutting through the fence to their right. He didn't want to stumble into the line of fire and be mistaken for enemy troops. Four light machine-guns were already blasting the two barracks with a twenty-four hundred rounds per minute, sheets of 7.62mm tracer piercing the soft skin of the buildings and any living thing they found inside. As the fence peeled back, grenadiers stepped inside the compound and began to pump rounds into the barracks, thermobaric grenades exploded inside, shockwaves shuddering the ground. The thermobaric grenades were the one thing they carried that the locals didn't possess. Ironically, they came from Libyan stocks—munitions the Russians had provided a while back. Stocks that had been stolen by a rival clan and were acquired by the Agency for deniable contingencies such as this.

"Inside!" yelled the element leader. Grenadiers and machine gunners ceased fire as the assault teams entered the buildings. It was individual shots now, occasional short bursts, as the teams cleared the buildings of the enemy. Flames began to lick at the windows, lighting up the compound outside. Sirwan ran to the first building where his element leader entered and followed him. Using their flashlights to illuminate the interior, the fighters worked their way through the smoke, but it was difficult to see. The inside of this building was torn apart, bunks upturned, ceiling hanging in pieces, bodies and parts of bodies in piles and scattered, resembling a flaming abattoir. All he could hear was crackling fire. "Let's get out of here."

The element leader gave the command and his fighters moved quickly outside. The men began to form up to head for the rally point.

Sirwan walked up to the first GAZ and fired a burst with his rifle through the hood into the engine bay and then did the same to the second.

As they trotted up the track toward the rally point, the assault force leader caught up to Sirwan from behind. "We lost Dushka."

"What happened?"

"Friendly fire, I think. He was hit in the back near the other barracks. We left him behind."

The fighter nick-named for his prowess with the truck-mounted 12.7mm machine-gun, Dushka was a bear of a man, soft-spoken, liked by all. It was Sirwan's first loss of this campaign. He looked back at the flames of the camp and began to recite a poem of Rumi's, "don't shed any tears, don't lament, or feel sorry. I have done my duty." To himself he said, "We couldn't carry him home anyway." He turned back to the track ahead. "The leaflet is on his body?"

"Yes, Sirwan."

"Then he will continue to serve our purpose. The Russians will find the propaganda on him." Sirwan began to walk then trot again. "Quickly now, to the rally point."

At a trot, one thousand meters is not so far, and the time went quickly. The Ural was where it was supposed to be with its tailgate down, the two left behind as guards stood on either side. One fighter began to climb into the back when Sirwan stopped him and brought them all in close to speak, a quick communion.

"Brothers and sisters. We have lost one of our best. Dushka died a soldier. But we must not mourn him. He will not lament us because he is ready to meet us on the other side as a comrade. But if we should live, say his name. Remember him." He paused, head down. Then he took charge again. "Load up." He turned to Arkady. "Get us out of here."

"IMAGINE THAT," said Jamie. "Seems the Azeri have violated the truce. Four attacks on Russian check points and barracks inside the so-called neutral zone. Heavy casualties." He was on his iPad reading the Early Bird briefing, the Pentagon's unclassified intel wrap-up. He'd already breezed through the classified briefs on his secure computer in the office before joining Joshua at the pub.

Daniel O'Connell's was one of Joshua's favorite haunts in Old Town for a good Guinness with corned beef and cabbage on the side. Second only to Ireland's Own. But Ireland's Own was long gone, so he had to make do. O'Connell was more his favorite because he knew Jamie wasn't one for fish and chips, being more a fresh poke kinda guy. But good Hawaiian food was rare on the mid-Atlantic coast.

"Heavy losses on both sides?"

"The Russians say so, but our sources say they were pretty lop-sided, about one hundred Russians and only a few attackers. Moscow is pissed off with the government in Baku right now. Naturally, Baku wants to blame the rebels."

"The Russians bought the deception?" Joshua asked.

"KB thinks so. For the moment at least."

The propaganda leaflets the teams carried and dropped around the targets outlined Azeri complaints and demands for territory, an aim to push the Armenians completely out of Nagorno-Karabkh. They were forged by a guy with a print shop in Mosul that KB had recruited.

"Where is KB now?"

"He's sitting in Yerevan monitoring things. Hopefully, he'll be able to extract the force in several days, but it'll be like going into a hornet's nest."

"And in the meantime, back to Europe?"

"Yes, but you first. I'll follow after you link up with Batman."

"Did I tell you he's not fond of that name?"

"You may have said something, but it's one of those nicknames that sticks once you get tagged with it."

"Did you ever have a nickname?"

Jamie started to say something but stopped himself. "I can't remember."

"Right, like I'm supposed to believe you. There are a few guys I can ask, like some of your old SOG buddies."

"We always end up talking about the old days and mostly about my time in Vietnam. Why is that?"

"Maybe I live vicariously though you," said Joshua.

"You have enough adventures to talk about. Why don't you write a book?"

"Not likely. You'd probably demand to clear it. Anyway, how do you suggest we proceed with Hammer? To convince him to get the modules inserted? It's not like we have any leverage over him."

Joshua sensed that Jamie didn't want to talk about his time in the service. Like many Vietnam vets he mostly wanted to forget about his previous life. Every vet Joshua knew said there were good moments, mostly off duty. Traveling. The teammates. It was the time in the bush they wanted to forget, the faces of lost comrades who haunted them at night.

Jamie was quiet.

"Gabriel should determine how to handle him on this one. Hammer is his asset, and he knows him best. Gabe has the most experience and more recruitments of key players than anyone I know. Moreover, he's handled some really hard targets. He's got the gift."

Jamie meant the gift of being able to not only convince someone to spy on their country, but to continue to handle that same person over the long haul as well. Most case officers could do one or the other very well, but both, not so much. A CO who could do both things well, that was rare. More importantly, he was not going to give advice to Gabriel. A guy with that many scalps didn't really need much coaching.

Once the work talk ended, a friendly banter ensued with Jamie wondering why Joshua would want subject himself to the Irish scene after the bad experiences he had there long ago. Joshua only said, "a little masochism is good for soul once in a while." But then he didn't want to talk details either.

Jamie looked at his watch and declared he needed to head back to the office. Although the days of the three-martini lunch were long gone, he still had the latitude (and rank) to do whatever he wanted. The only person who could call him out was Clairissa, but she was his wife's friend and cut him slack. They cleared out of the pub and stood for a moment on the street, mostly empty on a mid-afternoon weekday.

Jamie shook his hand, "I'll see you tomorrow morning at the annex. We'll go over the modules, so you can instruct Hammer."

"I am so looking forward to that. Hammer seems to have no patience for anything his minions could do for him." Joshua turned to walk away.

A couple of blocks from the pub, Joshua hopped, or rather folded himself into his car, which he'd parked off the main drag. For once, he was driving something he actually owned rather than a rental. His townhouse wasn't far and there he could put together his travel plan to link up with Gabriel again. Since Jamie had said to make things happen, he decided his contract provisions would allow him to book a first class set on the first thing smoking out of Dulles after the session tomorrow.

Sitting at one of the many ill-timed traffic lights on King Street in Old Town (a cunning conspiracy by city planners to dissuade motor vehicles), Joshua thought a bit about his chosen trade. Experience counted in the Agency. Left unsaid in the recruitment brochures, however, was that knife handling skills were very valuable to negotiate the corridors of power at Langley. Case officers, highly trained in the arts of spreading and detecting deception and disinformation, were formidable opponents in this regard.

He was starting to look forward to the end. One last job—this one—and he could punch out once and for all.

Although it might require Jamie's untimely death so he can't recruit me again.

THE ANNEX WASN'T FAR FROM THE INTERSTATE, hidden in plain sight among warehouse complexes, tiny businesses operating on a shoestring, and a huge tank yard, all roped together by roads crowded with eighteen-wheelers and Latino food trucks. It was not at all the picturesque vista afforded the residents of Langley or the Farm, but then its function was different. The annex was where toys got tweaked and things got moved in and out of the country. It was close to two international airports and one seaport.

Joshua saw the facility and knew instantly he was in the right place: military-grade security that surrounded the facility and a sign announcing the big aluminum-clad building belonged to FEMA. Outsiders might just ignore it as another waste of government money but what was inside told another story.

Joshua didn't use his own car to get to the annex. He put his car in for service and used the shop's loaner instead. Anyone who tried to track his car would have some serious digging to do. Jamie was already there, as was Gladys Thompson, Tom Hopman, and Mark Phillips, all there to see the newest gadgets, and one man who actually knew how everything worked. Garth Locke was one of those people who could build a super-computer from old cell phone parts and explain what he built in simple English.

A strange resemblance to Q's laboratory in the Bond movies made Joshua think he could find some interesting gadgets he could steal. Locke apparently sensed this and kept a close watch until his visitors were ushered into a small workshop, almost but not quite a clean room.

On the table in front of Locke was the printed Russian schematics and what looked to be a motherboard. He explained the set up and pointed to the key component, the American module. "We got twenty of the modules and reprogrammed them to shut down two minutes after the launch sequence begins. Half are marked like the originals, half are marked in Chinese, as if they came from one of their factories. We thought you might want a choice."

"What if they do an extended test on the modules?" Phillips asked.

"They will function perfectly. Shutdown will only happen when an accelerometer tells the module the missile has actually been launched."

Locke went through the method for replacing the module and presented instructions in English, Russian, and Chinese. "We may produce some more in Korean if this works. Might as well see if we can seed the world with defective parts."

Twenty modules individually packed and grouped by their supposed origin were on the table. "You want to take them now?" Locke asked.

"No. Courier them to Frankfurt Base so they'll be ready. We'll take them as soon as we're ready to pass them on," Jamie said.

Locke nodded. A courier could be moving within hours.

Joshua knew he couldn't carry the devices through an airport. The risk was too high, and he didn't even know when and where the next phase would begin. From this point on, everything would depend on Gabriel and Hammer.

Locke followed everyone out to the parking area. Joshua had the impression he was counting all his gadgets as they walked and was disappointed. He remembered that Bond never signed a Q-hand receipt for his toys.

Jamie sent the others off and walked with Joshua to his car. "I think I've said this already, but the next stage is critical and will be the most difficult. I told Gabriel he has full authority on this case. No need to ask permission. Commit whatever you need as long as it makes sense."

"Whatever we need?"

"Whatever. You'll need it if you're going to pull a rabbit out of a hat."

"Got it. See you over there soon then?"

"Soon enough, Joshua. Keep an eye on Gabriel and make sure you both come home alive."

As he watched Joshua drive away, Jamie said to himself, *"E hele maluhia e kuʻu kaikunāne."* *Go in peace my brother.*

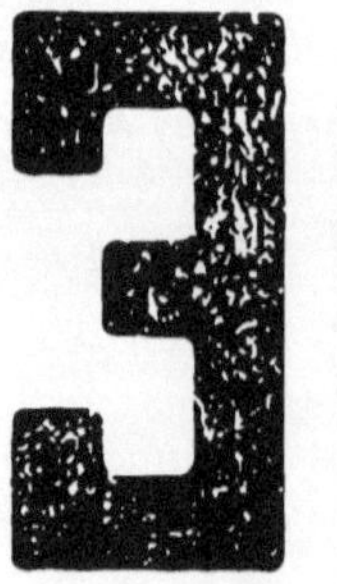

GABRIEL'S LITTLE DUMP, as he called it, was more impressive than Joshua had imagined. A freestanding, old stone house near Valletta's Triq Marina surrounded by an equally old wall, but the old seemed to disappear as soon as the front gate was breached. Once inside, it was modern Mediterranean.

Joshua rotated in place looking at the view, the house, and the marina beyond.

"Location, location, location," Gabriel said. "It was cheap, an estate sale."

"You have a boat down there too?"

"No. Boats are a hole in the water where you dump money. And I'm not a sailor, but I can charter one if I need to and kick back on the deck."

"Your career choices seem to have put you in good stead."

"Life is good and when I retired, I took my business private, so to speak."

"How?"

"I paid back Uncle Sam for all the stuff he bought and went solo, doing consulting work. And I get called back for special engagements like this one."

"And the Maltese citizenship?"

"Paid for with profits. No one could figure out how to make me surrender it, so they decided I could keep it with conditions."

"Conditions being…"

"Availability to do contract work for ten years. I like it here, so it was a good deal."

"I'll say." Across the inlet, a wave crashed against the sea wall with enough force to be heard two hundred meters away. A gaggle of sea birds circling above the marina answered with their cries. Dozens of sail and power boats rolled in the wave's backwash.

Joshua followed Gabriel inside. A compact house built around an open courtyard garden, water gurgled and splashed in an old fountain standing in a circle of stone. Next to it was a small orange tree. He looked up to see a second-floor balcony connecting the rooms in a square.

"There were twelve separate rooms up there, but they were too small for modern living, so I had them opened up. Now there are five. I thought you could stay here if you wanted."

Joshua had anticipated that and didn't make reservations at any old haunts where they knew him by another name from long ago. "I'd love to, thanks. Who takes care of the house when you're gone?"

"I have a person, Eva Maria. And don't worry about being assassinated or anything, I had her checked out."

"Good, it's bad form to let the staff murder your guests. What's for dinner?"

"Take your stuff up to that room." Gabriel pointed at a room on the side facing the marina. "We'll eat about half six."

As he climbed the wooden staircase, Joshua focused on the details. The well-scrubbed stones of the inner courtyard walls had been left exposed, while those on the upper floor were plastered over not long ago. The wood of the balcony, the balustrades, the floor to ceiling support posts, as well as the flooring was a deep brown, waxed mahogany, probably African and very old.

Whoever owned this house before Gabriel had taken took good care of it. But the new owner's touch became apparent when Joshua walked into his room. Spartan. He took off his shoes at the entry. Japanese tatami covered the floor, a raised sleeping platform with a futon was centered along one wall. Most striking was the grouping of woodblock prints on the opposite wall. Kuniyoshi, if he remembered the artist correctly. The tale of the 47 Ronin, as martial as anything the Greeks could devise, but more appropriate to Gabriel's origins.

He dropped his suitcase and looked out the long double window. A small balcony beckoned but only if he wanted to sit in the direct afternoon sun. It might be a good place for morning coffee before descending to the courtyard. He was always a bit envious of the places he visited. His own home, with its individual trinkets and pieces he'd gathered from around the world and haphazardly strewn about, had no style. But then he wasn't a decorator.

After a brisk rinse in the modern Italian rain-shower and a short nap on the all-enveloping futon, he felt relaxed enough to go down to the courtyard. There he found a table laid out with a pitcher of fresh-pressed lemonade, an ice bucket, and some cookies. He skipped the cookies and sat on a well-cushioned divan to contemplate the splashing rhythm of the falling water. Eyes closed, sipping his drink, he was reminded of a similar home in Damascus. A *mezuzah* had been affixed to the entryway of that home, which surprised Joshua until the owner explained how religious tolerance ruled the ancient Syrian city. He wondered how the Jews fared today in that war-torn country. Malta was by far a more peaceful country unless you happened to be a journalist who specialized in uncovering corruption. But today it was quiet.

A little later, Gabriel padded down the stairs. Joshua heard the tinkle of ice cubes, the pouring of juice, and a stir of the glass before he opened his eyes. "It's very peaceful here."

"It is. This is my safe haven and a good place to return to after work." Gabriel sat and stared into the water as Joshua had done. "It can be mesmerizing, but it's also relaxing. I like to listen to the fountain at night. When the city is quiet, that's all I can hear."

"Better than melatonin?"

"Non-addicting too." Gabriel smiled his inscrutable smile. He found humor in strange places. "How do like your room?"

"It's nice. Very Japanese. Did you study kendo?"

"Not so much. My core martial arts training was long complete—that is, I had little need of a teacher. I practiced and improved, but in Japan, I studied Bushido, the Way, the teaching behind my chosen path."

"You had time for that and a career?"

"It was my career. Then I came to the States."

"With your family?"

"I lost most of my family in Mongolia long before that. I escaped to China with an uncle. I studied there until I was able to leave."

"To Japan?"

"Macau. Japan after that."

"How did you end up in the States."

"An American was studying at the same dojo in Aizuwakamatsu. He convinced me to apply for college and I got a student visa."

"Where did you go?"

"Berkeley. I joined the Asian studies program, which was pretty easy because I knew the languages and the culture. I ended up being an intern, got a second degree in business and then this guy from Washington visited me. It's been downhill ever since."

"It makes sense that they hired you for your background."

"Of course, that and my connections to the Triad."

Joshua sputtered and coughed. "The Triad?"

"Long story. Better told later. But think Mongolia, China, Macau, and Japan. The Triad is the most efficient network in Asia has connections in all those places. Come, I see Eva Maria is at the door. That means dinner is waiting."

Supper was simple. Grilled marinated swordfish on a bed of vegetables with capers and olives. And lots of olive oil. White wine, a light one, not too sweet, appellation unknown, but tasty, came with the meal. Joshua knew only enough about wine to judge if it tasted good or not, Sarah had been his sommelier after all.

"I hope you like the capers and olives," said Gabriel.

"I'm Greek. Capers and olives are part of my DNA."

Polite talk coupled with the clink of silverware on china, then coffee. Joshua settled back and looked at the painting over the sideboard. It looked like a Gauguin, colorful, bright, a mountain landscape, not one of his more common depictions of Tahitian women. Gabriel caught Joshua's look, glanced over his shoulder, and saw what he was appraising.

"It was a gift from a client. I don't think it's an original," he said.

"Probably better that way. A real Gauguin wouldn't be safe outside a museum."

Gabriel's eyes briefly acknowledged Joshua's assessment of his painting.

"Agreed, that's why I tell everyone it's a forgery." With that he folded his napkin and tossed it on the table. "Let's go to my study."

A study. Not a library, an office, or a man cave. A study. And when Gabriel opened the door, he saw that it was indeed, a study. A desk, bookshelves along one wall, an oak table to sit four but with only two chairs, and in front of the desk, two tufted, green leather easy chairs. Between the chairs was a table with a decanter of what Joshua guessed was single malt. No artwork this time, just a large map of the world hanging over two map cases against another wall. Gabriel shut the double doors and the pressure on Joshua's ears increased.

Not a study—a war room.

"We've got a lot to do and not much time," Gabriel said.

"Have you heard from Hammer?"

"Not yet, but I think we should begin to put things in motion so we can spend as much time with him as necessary."

"You know what he must do for us then?"

"Jamie gave me the short version over my covcom, which was that we have to convince him to put the gizmos into the missiles."

"That as clear a mission statement as anything I could come up with."

"Okay, so how do we do this? I have some ideas, but you go first."

"We call him out on a pretext, that way we can control the terrain. Before that, I need to have the modules passed to me in whatever country we decide to meet him in, which will be where?"

"In the entire history of this case, we have never initiated a meeting. He's always said when and where. But I think we should do Lithuania again."

"You're not worried about meeting twice in the same country? Last time we had some unintended consequences. And the locals might be more curious to see us again."

"I'm pretty sure Hammer is being more careful with his staff after your affair in Berlin. We could have had that happen anywhere and it could happen again. Look at Baku or what happened in Sofia. If the

Russians want you, they have long arms. The locals … I'm not worried about them. They're our allies remember?"

"You make it sound like a Len Deighton novel… we'll call it *The Berlin Affair*." Joshua made air quotes around his words.

"His novels have it the other way around, they're art imitating life. Now, what's the reason for our meeting?"

"It's an emergency. We just need the right excuse."

Gabriel contemplated the wall across from him, adopting his best Auguste Rodin pose. "That's an idea, but the emergency will have to be something from our side, not his. We don't know enough about his world to make anything up about the Russians. But there just might be another way."

ANDRIY KUZNETSOV SAT in the conference room and listened as each of the men around the table lay out the reasoning behind their recommendations. Each and every man—for there were no women this deep inside the president's Novo Ogaryovo residence—was convinced he was right and his was the best way forward.

Volodya listened patiently at the far end of the table, and it was far. The president sitting at one end, his ministers at the other end of a ten-meter table, a firewall of emptiness between them.

Andriy couldn't help but think it was an appropriate metaphor for the situation. No one ever got close to the boss. There was: Petrakov, security council; Belyaev, FSB; Shoygin, Defense; and the dead Korlov's replacement, Viktor Solovyov, the new kid in town from the SVR. From the nonsense Solovyov spouted, he must have been educated by his witless boss. The only man missing was Ivanov, but the foreign minister usually had little to contribute. His foreign policy declarations had all been written by the president's staff under Volodya's direct guidance.

Each of the ministers present had an assistant to take notes and remind them of things when they couldn't remember, which was becoming common as more and more of the *Siloviki, Nomenklatura,* and *Apparatchiks* fell out of windows. *Defenestrate,* an occupational hazard resurrected in Czechoslovakia after the Great Patriotic War. It was a lovely French word probably written on the insignia of *Vega,* the SVR unit responsible for doing such things, so-called wet work or just special tasks.

Shoygin argued for a change to the country's first strike policy. Andriy would not interrupt or interject. He waited for a question from Volodya, otherwise he would remain silent.

Luckily, Petrakov pushed back. "What exactly would that accomplish?"

"If we destroy the American's nuclear strike capability first," Shoygin said, "then our plans can go ahead with no resistance."

"And you expect your first strike to take out all of their nuclear triad? All that needs to remain is one submarine, let's say the *USS Rhode Island*, a submarine from the smallest state in America. It carries twenty-four ICBMs… twenty-four! That's more than any one of our boats. And we have no idea where she is or, for that matter, where any of the American submarines might be in any of the oceans around the world. If any one of them survives your first strike, Russia will cease to exist."

There was an uneasy quiet around the table. The president tapped the table with his pen, signaling everyone to pay attention. Volodya spoke in measured cadence, his words carefully chosen and directed to Shoygin. "Nicolei, your spokesman may announce that Russia's current stance on the use of first strike is being discussed at the highest levels. That will alarm our enemies. I will also instruct Ivanov to immediately deny those discussions. Then maybe several news outlets leak stories of arguments at the highest levels. That will also confuse our enemies as to our true intentions. It is best that we keep them off balance."

Shoygin nodded and kept his head down a moment in subservience.

Volodya smiled at him coldly, as if he was forgiving a sin. "Now, I would like to ask a question. Why did our military and our equipment fail so badly in the Ukraine operation? Yes, we overcame the fascists, but at what cost? What are you doing to remedy this, Minister Shoygin?"

Andriy shivered at Volodya's use of the title minister instead of general. It was a sign of his disgust with Shoygin, who began to answer but was stopped short by Volodya's wave of the hand. Andriy saw his other hand under the table push a call button. *What now?*

The conference room door cracked open, and an aide stuck his head in. Another wave, this one a summons to whomever waited outside. The aide disappeared to be replaced by a ceremonial guard in uniform who held the door open for a bald man with a paunch.

Dressed in a bespoke suit, dripping privilege, the man sauntered in eyeing everyone present with disdain.

Everyone except the president.

Here I am, he appeared to say. *Here to save you all from yourselves.*

Andriy had a hard time believing what he saw. He was called the Chef, but his real name was Dmitriy Pritzkhin. He had been caterer to the Kremlin, but now he styled himself as the Chairman of Wagner: the biggest Private Military Company in Russia. It was all very simple, what the military couldn't do legally, Wagner PMC could do privately for a price. Except nothing was done privately in Russia, especially in the field of security and defense. Wagner was Volodya's private praetorian guard.

Shoygin turned red, even more surprised by Pritzkhin's appearance. A sight which normally would have amused Andriy, but not now. Pritzkhin's presence was unheard of—a civilian contractor in a national security conference?

Pritzkhin sat in a chair at the middle of the table, smiling his ingratiating smile, closer to the president than anyone. Andriy was directly across from him but not at the table. He sat against the wall with the notetakers, luckily removed from what he thought was about to erupt into a serious squabble.

Volodya took a sip of his private stock of chemically tested, pure water and clasped both his hands together on the table, leaning forward like a man with the weight of the world on his shoulders. "I invited Comrade Pritzkhin here today to announce that I have chosen his Wagner group to lead the SVO—our special military operation into Lithuania. He has succeeded in recruiting nearly one hundred thousand men and has begun to position them inside Belarus. I base my decision on the fact that Comrade Pritzkhin's brigade was the only successful unit in the last SVO. When it reached the enemy's capital, Kyiv, his forces completed the victory celebrations against the enemy's leadership in record time. Therefore, it is just, that his troops lead the upcoming operation." Pritzkhin beamed with pride.

Andriy scoffed inside. *Successful?* Perhaps, if you count over fifty percent casualties taken in the process. The only reason his force made it to Kyiv was because the Russian army fought a real war against real troops, while Wagner slipped around the rear and came in the back door. He shuddered when he thought of the so-called victory celebrations as well.

Defenestrate was mild compared to what happened in the city after its capture. The United Nations would hang Pritzkhin for the atrocities his quote-unquote soldiers committed there—that is if they ever had the balls to capture him.

Shoygin, who was now a shade of purple, looked to the others around the table. They all seemed equally surprised. *Volodya showed his true colors.* Just when he thought he understood the man or at least knew what he was about to do … Bam! a round-house to the head. He should have seen this was coming.

The president turned to face Pritzkhin directly. "Comrade, when will your forces be ready to begin operations?"

"Three weeks, Comrade President."

Volodya nodded and looked to the others. "We have delayed the Baltic operation because of the unpleasant situation in Nagorno-Karabakh and the requirement to deploy reinforcements to calm the situation there. With the Wagner's readiness for action, I think we can now plan on Day Zero, the initiation of operations, four weeks from today. Nicolei, I expect your forces will be able to support this operation?"

"Yes, Comrade President. And, if I may…" He seemed to expect the president him to stop him from speaking again. Instead, Pynya cocked his head to one side, he waited, listening.

Sweating and embarrassed in front of his peers, Shoykin took a breath and continued, "The deficiencies you noted have been corrected. Our material reserves have been built back up with acquisitions from outside the motherland and or training has accommodated the lessons learned from Ukraine. We are ready."

Andriy knew nothing of the sort had happened. The Russian Army fought old battles using techniques learned from combat with inferior adversaries in Syria and Central Asia. Little had been learned in the Ukraine debacle. Brute force was the military's mantra. Line up the artillery pieces wheel to wheel and pound the enemy into submission. There still was no competent non-commissioned officer corps and most of the promising young officers were dead. The equipment that Korlov was to have acquired during his trip to Sofia was nowhere in sight and now Russia was about to take on the Baltic nations and probably NATO with a mercenary force leading the way.

Volodya didn't bat an eye. "I hope so, Nicolei. I hope so." He stood and everyone in the room followed suit. As Volodya walked toward the doors to his office they opened as if someone knew exactly when he would reach them. Two guards took up their places, standing at attention in the opening.

The room emptied quickly through the door at the opposite end, principals followed by notetakers. Andriy followed behind then caught up with Petrakov. "Comrade Petrakov…"

Petrakov turned. "Comrade Kuznetsov. An interesting meeting, no?"

"Indeed. A question, if I may. Perhaps indiscreet, but do you think Shoykin maybe a bit far out from the shore?"

"Andriy, you always talk in riddles. Do I think he is incompetent or just a fool? Is that what you're asking? Because, yes, I think Shoykin is both. I wish we had a defense minister worth his salt because the next phase of this operation will test us all."

"You have no reservations about going ahead with this special military operation?"

"Absolutely none. It was I who suggested to the president that Pritzkhin be used. I think that will shake Shoykin enough that he gets his act together and performs. It is critical. Do you not agree with the plan?" said Petrakov.

"Comrade, I am here to only give counsel. I don't make plans, but I am not sure Shoykin is up to the task."

"Who would you suggest is up to it?"

"Marshal Zhukov is not available. Beyond him, I have no idea."

"We have no Zhukov these days."

"I wish that wasn't the case, but it seems to me that this timeline is rushed. Not all our military's problems have been rectified."

Petrakov regarded him for a moment. "Have you always been such a shrinking violet when it comes to offensive action?"

"No, I just wish our tools were sharper." Andriy was now certain that no one at the top would oppose the upcoming operation.

"We overcame the West's best weapons in Ukraine. After they saw how Wagner cleaned the fascists out, NATO will have no stomach to fight us in the Baltic countries," Petrakov boasted.

"You are correct, of course. We will be victorious, comrade." He watched Petrakov walk away down the hallway. *The Beast may be victorious, but I fear for Mother Russia.*

Another *Siloviki* with no conscience. The place was full of them. Andriy shook his head at the thought and turned to leave, only to see someone with a badge scurrying toward him. One of the staff he'd seen before, one of the nameless minions of the president. "Comrade Kuznetsov, President Pynya would like a word with you."

He smiled and thanked the young man. Asked his name. You never knew when a small connection might be useful. Followed him down the hall and through another set of ceremonial doors into an anteroom. He'd been here many times, sometimes in the middle of the night. The office held no special place in his thoughts other than concern for his country. The president could do whatever he wanted and would, but Andriy doubted he would end up on the sidewalk of ten-story apartment building. He gave advice, he posed no threat to Volodya.

There were no guards to be seen. They weren't needed. No one could penetrate the residence this far without authorization. The male secretary reacted to the light changing to green on his desk, stood up and directed Andriy to the second set of doors, the inner sanctum. He stepped inside.

"Welcome Andriy." A familiar smile from Volodya. More relaxed than a moment ago when the man dealt with his cadre of ministers. He stood in front of his desk—a good sign. If he sat behind it, that meant he was occupied or disturbed by something. Volodya motioned him to sit and followed suit at the table. Another good sign. If the meeting was to be hostile, a visitor remained standing.

Andriy found the president's office revealing and, although it was not as large as the one in the Kremlin, it was still ostentatious. It reeked of Imperial Russia even though it was built in the 1950s. A gold, double-headed Russian eagle on the wall, massive crystal chandeliers, and the huge Kazakh carpets on the floor. On the other hand, Pynya exuded the exact opposite. Subtly dressed, a dark gray suit and deep blue tie, without ornamentation, he appeared to be a simple man. Decorations and medals were for his followers.

Andriy thought of Adolf Hitler, who wore the simple Iron Cross he earned as a corporal in the trenches of World War I, while his minions designed their uniforms with ever larger medals they custom-ordered just for themselves. A seemingly common man, but egotistical and confident beyond measure. Like Hitler, Volodya believed in his infallibility. "I am Russia and I alone will make our country great again." His hero, Czar Peter the Great, couldn't have said it better.

"What did you think of our meeting?" the president asked.

"Enlightening. To be frank, I don't think Shoykin is ready for this next task. The things he told you were not true."

"In what way?"

"In almost every way. The military, especially the army, is poorly trained, fighting old wars, without good leadership. And the equipment we need has not yet arrived. Unfortunately, the death of Korlov slowed or stopped acquisitions through his channels and Solovyov has not been able to get the supply lines up and running again."

"That is why I chose Pritzkhin to lead the operation."

"I understand. A brilliant idea. To push Shoykin to perform. But doesn't your choice of Pritzkhin serve another reason as well?"

"What do you think?"

"To exact vengeance. Vengeance against NATO, vengeance against the petty leaders of the Baltic nations…" Andriy knew exactly what Volodya wanted to accomplish, and Petrakov had confirmed Pritzkhin was part of it.

"Comrade Kuznetsov, you understand me well. Yes, that is my goal. The West has pushed us far enough and now we will push back. And Pritzkhin's troops will make them regret opposing us."

"Comrade President, it is time, I agree. But Pritzkhin leading the assault is only a half-measure. Better leadership is required but if we are to win conclusively, we need better equipment. I have an idea that will help us achieve that goal."

"What is that?"

"The weapons that give us grief on the battlefield are not Russian, they are western. Simply put, there are too many different types, shapes, and sizes for us defeat them all easily."

"And what do you propose as a solution?"

"A suggestion, Comrade President. We should acquire the same weapons and turn them against their masters."

JOSHUA WAS BACK IN VILNIUS, thinking he might be part of some strange travel group. A different tour in a different foreign city every couple of days, and now he'd returned to the start point again. The good thing was the first round of Russia's new operation didn't seem ready to go off just yet. The only other thing to consider was whether this would be the final mission with a happy ending or, he supposed, a mission with a lousy ending.

Can't let that happen. Too many friends are counting on a happy ending.

The little bar was busy. Something was in the air like before a well anticipated football match or the holidays. Not quite the day of an event but getting close. The people appeared in good spirits, so Joshua wasn't worried that he would re-read the news later and find he'd missed something.

Maybe Gabriel knew, but he wasn't here yet. There were some nice-looking women, some even close to his age, but he wouldn't ask them. One even spotted him in the crowd and with a smile and a nod told him she'd noticed him. Joshua knew he was in reasonably good shape and not hard on the eyes for his age, but he didn't want to get conversationally entangled with a woman when a meeting was about to happen, that could be awkward. He smiled back shrugged to show that he was waiting for someone and stayed rooted to his table. He played nursemaid to two glasses of a not bad local brew, his half-liter growing smaller while the still absent Gabriel's remained the same.

It had been a while since he'd been in a bar overseas and he wondered for a while why he could see so clearly. His memory was of dark places, fogged with smoke. There had been a lot of that in the subterranean bars of Berlin and elsewhere.

That was it, no one was smoking. New health guidelines and rules, clear air, he could discern details, like the look on Gabriel's face as he walked in.

Gabriel took his place at the table and immediately grabbed his beer and quaffed a third of it before he looked at Joshua and gave him a conspiratorial grin.

"What did you do now?" Joshua asked.

"Some idiot outside said something about slant eyes, it doesn't translate well. Anyway, you know this country is racist, don't you?" He didn't allow time for a response. "I said something back."

"What?"

"Nothing much. Just that we Mongols would have occupied this country, but it was filled with too many shitheads."

"I imagine that went over well."

"I don't know, I said it in Lithuanian and they pretended not to understand, so I said it again in Russian. That surprised them."

"They try to move on you?'

"One almost did. There were three of them, but I wagged my finger, and they went away."

"No bodies in the streets? You did well in the conflict resolution class, I see."

"I don't remember any bodies. I just hate assholes. What's up with you?"

"Not much. I was thinking about practicing my elicitation skills with the women but thought I'd better wait for you."

"Go for it, Grasshopper." He looked over the prospects.

"Nah, you're far more interesting. We have things to talk about anyway."

"Like?"

Gabriel could be fun when it suited him. They'd just traveled across Europe to work, and he wants to pretend it was boys' night out.

"I dunno, maybe seeing your boy."

"He's yours now too. Have you picked up the stuff?"

"Not yet. The office is standing by. When you tell me we're on, I'll call for them." Joshua thought it smart not to have the modules on him until absolutely necessary.

"I sent Andriy a message and am waiting for his reply."

"What did you say?"

"I told him we have information of great import to give him, and that we need to meet."

"That's it?"

"That's it."

"Stunning in its simplicity." Joshua wasn't sarcastic. "I should have thought of that."

"You did, kind of."

"By suggesting nothing? You're too kind with your praise. Has he answered?"

"Not yet, I only sent the message this morning and it usually takes several hours to go through the system each way. Then he'll have to arrange travel. Hopefully, he won't balk at meeting at the same place. That means we should have some free time. Have you seen your son yet?"

"I hope to see him tomorrow, unless something else comes up."

"Then you can do it with a hangover." Gabriel took another large swig of beer.

"I have a feeling I've seen this movie before."

"You probably have. We tend to do this a lot. A friend once told me that this job was mainly about solitude and time-wasting. Both are occupational hazards."

"Smart man. Who was he?" Joshua said.

"He's still with us. A fellow NOC."

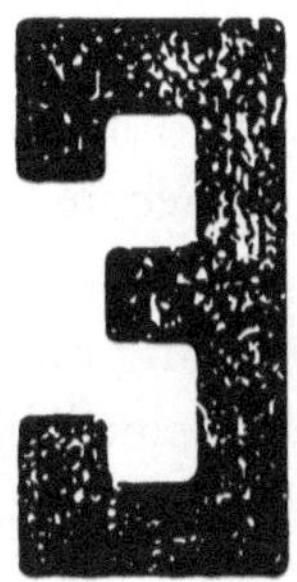

LEAVING THE BASE WAS ALWAYS the weak point in Matt Devlin's extracurricular activities. The guards knew him on sight and any thought of using a disguise was ridiculous. He was convinced that the moment his taillights went through the gate, his absence was reported to Commander Melis as a priority requirement. "The American has left the compound," could be the message, just like Elvis. There were two other American captains on the base, two other team leaders, but as they related their stories, he realized he was the only one Melis gave a damn about probably because the others hadn't irritated her yet.

This evening would be different. The three captains, along with two of the warrants—one warrant stayed behind to do his laundry, read a book, babysit the troops or whatever excuse he used because he was the loner—hopped in the unit van. No matter. Five was a good number for what Matt had in mind.

Their van left the base and followed a simple route for the old town section of Vilnius. No evasion, sudden lane changes, randomized routes, or stair-stepping through the neighborhoods. It was all above board. Follow us and know exactly where we're going and what we intend to do. They didn't need a surveillance team or police chatter to tell Melis where they were located. They arrived in the city center and parked in a hotel garage to keep it off the street. Matt made sure he stared into the CCTV when they drove in. *Here I am, commander!*

They clambered out of the van and headed for their target—Popov's, a bar of some repute. Usually there's nothing like the raucous scene five American soldiers cause when they arrive in an overseas bar. They tried for the opposite effect and disappeared into the crowd. Popov's was chosen because it was well known, already surveyed, and the back exits known. The owner, a friend of one of the team, was cooperative to a degree. He agreed to hold a table for a small contribution to his building fund, which acted as their secure base. Initial rounds of alcohol were ordered and the five became part of the scene, moving about, practicing card tricks, and engaging everyone present. In the confusion, the crushing melee inside helped hide Devlin when he made a call of nature and slipped out the back door—he'd told his team he only needed an hour.

The park wasn't far. Matt walked with determination. His footsteps echoed on the narrow streets despite the rubber soles of his shoes. He wasn't alone. He shared the streets with the occasional pensioner heading home with a grocery trolly, university students heading out to the bars, and solitary cars passing by. No repeats, no coincidences, he managed a somewhat logical route to confirm Melis's trackers weren't on his tail.

Whomever they were—military intel or VSD—he counted on low-level competence. He couldn't see the national service being called in to follow a man who was not a threat to the sovereignty of Lithuania. But then, Melis may have made the case that he was such a problem. Matt Devlin was not a fearful man, nor did he dread confrontation, but the last thing he wanted, besides witnessing a Russian invasion, was another confrontation with the woman. He wasn't ready to explain why he furtively met with a foreign national at night, even if it was his father, although he couldn't prove that either since his dad used alias documentation. Better to not give her the opportunity to question him.

He entered the park and took a circuit along the track he'd visited before. Then he took an even smaller track through the bush to the back side of a small pavilion where a familiar figure waited.

Joshua looked at his watch. "Well inside the window."

"Hi, Dad. How are you?"

"Doing well. Do you think the precautions are necessary?"

"Yeah, I do." Matt gave his father the details on the ghost asset incident and his current, probationary status with the colonel and

Commander Melis.

"She sounds formidable. Sorry my idea didn't work. I guess I won't be able to give you anymore anonymous tips. We'll have to work on getting you information quicker through the attaché. What else is happening?"

"Nothing unusual. Training and watching the eastern horizon. I'm not sure if our hosts have taken your warning seriously or not. The troops are concerned, but that's kind of normal for them." He could have described his days in detail, but that wasn't what his father wanted. His father wanted to know that he was of sound mind and body and not contemplating anything remotely suicidal. Being a former Green Beret and the father of a current one gave him some insight into the mind of the younger snake eaters, even if a generation separated their service.

"What happens if the balloon goes up?" Joshua said.

"Not sure. Some folks say we'll get pulled back. Others think we'll work alongside our partners."

"Planning for guerrilla warfare?"

"We are planning for it, in good old Jedburgh style."

Jedburghs—teams of Allied special forces that lived, trained, and fought with resistance fighters in German-occupied Europe during World War II. It was a hard life, and some didn't come back. The difference was they came into the fight just before D-Day, toward the end of the war. This time, the Americans might be in the middle of the fray from the beginning.

"That's kind of what I was afraid of. If that happens, you'll be in the thick of it. From everything we've heard, we have about a month before anything serious happens. The uprising in Nagorno has slowed things but not that much. My partner and I will be in-country maybe another week, I'm not sure. After that, it's all up in the air. But I'll try to keep you in the loop as to what's happening and where I'm located. We'll use our brevity codes, right?"

"Right, Dad."

Fathers always seemed always ready to teach and counsel when they encountered their kids. This time Dad played the encounter like a cross between a concerned father and an asset handling meeting.

"How are you doing, Dad?" Agents never asked their case officer a question like that, but sons could.

"Well enough. The main thing is that I want you to know I support everything you're doing here, you and your men, no matter what I said before. I'll do my best to help you succeed." Joshua wiped away whatever it was bothering his eyes.

"I don't remember, what did you say before?"

"Back home. When I was mumbling about giving it all up. I know we can't … you can't give it up. You're the sheepdog now."

"We're good, Dad. But you're right, sometimes it's good to question the gods." Matt saw his father's dissembling behavior for parental concern and knew he'd better go before someone got emotional. "Listen, I better get out of here. My buddies are covering for me."

"Yeah, do that. Go. Stay safe. I love you."

"I love you too, Dad." Matt turned and began to walk away but when he looked back, the pavilion was empty. His father had vanished into the night.

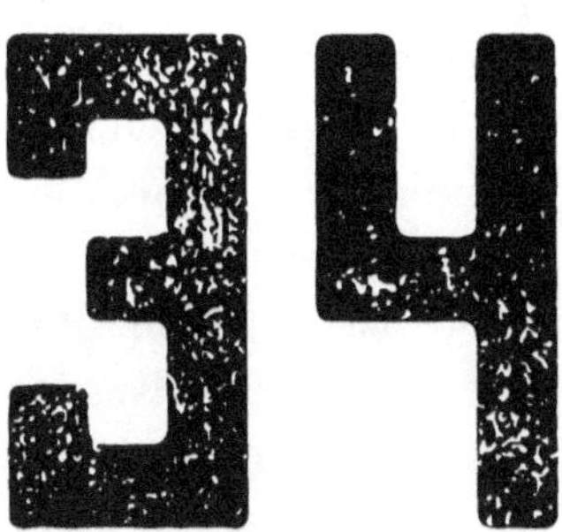

AS THEY DROVE INTO THE RETREAT, Joshua felt the forest close in around him. The dark green pines shut out all the sunlight except in the small patches where a ray penetrated the canopy, falling to the floor in a bright shaft. It was in those circles of light where he sensed movement, a shadow that moved too quickly, an edge that was too straight for nature, and then a glint, a reflection off glass or shiny metal.

Whoever was out there was either poorly trained or complacent, like a fox that assumes the rabbit doesn't see it or isn't fast enough to escape his jaws. His hand went involuntarily to the CZ stuffed between his thigh and the car seat. It wasn't much good against a rifle at long range but at least he could show one last act of defiance if they didn't hit him first. "I may be paranoid, but the woods have eyes. They're out there."

"Just because you're paranoid…" Gabriel stopped. "But we'll ask Hammer. Hopefully, they are his minions." He and Joshua had agreed that minions was the technical term for Hammer's employees. Like-minded, loyal followers who did what they were told. Except when a bad one got into the system and ended up getting wasted, like what may have happened to Milatovich's tattletale. Joshua hadn't always been worried about getting himself killed. He certainly wouldn't have stayed in this line of work if he had. He just felt—especially since he lost Sarah—that he really wanted to live for his son. His son was in the real danger. He had to do his best to eliminate that threat even if it meant dying himself.

Two nights ago, Gabriel told him the game was on. Hammer had accepted the invitation and the condition to come to the Lithuanian spa. He gave a simple reply, which made Gabriel wonder what Hammer was thinking. They would soon find out.

The compound hadn't changed much, which made it easier for Joshua to assuage his paranoia. No new buildings or cars parked along the road, no deviations. Though maybe that's what they wanted him to think. His paranoia rose. He had to get out of this business.

Hammer waited. As aristocratically Russian as ever, but this time without a cigarette. He was effusive in his welcome, though Joshua caught a hint of concern in his eyes. "Welcome, Peter! Welcome, Thomas! I'm glad to see you again."

Joshua thought he could have added alive after the Baku incident, but as Hammer was probably the target, Joshua was happy his own skin was intact.

Nothing had changed inside either. The place was overwhelming and quiet. Soft light filtered by window shades showed tiny specks of dust glistening as they drifted through the air. Flames danced in the mouth of the fireplace. Joshua took it all in reverentially, even though they'd experienced it once before.

"I'd like to have a library like this," Joshua said.

"Not likely on your salary," said Gabriel.

"If I come to America, I should like a house like this in a forest somewhere," said Andriy.

"Right, I'll alert the office. That'll give them time to buy the Banff or El Tovar for you."

A confused look came over Andriy. "What are they?"

"Two of the grandest hotels in North America. Only slightly bigger than this place," Gabriel answered.

"You are being facetious, Peter?"

"Only a bit. A place like this would cost at least twenty million to build."

"Forty in Jackson Hole," Joshua said.

Andriy looked around. "Maybe I could have something only half this size."

"Let's see how our project goes first. But if we don't succeed, property values may be going down all around the world," said Gabriel.

"Fine, we will talk property later. What is so important that you pulled me out of Russia so quickly?"

"The missiles, Andriy," Gabriel said. "You provided us with the plans, and we have come up with a solution. The only solution as far as we can determine."

"What is it?"

Gabriel motioned to Joshua who pulled a module packed in a clear plastic box from his pocket. "This. It's an electronic control unit identical to the one in the plans."

"What do you expect me to do with that?" Andriy asked looking from Gabriel to Joshua.

Joshua waited for Gabriel to answer. "I need you to replace the ones in the missiles with ours."

He stared at the box. "And this, I suppose, will make the missiles somehow useless."

"They will cause all of them to malfunction. But they must be installed in each missile."

"Me? A senior official in the president's office installing these things in missiles? Your idea makes no sense."

"You got the plans to us. You must have someone who has access and can install them."

Andriy began to pace. Agitated by the proposal or perhaps Gabriel's audacity in asking him. Gabriel began to speak and was cut off by Andriy's wave of the hand. A typical gesture of those accustomed to power. Both Americans settled back into the shadows to wait.

"I am thinking," he said, "but while I'm thinking, look at this." He pulled a single, folded sheet of paper from his pocket. "This paper has details of two things of interest for you, I think. The Turkish government is shipping twenty-five Bayraktar UAVs—drones I guess everyone calls them now—to the Azerbaijanis at Ganja Airbase. At the same time, the Iranians are shipping the first fifty of one hundred Shahed 136 drones to Russia through Armenia via Yerevan. All the dates and flights are in there. I just thought it curious it was happening at the same time there is an uprising going on in Nagorno-Karabakh, especially the latest attacks on Russian forces there. Don't you?"

"I heard it was Azeris who attacked the Russians," Gabriel said.

Andriy stopped pacing and looked at Gabriel. "That is what the army thinks. I think the attack was too well planned and coordinated for simple Azeri rebels or whomever they were. Also, curious."

Gabriel didn't know all the details of Operation Honey Bear, just that the drone shipments could be a potential complication on both sides of the border. But it was a problem well above his paygrade, he just needed to get the info sent home once he was done convincing Hammer to do his job.

"I don't know anything about the rebels. Our last visit to Baku was the first time I've been there in a long time, and I know little of Azerbaijan or Armenia."

"Thomas, how about you?"

"Nothing. All I know is that it's a place like Afghanistan where Westerners go to die."

"Many people die there. The only people who make it romantic to die there are poets like Kipling. Now as to your proposal, I think it can be done, this implant. But, and you may think this is a big request, I need something. Two things, actually."

"What?" said Gabriel.

"First, I want you to get me one hundred Javelin missiles."

"How the hell am I supposed to do that?" Gabriel asked.

"Russia will pay for them. You must set up an account in Switzerland or somewhere to receive the money. Then you ship the missiles to, say, Poland. Of course, you don't tell the Poles, just your Congress in a secret memo, however you do that. Then you put them on a boat, and we do a mid-ocean transfer. I know your people have the experience to make it happen. That's how you stole our T-72. But I digress. What do you say?"

"I don't say anything. I have to run this by headquarters. Why do you want them?" Gabriel said.

"Have you seen what the Russian army uses? Javelins work."

"That's exactly why my government will not want you to have them," Gabriel said.

"Well, tell them it's that or no implant, install, whatever you call it. I need them to show Volodya that I can acquire something extraordinary for him."

"What's the second thing?" Gabriel stood feet apart braced for the worst.

"You go with me to Russia. To the missiles. Both of you."

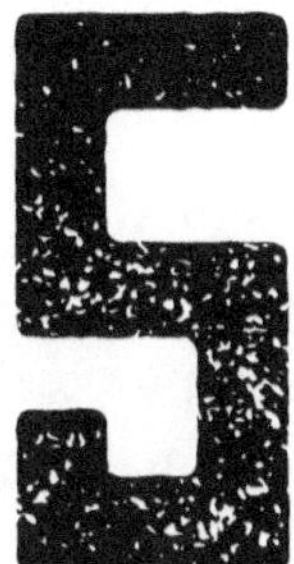

Gabriel looked around, a park with children being chased by babysitters, or being ignored by mothers. Dogs walking their owners, while the music from an old-fashioned carousel drifted lightly by. A typical weekend in Vilnius, quiet considering what was happening in the world. Or maybe people just wanted life to be normal. He pushed call on his cell and waited, then did a series of keystrokes to activate the secure mode. Jamie's voice came through scratchy and distant.

"Hello, my friend." Never names even though it was a secure line.

Gabriel explained the situation and their destination and waited for the explosion.

"Where?" Jamie asked. He was doing a good job of concealing his emotions, thought Gabriel. He should be screaming.

"To Kosvinsky. The good news is that he can get access to two of the missiles. The bad news is the third one is hidden, but you knew that," Gabriel said.

"Now you're soft-pedaling the fact that you would be inside Russia. Where is Kosvinsky exactly?" A rational question.

"In the northern Urals."

"You're out of your fucking mind, Batman."

The truth comes out. Considering the direction of the conversation, Gabriel decided to ignore the nickname.

It was several seconds before Jamie's voice came through to his mobile again. "What does your partner say?"

"Said he's never been there before. Wondered how the food is, et cetera."

"The boss will flip out."

"Tell her it's our only chance."

"What else?"

"I need one hundred Javelins."

"How exactly is that supposed to work out?" Jamie asked.

Gabriel explained the proposal, which was met with a stony silence. "Russia will pay full black-market price which is around three hundred million. I sent you the bank account details. I set it up as a proprietary. It's well covered through about seven cut-outs in the Seychelles, Trinidad and Tobago, like that. My office lawyer helped. I didn't tell him what it was really for. And you'll have to get the approvals."

"You realize of course that the boss may have all our heads before this is over."

"Just as long as it doesn't affect my retirement pay."

Jamie stood in front of Clairissa's desk, to lay out the two issues. She sat quietly as he finished. *She is surprisingly calm.* Possibly she was in shock. Sending NOCs into Russia wasn't a normal occurrence these days.

"If anyone but you brought this to me, I would have them drawn and quartered. Why do you think it makes sense?"

She wasn't shocked. She expected things like this from him. A less forward-leaning director of operations wouldn't have had the guts to present this to her, afraid to rock the boat. Not Jamie. She was sure it was his background. That's why she liked him. His wife was nice too.

"Sheepdogs," she said.

"Pardon me?" Jamie said.

"You are those people, someone once said, who do bad things so ordinary people can sleep peacefully in their beds—Kipling, Churchill, Orwell, or Le Carré, one of them anyway." Clairissa said.

"I think they all did," said Jamie. "Gabriel and Joshua each have more experience at denied area operations than anyone else in the Agency. That's no guarantee of success, but it's a start."

"They've both been inside Russia?" She asked.

"Gabriel several times. Joshua never, but they've both been to other hard places."

"You ran this by Gladys in Russia House before you came to me, I hope?"

"Yes, she said she'll support it but it's my fault if it goes bad."

"That won't help them if it does. How do we know Hammer isn't delivering two of our best case officers to the SVR?"

"We don't. All we know is that his track record is good."

"Except he almost got everyone killed in Baku and Joshua almost got kidnapped in Berlin."

"Hammer could easily be killed inside Russia. If Pynya wanted him dead, he would have been dead already."

"Maybe he cut a deal with Pynya and the price is one hundred missiles and two Agency case officers for his life."

"Maybe, but have you ever heard of Project Eldest Son?"

"No."

"It was a devious thing. My boss, Jack Singlaub, thought it up. We, as in Studies and Observations Group in Vietnam, seeded defective ammunition into the Viet Cong's and North Vietnamese Army's supply lines. They used it and got themselves blown up. Worked very well."

"We can do that with the Javelins?"

"The techs say yes. And we can fix the guidance systems so no one gets any technology bump ups. The Russians already got hold of some when they took Ukraine anyway."

Director Hall looked out her window and sighed the sigh of someone who knew she had only one way to decide. The die was cast. In the cool blue sky, over the trees in the distance, the spires of Georgetown University stood out on their hill. A farther off was the Washington Monument, the dome of the Capitol behind it.

"It appears so easy here. Making your plans and overturning others. Rarely does anyone think about the lives behind those plans, who will live and who won't. Could be four hundred lives or it could be just one. Or maybe two. You know what I mean, Jamie?" She said. "Okay, it's a maybe on the Javelins. I'm still thinking about the Dynamic Duo's travel into bear country. But don't do anything yet."

Jamie nodded and said, "He gave us one more thing, the coordinates of at least fifty Iranian UAVs being shipped to Russia through Armenia and a bunch of Turkish Bayraktars going to Azerbaijan."

"As a tradeoff that's chump change. What are we supposed to do about a bunch of UAVs going to Azerbaijan and Armenia with the Honey Bear team inside one country and our Kipling in the other?"

"I'm not sure yet. This is beginning to look like a three-level chess game. Everybody has some leverage over everyone else."

"And we still have no idea where the third Perimeter missile is located?

"Not exactly, no."

"Thank you, Jamie. You just made my very complicated life even more so … go away, I'll call you when I need you."

He looked to see if anyone else was in earshot. "It'll be long distance, Clairissa," He only called her Clairissa when she was at his house, or no one was around. "Storm clouds are gathering so I'm leaving for Europe this afternoon."

Clairissa looked at him sternly through her owl-eye glasses. "Good. You need to be on the front lines with your troops. Permission granted whether you asked for it or not. Get out of here."

Jamie walked through the outer office and into the corridor. He looked both ways, not a person in sight. Only people who had business here walked down this hall, otherwise they avoided it. No one wanted to get their soul sucked into the black hole. His own office wasn't far away and as he walked, he wondered what would be different if they were in a war zone. Would decisions come faster, would they be any clearer if they didn't have time to war-game each decision or run an idea by subject matter experts? He wasn't sure but he knew it certainly wouldn't be this quiet. Thankfully, Clairissa made the job simpler for everyone under her. Since becoming director, she didn't test the waters with the White House or Liberty Crossing before making the hard decisions. Where a school-trained bureaucrat would waffle for days, she just made the choice.

"Don't try to scare me, Jamie," Clairissa said. "Just tell me why."

Jamie's call came out of blue that morning. She hadn't even had her first cup of coffee. They were talking on a secure video channel via a satellite that was probably in a geo-synchronous orbit right over the Berlin Chancery because the feed was so clear. Jamie was alone in the perspex bubble box. He'd left Bob in his office a floor below him, the station chief, wondering what was happening. Clairissa was in her own private sanctum on the seventh floor of headquarters overlooking the Potomac, which was as impervious to electronic interception as she was to a bullying senator.

Ordinarily, Jamie would never consider setting foot inside a NOC's operational area, but this case was anything but normal and became more unusual by the day. He might have said more complex, but it really wasn't any more complex than previous years, except perhaps those few easy days after the Iron Curtain came down when America and NATO Europe thought there would be peace; militaries were reduced in size, budgets cut, and some countries even decided Russia might be a friend. But then came Pynya. No one realized the Russian leader was a spider weaving his personal web in secret, pretending to be a nice guy. He wasn't a communist and he wasn't a democrat. Driven by his pathological dream to be Czar and regain the Motherland's lost territory, he slowly pushed west—give me this and I'll be happy, give me a little more and I'll stop. It was time to end the game.

"I need to give them the news in person. No cut-outs. I don't trust our communications to be passed by an intermediary from Vilnius Station. I trust them, but it's just one more link that can be broken. I'm going. They don't know me there and I'll be traveling with cover docs."

"How long will you be operational?" She said it like he was going into kill mode.

"Operational? It's not like this is a denied area … just low key. But I'll be out for three or four days, five at most. Drive overland, make the meet, and get out."

"Will you be out of pocket the whole time?"

"I'm carrying the same commo as Gabriel. I'll send SITREPs."

"All right, Jamie. But if you are caught or killed, the secretary will disavow any knowledge of your actions."

"Ha! But really now, do I look like Jim or Ethan?

"Better than either. You're the Rock."

"Okay, I'll admit I'm good-looking but I'm not as rich as any of them. Do me a favor and go see my wife. I don't think it would be a good idea for me to mention my travel on an open line."

"I'll do that, Jamie. But for both our sakes, be sure and get your butt back here soon. And by the way, I have a plan for our Mister Kipling. I'll fill you in when you get back to Berlin."

Jamie picked up the car in an underground hotel parking lot. The keys sat on top of the left rear tire, which had been arranged between Frankfurt Base and Berlin Station. The location was a well-thought-out choice. No surveillance cameras covered the stairwell access or inside the garage itself. The only cameras were fixed on the entry and exit points. The disguise he used to get out of the garage went in a roadside bin on the way to Poland later that day.

He had barely thought about his cover legend. His language skills were oriented on Southeast Asia, but he didn't think he could pass himself off as a Thai or Vietnamese businessman. Maybe a retired professional wrestler from Guam, but that was also pretty thin. If his wife had been with him, he could probably just say tourism and get away with it. Ultimately, he decided a loose cover as a retired teacher now freelance photographer would have to do. A specialist in the office of technology back home put together a website extolling his imaging skills using some of his travelogue photos and others borrowed from the Agency's archives. That would provide him with about twenty minutes of cover explanation if he was ever interrogated by the police. He would have to hope that wouldn't happen. Plus, an authentic American travel document issued by the passport folks in Washington was hard to dispute. Unless, that is, he was caught in the act of subverting a country, which he had no intention of letting happen.

For the most part, living a cover was about adopting a mental attitude, existing totally in the role you are supposed to portray. Not playing a role but being the role. Well beyond remembering birthdates, schools, training programs, childhood friends, one had to become a life imagined. Just as a good actor assumes a character in a play, the intelligence officer must give life to a person who doesn't exist. But there was no script in real life and there was never a moment to step off the stage and accept a bouquet of roses for the performance.

But Jamie was used to it. It had been several years since he had to worry about cover mainly because his position didn't require it. He wasn't in the field and he often had to meet with senior officers from other countries. But his photo wasn't published in the newspapers and his name wasn't advertised either. The Director was the only one who had to deal with that burden. As such, there were still places he could go and not be himself.

In Vilnius, Jamie found himself doing what he imagined Gabriel and Joshua had done, walking the city streets. He carried a nice Canon EOS digital that Frankfurt had rustled up along with two lenses—a wide angle and a telephoto zoom—which were great for photographers who traveled light. He found things to shoot, images to capture from different points of view and in different light. He made notes and remembered routes and angles, things that would give him reason to come back later. Vilnius was full of interesting vignettes, so it was good for Jamie to have a meeting close to one of those. A place where his two officers could be inconspicuous as well.

Jamie decided Gabriel got tagged to make the approach when he spotted him on the edge of the park. He was behind the camera struggling to hold still while he shot a long exposure. The cable release helped, but the spindly tripod the office gave him was all over the place. He half watched Gabriel as Gabriel watched him compose the scene, the old castle on the hill as the photogenic half-moon climbed up in the background. He fired off a couple of exposures when Gabriel finally decided the time was right. Jamie panned the edge of park with the camera looking for strangers. A last glance around told him they were alone.

"Is this where the Boston Lobsters train?" Gabriel asked.

Jamie straightened up, cable release in hand and looked around. He towered over Gabriel. "You talking to me, chump?"

"That's not the proper response, Jamie."

"I guess I can't talk to you, Gabriel."

"Okay, close enough. What's up?"

"There's a pub called the Piano, about three blocks away. Meet me there with your wing man in forty-five minutes."

Gabriel walked into the bar first and pantomimed a gorilla to the waiter who pointed back to Jamie's booth. Jamie saw him and frowned.

"That wasn't very nice," he said when Gabriel sat down.

"Sorry, I couldn't think of the word for big Kahuna in Lithuanian."

"Are you going to get serious about this?" Jamie asked.

Joshua stepped into the bar a moment later and did not require direction. He joined them at the table after ordering a drink from the barkeep.

"So, Batman and Robin walk into a bar—" Gabriel began.

"Stop it. Now." The look on Jamie's face stopped him dead.

"Sorry, but you started it in the park."

"Fine. Clairissa sends her regards and what I am about to say comes from her. Got it?"

Joshua and Gabriel nodded, their attention captured.

"The reason I'm here is because I didn't want anyone to play telephone with her message or have them misinterpret the instructions. You have authorization to travel, and you are fully covered if anything goes south. In other words, we are behind you all the way. Do what you need to do to get the modules in and then get out. No side trips, no expedient intel collection, no extracurricular sabotage. Got it?"

"Okay, but what about the Javelins?" Gabriel asked.

"They're shipping out of Baltimore. It won't be right away but maybe that's a reason to slow down Zero Day."

"Day Zero, you mean. I need to tell him something. Is there anything I can use to verify the shipment? They'll need specifics in order to conduct a transfer."

"I'll send you a shipping doc you can use with him. It will look like farm equipment or something but it's too early yet for tracking data."

Gabriel looked at Joshua, who was just absorbing the moment as the silent partner. "I guess this means we're off the see the wizard."

"You are indeed. Keep me posted when you can. And please don't get caught."

EARLY THAT MORNING, they had to answer the question of how to prepare for their denied area trip. They each brought one carry-on and a shoulder bag. Nothing was of any sentimental value and all the bags were electronically tagged with AirTags. If security objected to regular, commercially available tracking devices, so be it, they would explain they were normal for travelers these days. The one thing Joshua didn't want to give up was his pistol, so it went into the cache site in a park near the castle. He doubted anyone would find it as it had already gone undetected between the last trips.

The Mercedes picked them up at the hotel and, once out of the city, time and distance flew in the comfortable cocoon that insulated them from the outside world. The driver presented three diplomatic passports to the Lithuanian border guard who scanned them quickly and handed everything back. The second gate on the Belarus side went even quicker and the guard waved them on. No need to check a known *Siloviki* vehicle. Not if he wanted to remain employed at least. The driver stuffed the passports into a satchel on the front seat and then eyed the passengers in the back seats who had never seen or touched the travel documents. Their real ones were still tucked inside their own pockets, which meant no record of them crossing the border into Belarus.

It was the same at the airfield. Dropped at the base of the Sukhoi business jet's boarding stairs, Joshua and Gabriel looked in vain for guidance. Attendants or ground crew were nowhere to be seen. The pilot looked down at them from the cockpit and went back to his checklists.

"I guess the pilot thinks we're cleared for travel." Gabriel clomped up the steps and left Joshua to follow.

When the far engine began to spool up, Joshua thought it a good idea to climb aboard or be left behind. Preparations for take-off were well advanced as an attendant grabbed his bag and wandered somewhere in back to store it. He sat down near Gabriel and Andriy—already deep in conversation—in a lounge chair across the aisle and turned his attention to the game unfolding ahead of him.

"Peter has been telling me that you are an aerospace engineer," Andriy said, "and together you two facilitate the purchase of specialized military equipment for certain unnamed countries."

Playing the game, Joshua said, "That's correct. He brings his expertise and language skills and I bring mine, which mostly center around weapons design. He's been at it much longer and in more—how do you say—diverse locations." He was feeling around his new legend. It would get them through the trip if it held up.

The Sukhoi rolled down the taxiway, past an old Antonov An-26 parked on the grass, which had seen better days. One wing drooped and a prop was missing from one of the engines. Nothing else on the field was visible, which, despite Jamie's warning that no collection, even passive, was to be done, led him to deduce this airfield would see use only at the last minute when and if a Russian offensive began. The plane shuddered and dipped when the brakes bit and took hold. The plane pivoted on the runway as the twin turbojets ran up, then power went to full, and they began rolling. It didn't take long for the powerful engines to get them to transition, and the plane angled up off the runway. They turned east toward Russia. Joshua turned back to Andriy and Gabriel who were also captivated by the view.

"Seems to be a nice aircraft," Joshua said.

"It is," said Andriy. "All Russian-made with more features and half the price of a western business jet. Now, may I see the replacement modules?"

Joshua pulled them from his bag and placed the sealed containers on the table.

"The original set of modules for your RS-28 missiles came from the Chinese Military Corporation who acquired them from the United States," Gabriel said. "CMC subsequently discovered the Americans had engineered them with a built-in fault. CMC redesigned the modules and manufactured their replacements under controlled conditions inside China. These are the replacements. You can see the markings on them." That was the story they had decided on.

Andriy smiled. "I have notified our people of the problem. They will meet us to discuss how it can be resolved. I know you are prepared to show them."

Joshua was not convinced that he wasn't looking at a hyena, but it was too late to back out.

"I almost forgot, Peter." Andriy said, "What of the other transaction?"

Gabriel unfolded two pieces of paper from his pocket and handed them to Andriy. "The first is an invoice for the Javelins. The second is the export packing list, one hundred single-use tubes and twenty control units, labeled as agricultural equipment. We will have the bill of lading once the shipment moves. That will show the carrier and ship it has embarked on. I should add that the shipment won't be loaded until the invoice is taken care of, and we have all the bank details including a confirmation of deposit."

"I think maybe you don't trust me to pay, Peter. It is true that money is a bit tight at home, but this shouldn't be a problem to make happen. We don't want any delays."

"If anyone can do it, I'm sure you can, Andriy. One question though, once I provide you with the navigation data, you will be able to arrange the ship-to-ship transfer?"

"We must be able to, mustn't we? Sea transfers are actually quite normal for us even on the high seas, mostly petroleum products, but a small shipment like this will pose no difficulty. We just need a rendezvous location and the communications protocols."

"Those will be forthcoming," Gabriel said. "Once the payment has been verified. My masters were quite firm on that."

"No worries, Peter. This is quite important to me personally, so it will happen." Andriy reached forward to pat Gabriel's knee as if his personal touch would guarantee his words.

Andriy's settled back into the lounge chair, signaling a break in the conversation. Joshua was content to close his eyes and review how he hoped things would unfold. Their plan could go many ways, but he tried not to dwell on the negatives.

The plane touched down at a busier airfield than they started from. Two propeller-driven transports were parked on the tarmac in front a row of hangars. There was a proper, if small terminal.

"Is this Kosvinsky?" Joshua asked. A reasonable deduction but he thought it better to confirm.

"This airfield is part of the Kosvinsky restricted area. We're about thirty kilometers from our destination," Andriy said.

"Which is?" Gabriel had his face against the window trying to find reference points.

"The missile support facility. The place where all the maintenance work is completed. Not the command post, if you're wondering. Your presence there would be hard to explain."

"That's just fine, Andriy. We have one thing to do and then we can get out of here," said Gabriel.

Met by a Russian Army officer at the foot of the stairs, they loaded their bags into the UAZ Patriot, a civilian SUV version of a military truck. Joshua thought of it as a cheap Toyota Highlander, not even on par with an old Defender. *But when in Russia…*

No BMWs as escorts this time, just more UAZs, two each, painted matte green with emblems on the doors, the double-headed eagle with flags and an inscription that translated roughly as Russian Army Forces Facility 3902.

In the lower altitudes of the Urals, the conifers were tall, thin, and deep green. It was not virgin forest, far from it. From his window, as the trees blurred by, the depth of the well-manicured forest was apparent. It was almost like Germany, where the animals and trees were all counted and cared for with great precision and efficiency. In this place, it was probably to help ensure no one attempted to infiltrate —it kept the fields of fire clear. Cameras on poles along the road assisted as well.

Joshua was filled with a combination of dread and elation, in awe of the fact that he was in one of the most secure areas in Russia, and worried that he was deep inside the bear's lair. There were many things that troubled him. For one, his telephone hadn't been taken. It was in his shoulder bag and, granted, it was turned off, but that was very strange for such a security-minded country. Andriy's presence must explain that. He doubted that his bag-tracking devices were of much use here, there didn't appear to be any cellular telephone towers and he was pretty sure that was a requirement to get a fix. Maybe a low-flying satellite would pick them up. Not that the guys with guns (GWG) would be able to save their chestnuts from an open fire this far from home, but it was one of those better than nothing ideas. A flashback to a time long ago in Northern Ireland appeared for a moment before he willed it to go away.

It a little less than an hour to reach the compound. More buildings surrounded by another fence. There were big buildings with big doors that looked like they could accommodate the largest transporter-erector-launcher vehicles, but nothing outside to give away the contents to the spies in the sky—the satellites that overflew this compound on a daily basis. Just the analysts would measure tire marks and debris on the ground then calculate to the nearest fraction and guess what might be inside. Joshua imagined the Russians would have restricted all the missile launcher movement would be done at night to avoid those pesky camera-laden birds. They parked in front of a low, long building, not unlike the one he'd visited at White Sands, and climbed out to find a man waiting for them.

"Leave your bag in the vehicle for now. We'll just need the modules and whatever tools you have for this," Andriy said. Andriy spoke Russian, Gabriel translated Andriy's Russian to German, while Joshua was just mute, understanding in duplicate.

Andriy met their host at the base of the stairs. He looked officious, drab suit, with an ID card pinned to his breast, but he smiled at Andriy, shook his hand, and gave the required cheek to cheek greeting twice. Gabriel stood with his back to Joshua while Andriy exchanged pleasantries and words with the official about the strangers. With sidelong glances at Gabriel and Joshua, the Russian looked a little skeptical but nodded and finally smiled and welcomed them.

"This is Chief Administrator Yevgeny Garov, our host. Now, we go to meet the technicians," Andriy said.

Garov turned and, with a gesture to Andriy, opened the door to motion them inside.

Joshua couldn't stop himself from noticing the details and was surprised by the lack of security. No visible guards and only one security door. The eastern bloc architecture was sterile and simple. Cheaply constructed but utilitarian and a single color of off-white paint. Garov led them down a hallway to an open room, a laboratory, maybe a demonstration room. There were video screens on the wall, all blank, metal tables, and men in white coats. No women, but then that wasn't unheard of in the strategic missile industry, especially in Russia.

Andriy introduced Gabriel and Joshua as specialists. No mention of nationality, affiliation, or other identifier. Then he asked Gabriel to explain the issue while Joshua set out the ten sealed boxes containing the ECU modules and a nice German four-ring binder filled with schematic drawings and notes. The technicians crowded in close to listen and look—like little kids shown something new and special.

When Gabriel finished, he asked if they had pulled a motherboard as requested. Blank looks. Gabriel looked at Andriy. "We need a motherboard to show how the modules are replaced."

"Are you sure they can't do it on their own?" Andriy asked.

Gabriel shook his head.

Andriy looked at the official. "Yevgeny, I think there has been a miscommunication."

Joshua held the single ECU demonstrator, the only one that had been exposed to the open air, dust, static electricity, and human essential oils. He was ready to plug it into a test board, but without the board, he would not be able to easily talk them through the steps.

"Do you not have a test board, a spare?" he asked in German. Gabriel translated.

"Our spares are sealed. They are only brought out to replace a bad one," a technician said.

"Your boards are all bad," Andriy said. "That's what this is about. Sacrifice one for the Motherland," he ordered. The technician looked to Yevgeny. He nodded and another technician ran off to the storage room.

Joshua flipped open the binder to an instruction page in Chinese. The same page stared up from the other side in Russian. He turned it to the technicians. "This is what needs to be done." He let them look at the pages while they waited. "Maybe they should do the work on two," he said to Gabriel and Andriy, "and we could watch them install the new boards on the missiles. Or at least one of them."

Gabriel translated for Andriy again. They were his people after all.

"I will suggest it." Andriy grabbed Yevgeny by the shoulder and walked away from the crowd, explaining what should happen. It took a moment of back and forth, but then Yevgeny nodded.

Andriy came back. "They will fix two motherboards and then we can observe them installing one into a missile."

The technician came back with a sealed package and proceeded to open it on the table. With Gabriel translating, Joshua showed them the procedure. "Simple," he said, "even the Chinese can do it." Gabriel translated as he stared menacingly at Joshua. It got a laugh.

"Now," said Andriy. "You need to do two more."

The technicians took the sealed modules with the instructions and left.

"They're going to do it in the clean room," said Yevgeny. "We'll go with them to a site in the morning, but tonight we celebrate."

Gabriel had warned him before he went to get ready for the event, but Joshua couldn't find any butter to coat his stomach before they arrived at the mess hall converted to a party room. He decided the Russians must use the place often because the conversion had taken place quickly. Somewhat stainless-steel serving tables were pushed out of the way to line a hall or covered with cloth. The lighting was institutionally garish, and the sickly green wall tile added nothing to the decor other than maybe to hide what he expected would come after many rounds of vodka.

Seeing the crowd, Joshua felt his gut churn. Anxiety over the prospect of his cover being tested repeatedly by so many people. He'd stick to German and a beginner's level of Russian to feign ignorance, leaving the heavy lifting to Gabriel who had more experience at playing the con.

We are Andriy's hostages. Getting out of this place without incident would be totally in his hands. They were trusting a Russian asset of unknown motivation playing a long game that they hadn't yet begun to fathom.

And here he was, amateur NOC compared to Gabriel. Allegedly a journalist, now a weapons technician. The only thing he had on him remotely genuine was his passport, which he assumed was issued with the connivance of the German intelligence service as part of some Agency—BND deal brokering. His name wasn't real, it was issued, in fact all his operational names had been issued. But it felt surreal to be playing this game deep inside Russia at this moment in his life. He was beginning to feel sick. He needed a drink. The Russians obliged.

Joshua shook his head, I volunteered for this, get over it.

Andriy introduced them to the commander of the facility, a pudgy, bear-like colonel, if Joshua remembered his rank recognition tables correctly, but he didn't get the name. The colonel didn't get theirs either because what Joshua heard had little resemblance to his cover name. Must be the transliteration.

Luckily, there was food. Joshua stuck to carbs. Greasy proteins would not do him well later. Russian hors d'oeuvres typically didn't include carrot and celery sticks. But if there had been a baked potato, he would have eaten it between the shots. Instead, he relied on some deft sleight of hand maneuvers, palming his glass and consigning his drink to the fake rubber plants along the wall. But that was difficult during the one-on-one toasts, so he tried not to count.

Another Russian officer approached and stood on the edge of their group for a moment. "Why did you decide to come here to Russia?" More questions. Were they chipping away at the story or just curious?

"I work all over. There isn't much call for rocket scientists in Germany anymore."

"Germany, the richest country in Europe, has no work for you?"

"Maybe you have heard of Werner von Braun?"

The Russian nodded. "Of course. The V-2 and Saturn rockets. The only way America got to the moon, with the help of Nazi scientists."

"Well, I suppose so. I'm a little like him, I go where there is work and money."

The man appeared satisfied.

A little while later, Gabriel elbowed him discreetly. A man of obvious Asian descent approached. Medium height—about the same as Gabriel—tending to fat, with shiny, black hair. Joshua wasn't sure if he might be from the eastern districts of Russia or farther east. He walked straight up to Gabriel.

"Where are you from?" The plump man asked Gabriel in Chinese.

"Who are you?" Gabriel responded in the same language.

"Cho Jae-sung."

"I thought maybe you were Korean. You learned your Chinese from a Cantonese, no?"

"My mother was from Guangzhou. So, I guess so. Why do you ask?"

"I thought I caught an accent." Actually, Gabriel was struggling to understand the man because his Mandarin sucked.

"Would you prefer I speak Russian?" Cho said.

"It might be a good idea." Waving his hand to indicate the Russians. "Our friends get nervous if they can't understand us, you know what I mean." Gabriel gave Cho a conspiratorial wink, then added in Russian, "I am called Peter, Peter Liu, and this is my partner, Thomas." Keeping his eyes on Cho, Gabriel said in German, "This is Cho. He is Korean." Cho appeared to have no idea what Gabriel had said, so he smiled pleasantly while continuing to describe him to Joshua, "He's rude, not even a proper greeting, he used the informal, and his Mandarin is really bad."

"So, you two are going to get along really well." Thomas gave a slight bow to Cho who smiled back.

"I doubt it. He's from the North."

My first trip into Russia and we meet a Nork missile guy, thought Joshua.

"Why are you here?" Cho continued his probe in Russian.

"We were invited." Gabriel wasn't about to surrender ground.

"But why?" Cho had begun to sound like a petulant child.

"I don't think I'm authorized to say. Perhaps you should ask the commander there."

Cho looked where Gabriel had indicated and then back. He huffed a bit in frustration, but Gabriel had turned away, leading Joshua to another, easier conversation.

Andriy found them again. "Enjoying yourselves, I hope. The commander is pleased that we were able to prevent a possible problem. His only question was why it developed at all. I could only tell him supply chain issues and the reliance on foreign technology and technicians."

"Sounds familiar," said Gabriel. "I see you have other outsiders working here."

Andriy followed Gabriel's gaze. "Yes, unfortunately our systems have become intertwined and crossbred. It seems we have a symbiotic relationship with China, Korea, and Iran. Therefore, we have a hard time producing anything original on our own." Andriy spoke in a low voice to Gabriel, so low that Joshua couldn't hear.

"I'll tell you later," Gabriel said in Joshua's ear when Andriy was finished.

Gabriel finally decided he had enough of the party. "It's time to bail." With much smiling and back-slapping, they made their way out. Pretending to be present but disappearing slowly until they made the exit corridor and eventually the outdoors.

The sky was bright with stars and the mountain air was cold and damp. Half a bright, white moon illuminated the way as they walked toward their quarters, hoping the night chill would clear their heads, leaning on each other to make it home.

A lot of water and aspirin would help, and the pierogis Joshua had managed to wrap in napkins and stuff into his pockets might get him through the night without too much pain. Inside his utilitarian room, Joshua shed his clothing and managed to step under a lukewarm shower, the water drumming a roaring beat into his head. He quickly toweled himself off, turned off the light, and jumped under a luckily fat duvet. It was just after two in the morning.

The next morning early, Yevgeny and two technicians gingerly carried a silver, aluminum case containing what Joshua presumed was at least one mother board out to the vehicles. Joshua scuffed his shoes about in the gravel as he watched them load the case, hoping they weren't going to dump the modules and their bodies in a pit somewhere in the forest.

Yevgeny walked over and shook Andrey's hand. He looked at

Gabriel and Joshua perhaps assessing how they had made it through the evening before smiling and greeting them as well.

"A beautiful day in Russia, no?"

He must be impervious to drinking rocket fuel.

Once in the vehicles, Yevgeny led in the first SUV, while Andriy, Joshua, and Gabriel followed in the second driven by someone who appeared to be a conscript. This journey was more of a challenge for the SUVs as they left the paved road and ventured into the forest. It wasn't Paris to Dakar by any stretch of the imagination, but it wasn't an easy track either, heavy vehicle traffic had left ruts in the dirt and mud.

The small convoy wove its way through the trees. It looked to Joshua like the Russians had deliberately camouflaged the trail because he could not see the sky. The trees looked like they were tied together at the tops to conceal the track. Then they arrived at a small quadrangle carved out of the forest. The ground had been completely cleared of vegetation and only small patches of weed remained. There were several silos visible with a bunker in the middle. As they climbed out of their UAZ, Andriy gave a quick run-down. "There are three missiles here. Only one is Perimeter. The others have warheads. To get to the one silo we're visiting, we'll go into the bunker."

"They're all connected by tunnels?" Joshua asked.

"Yes, with security doors controlled by the command post inside the bunker."

Joshua was trying to remember which 007 movie this had begun to look like, when Yevgeny motioned them to hurry on. At the entrance, he picked up a telephone encased in a metal box, pushed a button, and asked permission to enter. A couple of minutes passed before the wheel on the door began to turn, much like a watertight door on a ship. A soldier poked his head out and then pushed the door open.

Joshua had expected drab concrete and chromate green paint. Instead, he found polished gray floors with industrial carpet and off-white walls displaying instructions, warnings, and patriotic posters.

Gabriel translated as Yevgeny spoke. "We will not enter the silo interior, but we can observe the technicians do their work."

They walked down a long hallway with several doglegs that intersected another hall, this one was circular and wrapped around the silo itself. Entry doors and an elevator faced them, and silence enveloped them.

Yevgeny must have paused for the effect. "Now we descend two levels, about twenty meters, where the work will be done."

The elevator was standing by, but it was small and they had to go in two groups. The technicians and Andriy went down first, while Yevgeny waited with Joshua and Gabriel.

"Is this your first time inside a silo?" Yevgeny asked.

Gabriel smiled. "This is my first time inside a *Russian* silo."

The elevator reappeared and they climbed in. A smooth ride down followed. The technicians and Andriy were putting on white overalls as they stepped out onto the deck. When Gabriel and Joshua had also dressed, Yevgeny patted them down to make sure no extra tools or hard objects had been inadvertently left in the pockets of their borrowed overalls. Then he opened the silver case, apparently checking that only necessary items were present. As they prepared to open the hatch into the silo, Yevgeny moved them to a thick glass portal nearby. "We shall observe from here."

Joshua felt like he was observing a NASA test run, where the astronauts practiced their assignments in a pool while the world watched. He saw why they couldn't go inside. Apart from keeping contamination out, the technicians stood on a small platform attached to the wall of the silo. There was room for the two of them and their case and that was it. One technician popped open an access door with a short wrench and then placed the tool back in its rack and latched its hold down. Every step was choreographed to avoid an accident. The other watched. Once he finished, the second man stuck his head inside the access door and began to work, finally pulling a board from inside the missile body. For the first time, Joshua looked down into the void below, and then up to see the olive green cylinder disappear out of sight.

How many have seen this view before?

The technicians never did anything at the same time. One worked, the other watched. The replacement board came out, was unwrapped, the trash stowed in a bag, and then was swapped places with its predecessor.

Simple.

The techs buttoned up the missile and cleaned up their space. Nothing could be left behind, debris or a tool in the wrong spot could be disastrous. Then they exited the silo space. "We are finished here," one said.

The technicians walked ahead as Andriy and Yevgeny conferred quietly. Then, Yevgeny led them back to the main hallway.

"We will go now," Andriy said. "Our work is complete; the technicians will do the rest of the repairs on their own."

A voice came out of the silo area, speaking in Chinese. Cho stepped out of the shadows. "Peter Liu, wait. Come back. I need to speak with you."

"Cho! What a surprise." Gabriel stepped back into the silo hallway. "How can I be of help."

There was an edge to their voices. Joshua turned to Andriy, whose concerned look was apparent. "Maybe we should walk," Andriy said.

Yevgeny hesitated but Andriy urged him on. "They'll be okay."

When Joshua turned, he could see Gabriel still speaking, but Cho was out of sight. Then Gabriel disappeared and for a moment all Joshua could hear was a conversation. Then the tunnel swallowed the sound as well.

They made the first dogleg when a shout echoed down the hall. Joshua heard one voice in Russian, "Safe journey!" and another yelling, "Goodbye" in Chinese.

"I guess we're finished here," Joshua said to Andriy, who smiled a grim smile.

Scurrying steps approached as Gabriel caught up with them. He looked pleased with himself, but his eyes showed he was troubled.

"Good?" Said Joshua.

"All good," said Gabriel. He was sweating a bit, but calm and his eyes reflected an energy that Joshua hadn't seen since Baku.

Once they gained the main road, it was a straight shot to the airfield. The polished Sukhoi waited for them on the tarmac and once again it was quickly rolling for takeoff.

As they cruised above Russia, Andriy briefed Gabriel and Joshua. "I won't return with you to Lithuania. A car will take you to Vilnius from the airfield and I will proceed home. I must report the acquisition of the Javelins to the boss. The money should be in the account shortly, so once you have verified that, please let me know the shipping details,"

"That was quick," Gabriel said.

"I had authorization already, so an interbank transfer was ordered. Like I said, it won't take long."

"Then you shall have the goods quickly," said Gabriel.

Andriy seemed pleased and poured three single malts from a crystal decanter he produced out of a cabinet. "I am sure you've had enough vodka to last you a while. This is better than distilled potatoes anyway."

"What is it?" asked Joshua.

"Glenfiddich 50-year-old," said Andriy.

Gabriel looked at Andriy askance. "So, this is a pretty expensive shot?"

"Yes," said Andriy. "The bottle cost more than my Mercedes."

They drank and settled back in their seats. It would not be a long flight, but everyone needed decompression time, some more than others. Gabriel seemed to be meditating, his eyes closed and his breathing slow and shallow.

Thirty minutes into the flight, a crew member came in and whispered to Andriy, who got up and followed him forward. Several minutes later Andriy came back and sat down heavily. He was quiet for a moment. "Yevgeny sent a message. It seems that Mister Cho fellow was found at the bottom of the missile silo. Cho either fell or jumped after we left. Headfirst, very messy. Yevgeny said it was a terrible accident, he is sure of that because he heard both your voices in the hallway before you rejoined us."

Andriy looked at Gabriel, a question in his eyes.

"Indeed, a terrible thing," Gabriel said and closed his eyes again.

They had just hopped out of the Mercedes in Vilnius when Joshua asked what happened.

"Cho said he finally recognized me. He met me at Chamjin-ri, a missile factory in NK."

"Were you there?"

"Yes, but under a different name and he knew it."

"Not good."

"No, not good, but no longer a problem, Grasshopper."

"He fell?"

"Yes. He said he would tell the Russians. What he was intending to say I have no idea and we don't need the complications. So, he fell."

Joshua imagined the moment when Gabriel acted. Maybe it was a punch to the heart. He knew Gabriel liked that one. He had seen the punch before, the master's bent legs straightening, a turn of the shoulder as the arm thrusts forward, elbow extending, the fist impacting and, equally quickly, pulling away. But it wasn't just muscle, it was the mind coordinating everything into focused power. It doesn't kill right away. The one-inch punch disables. The victim dies later. In this case though, the two-story drop would have finished the job.

"A terrible tragedy," said Joshua.

Gabriel was distracted, playing *Call to Honor* on his cell phone. "Yes, terrible."

Joshua turned back to the scenery streaming by the window to the tune of "Another One Bites the Dust" playing in his earbuds.

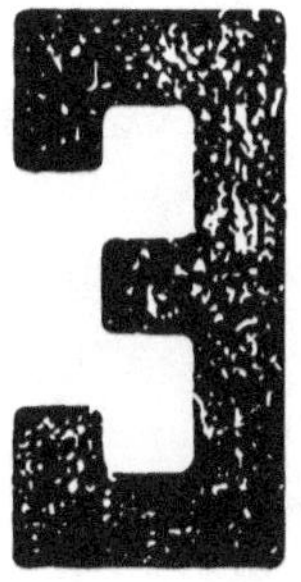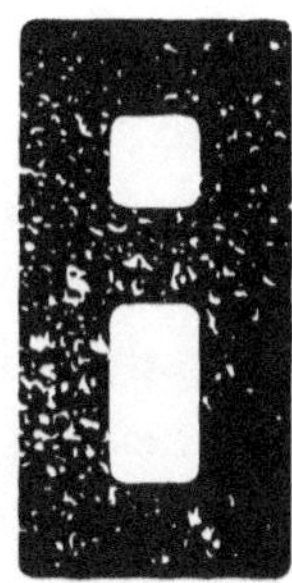

"WE'RE OUT." Joshua was talking on the secure cell walking along the river.

"I know. We've been watching," said Jamie. "You have any problems?"

"Nothing we couldn't handle. Most importantly, I think the main issue has been resolved," Joshua said.

"Except maybe for that one outlier."

"Well, yeah, there's that. When and where do we see you?"

"Can you get to Berlin?"

"Probably, but do we have to meet there? I'm not really keen on that city after what happened last time."

"You'll have to get over that. See you day after tomorrow. We have some stuff to discuss and not much time. Bring your partner."

They chose separate flights to Berlin. At least the gesture made a bit of sense cover-wise. Joshua got the short end of the stick and flew to Frankfurt, because there was only one direct flight. That cost an extra three hours. By the time he checked in it was late afternoon and when he got into his room, he had a text message waiting for him on his phone:

Tomorrow 2pm. Zoo Cafe. CC:G.

Which meant Gabriel had gotten the same text.

In the meantime, he settled back to read his *Berliner Morgenpost*, having decided cable was too annoying. It didn't take long before his attention wandered and he started into the puzzles and word games, which pushed his German vocabulary to the extreme. Tiring of that, he read the police blotter to see if he was wanted for any crimes, then he checked to see what movies were in town.

He walked out of the hotel and into the streams of people on the Ku'damm. It was mostly pairs and groups walking the street, businesspeople swinging their bags through the throngs heading for offices. He knew this neighborhood having lived nearby in the Uhland Straße some years before. Nothing looked the same at ground level. The stores and hotels had all changed ownership several times over since the Wall came down and the city had become even more frenetic.

He crossed the avenue and turned up heading for Kantstraße and saw the Delphi-Filmpalast. He was taking a roundabout tour of the city he knew so well. He wasn't going to tempt fate. Even in the light of day, he paid full attention to his surroundings. Gabriel should be underway as well, though Joshua would only see him if Gabriel wanted him to.

The cafeteria was a letdown. Small, clean, and efficient with all the food groups Joshua despised. It was cafeteria style, so he settled on a *Brotchen* sandwich, which appeared to be fresh, and took it to sit next to Jamie in the corner who was occupied with a big pretzel schmeared with extra sharp *Löwensenf.*

"Where's Gabe?" he asked.

"No clue, I assume he'll be here. He hates being left out."

"How are you doing?" Jamie might as well be Joshua's big brother as often as he'd asked him that question over the years.

"I'm happy," Joshua said. "Our boy didn't have us shot in the basement of Lubyanka and we got the job done. I think."

"You think? Why the hesitation?"

"We only witnessed the install of one device, and they said they were going to do the second. I'm hoping that's two out three. Any luck on the third one?"

"Getting closer. Belarus is still fairly easy terrain, and we have some good leads. Your tracking devices never showed up, but your cell phone talked to a tower near Kosvinsky, so we got a fix on that. We tracked your airplane after that."

Gabriel came up to the table carrying a plate with a couple of pizza slices and a Fanta, said something in what sounded like Korean, and sat down.

"Hi, Gabe," Jamie said.

"Hi. I need you to run a background check on a Korean we met. Cho Jae-sung, he's a Northerner. Mother from Guangzhou. He worked at the Chamjin-ri factory. Anything you can find, but there may be some chatter on the Russian side."

Jamie looked at Joshua while Gabriel tore into his pizza. "Right into things today. Why is this Cho important?"

"He's not anymore. He made me, recognized me from a trip I made to the factory several years ago. I'm just hoping there won't be any backlash from his accident."

"Accident?"

"He fell inside the silo. He's dead. Might have slipped."

"What does Hammer say?"

"Nothing other than it was a tragedy, so I assume we're okay."

"I'll ask folks to monitor things. Maybe something will show up if they send him home. I think Clairissa just needs the overview, not the details."

"What details? We weren't there. Hammer told us Cho must have done a swan dive. He got that from someone after we left," Gabriel said.

"What you're saying is there's no case."

"Right."

Jamie looked at Joshua again.

"Don't look at me. I know nothing," Joshua said.

There wasn't much else to say on the subject. Joshua thought back to the beginning of this operation. So far, at least six people had been waxed, not counting KB's soldiers in Azerbaijan.

"What else?" Jamie asked.

"I checked with the bank. All the money has been deposited," Gabriel said.

Jamie wiped his hands after swallowing some of his tough pretzel. "Which makes this all the more interesting. Our friend has led you around on quite an expedition and given us good information, but why? Especially, when you consider the Javelins."

A noisy crew of Japanese tourists came into the café and kept the single server busy spreading Nutella on cold Belgian Waffles.

Oh, wait, she threw them in the microwave first, even better. And for dinner they'll go to Burger King and have a Hamburger Royale, thought Joshua.

Gabriel polished off his pizza and drink. Jamie had given up on the pretzel and Joshua decided his sandwich wasn't at all what he needed. There were good restaurants in Berlin, many of them near-by. This wasn't one of them.

"The Javelins are curious," Gabriel said. "If he is trying to stop the conflict, why fuel it with more weapons? On the other hand, helping us disable Perimeter gives us a slight advantage. I'm just not sure what the next step should be."

Jamie stretched. Hands over his head, he worked his neck back and forth. "Tight," he muttered.

"You're spending too much time at your desk," Joshua said.

"Maybe. But we do have a couple of next steps. Clairissa already instructed the office in Yerevan to work with the locals and stop the onward drone shipment."

"How will they do that? The Armenian *Siloviki* must be taking its cut from the deal," said Gabriel.

"It's called quid pro quo and it's already underway," Jamie said. "The other step is for you to handle, Gabriel. Tell Hammer to send something provocative across the border before the army moves."

"Send what?"

"A harbinger."

KB HAD MUCH TO DO and didn't relish spending his precious time with the Chief of Yerevan station explaining himself. KB was certain the man had been chosen because of some diversity program that valued under-qualified idiots with little field time and zero recruitments, but he didn't say anything because he'd probably get slapped with some HR violation.

Instead, he listened to Chief Yerevan with no small amount of skepticism while sitting in the man's office, decorated as it was with pictures of him shaking hands with people KB had never seen before.

The chief was lecturing KB. "We do this, you do that," he said. What he meant was, "You get your boys to do that messy stuff." But this job was beyond anything headquarters had asked of KB or, for that matter, Sirwan before, and he knew what that meant—he needed to get personally involved. The chief thought the Honey Bear team could handle things on their own and said so. KB knew better; they needed an American on the ground to ensure they did what would be necessary. If he wasn't there, they might just say "Why should we risk our lives for them?" He needed to be with them. That wasn't anything he was afraid of, on the contrary, he'd gotten his hands dirty a number of times. It was, however, something that made the seniors very nervous and made them ask questions like "what if." They would try to stop him if they could. But there were ways around that. It was simply a question of risk versus gain. If he didn't go in, Sirwan and his comrades might even refuse. So, it would be up to him to lead the operation.

Once long ago, KB asked a man he respected if he'd ever disobeyed an order.

"Plenty of times," the man said, "especially in Vietnam."

"Why there?"

"War zones are nebulous places. An officer told me to break contact and leave my wounded people behind. That wasn't gonna happen. What about you?"

"I wouldn't call it disobey but I did mold the wording to fit my purpose."

"How?"

"It was Mogadishu. There was a standing order not to go anywhere near K4 Circle—a very bad section of town. We had a line on a terrorist we were looking for at a house two blocks from K4. I committed a map reading error and went along."

"Did you get the guy?"

"Unfortunately, no. Our folks went in with a snatch team, but the guy wasn't there. It turned out to be a hornet nest. We caught the bad guys unawares and blew the hell out of the place. A lot of baddies died, but not the one we were looking for. I reported the firefight but forgot to mention that I was there."

"And no one found out?"

"I think the chief suspected, but he never said a word."

No one would know this time either, KB thought.

KB said he planned to fly in and out in one night. A single MI-19 loaded with more ammunition and rockets for one last job before the element was pulled out of country. He'd ride in with it, just to make sure the stuff made it to the right people and come right back. *Scout's Honor.*

"You know how foreign contractor pilots are, they might just dump the stuff or sell it on the black market and tell us all was well," KB said.

The chief gave him the side eye but had to admit he was right. KB didn't mention that his pilots were the best contractors around and he trusted them implicitly. He loved guys that played "Ride of the Valkyries" over the sound system on infil.

Sirwan waited on the LZ with his people. Altogether they were sixteen with KB. The other groups were far to the south getting ready to hit their last target, hopefully at the same time that Sirwan's group hit theirs. And then out and back home for R&R, whatever that might be in Kurdistan these days.

KB hadn't explained the target to Sirwan in detail yet. He only said it was a surgical strike. Sirwan saw the tools his boss had brought for the job. More ammunition, grenades, and rockets. When it was all off-loaded, KB waved off the helicopter. Sirwan yelled at him as the chopper's rotor wash made talking impossible. He wanted to know why KB stayed. The bird lifted off and turned to go home, but KB waited until it was quiet.

"This might be a tough one and I need to be here."

Their burden was cut to the bare essentials. Two canteens of water and enough food for two days—the minimum daily requirement. Basic first aid kits for trauma, water purification pills. Even if it looked like clean, mountain water, it had to be treated because the goats carried bacteria inside them that does bad things to humans. And two radios. Everything else was meant to do damage to the enemy.

Half a day later, they reached their two trucks. Now they could save energy. Their target was a place called Ganja. An airbase, not the weed, KB said, although Sirwan was the only one in the group that understood the joke. KB said that the Turks had sent many Bayraktar drones, and their mission was to take out that capability.

"How many drones?" Sirwan asked.

"At least twenty-five."

"So, we destroy them all?"

"Not quite," said KB. "I've another idea."

In one day, they'd reached a line of hills about five kilometers short of the objective, a tiny village called Hachagaya where friends waited. That night, from the roof of the home that they hid in, KB showed Sirwan the target across the valley.

"The drones are in the two big hangars on the western end." KB pointed them out through binoculars. "The security level is pretty low. We'll approach from the west and breach the perimeter here." He pointed to a photomap, weighted down with rocks on the roof.

"We will attack the hangars?" Sirwan asked.

"No, we'll attack this building." A small square near the runway. "That's the control facility. If we destroy that, the drones are useless." Critical node 102.

Their planning was based solely on the photomap and the view from across the valley. The many small villages and suburbs of the larger city would prevent them from getting closer until the next evening. The attack would be reminiscent of a British Long Range Desert Group raid in Libya—hit and run.

They rested through the day, but sleep wouldn't come to anyone but the most determined. To make matters worse, the guard duty schedule kept everyone's body-clock out of sync with the real world.

KB was awake and roaming around before anyone else started to move. He went back up to the roof, nodding at the two women watching the approaches. They were the early warning sentinels, wearing robes over their combat utilities, weapons concealed. He looked at the airbase through his binos, well selected for their light-gathering abilities. Then he scanned back along the route he had worked out from the maps in Yerevan. KB and his team would be on their own after this. No friends north of here.

Drive the route, crash the gates, do havoc, and then escape. Hopefully they would make the pick-up zone beyond the reservoir and Yenikand Dam about twenty kilometers away. If the trucks held up, if they could get across the dam, if the bad guys just rolled over, all the usual hazards.

He was ready. He'd been ready since his father had encouraged him to follow in his footsteps as a soldier. Born and raised in India, KB emigrated to the United States with his mother after her husband was killed in a clash with the Chinese on the border. He'd been soldiering since the day he graduated from college, first with the army and then in the shadows. *Once more into the fray.*

KB went over the plan one final time in his head. Given the size of the unit and with only two trucks, it was the best they could hope for. The trucks were loaded as last light began to settle in. Last minute instructions were shared. Sirwan would ride in the second truck, he'd take the lead. They had the radios to stay in touch, but he didn't expect complications. The airfield had been attacked two years before but since the 2020 war with Armenia, security had gone lax. The Azeri military was mostly concentrated in the south, chasing shadows, trying to figure out who was attacking the Russian peacekeepers. Tonight would be the Azeri's last chance to resolve that conundrum. KB's job was to make sure they didn't.

They threaded their way north. First through the hills, then down into the river valley. Ganja, the second largest city in the country, more a collection of villages than anything else, stretched out before them. They were on a two-lane asphalt side road, one of the few that cut across the valley. It would bring them close to the airfield and, hopefully, take them out to the north after they completed the mission.

The countryside looked peaceful enough. Evening light had turned to dark, but lights shone in the windows of the homes. There was a streetlight at almost every junction that told him what to expect to his front and the answer was clear roads. The side road they used paralleled a larger road and it now turned toward the main terminal area. They were heading for the back door because, while there were nice fences around the front, his satellite imagery showed the far perimeter unguarded. They proceeded past the western end of the runway to take a look at their target: a one-story building surrounded by low trees and brush. It lay about one hundred and fifty meters from the hangars and the same distance from the runway to its north.

KB saw only one aircraft on the parking apron. Its tail was just visible from behind a building. Maybe cargo, maybe passenger, they'd find out later. He had hoped to see several to give his team more targets.

He directed the driver into an open, dusty field on the outskirts of the next village. Both trucks stopped on the edge of a grove of trees. Farther on, another truck was parked with its lights off. Probably of no consequence, but he told the driver to check it out anyway. Then he walked back to Sirwan's vehicle and climbed up on the step. "You saw everything?"

"Yes. We don't even need to cut a fence. This is too easy."

"Don't count on that. We go in as we planned. If we have time and no opposition, there's an airplane to knock out as well. But for now, we wait. We don't want to get to the pick-up zone too early."

KB used his binoculars to look at the road as far back toward the airfield as he could. It was so quiet, he started to wonder if the intelligence on the timing of the drone delivery might have been wrong. He shook the thought off, collateral had mentioned the Turks were helping build the control facility months ago. They must have just completed it. *The drones had to be here.* He wasn't going to dwell on it, the main target was the ground station.

Behind him, he heard a rustle of plastic. Behind him sat rows of greenhouses, their opaque plastic skins buffeted in the breeze. He would like to see what grew inside, but the mission came first.

Sirwan joined him. "Everyone is clear on the plan. We are ready."

KB pulled back his jacket sleeve and looked at the luminous hands of his watch. "We go in ten minutes."

Sirwan nodded as he checked his own watch, then went back to pass the word.

Minutes passed. KB thought he was doing well not checking his watch every thirty seconds. One final check. *Time.*

He whirled his finger in a circle above his head as he walked past Sirwan's window—*Let's go*—knocked on the tail gate and climbed into the cab of his own truck.

"Go." He picked up his Kalashnikov and tapped the magazine one more time to make sure it was seated.

The trucks did a slow, sweeping turn across the field to get back to the main road, then turned south. KB pointed at the path that left their road. Little more than a cart track, it led straight to the end of the runway. Remnants of fence, long fallen, stretched out in the weeds to either side. Once on the tarmac, Sirwan's truck pulled up alongside, a momentary pause, and a hand gesture. *Advance.*

Both sped on, spreading apart as they headed for the building. KB couldn't believe they hadn't been confronted yet. The house was surrounded by a chain-link fence. He hadn't seen that in the photos, or it came later. *No matter.*

KB's driver smashed into the gate and stopped. He backed out and swung the truck to the side and slammed on the brakes.

KB yelled, "Go, go, go!" But the troops were already bailing out the back. Two men with RPGs ran as far as the gate and fired at the front of the building. Smoke and dust immediately taking visibility to near zero.

Sirwan's truck stopped thirty meters away, parallel to the fence. His troops were also out, and two more RPGs slammed into the building. The assault team ran forward as the front door opened, a man staggered out, trying to escape the maelstrom inside. The first bursts of an AK and he fell. Grenades tossed inside, the grenadiers stood to the side, with the wall as a shield. The building began to burn, but KB had to see what was inside to confirm its destruction.

He followed the four assaulters into the front room where a pall of smoke greeted him at the door. They moved deeper into the building, a second room was untouched, full of computer stations and large monitors, the kind used to watch ground targets from a drone's camera. Bursts of machine-gun fire wasted much of the equipment, but he needed it all gone. More grenades and everyone backed out, the concussion shaking dust and smoke down on top of them.

KB yelled at them to get out as he pulled out his own special toys—something called "Willie Pete." He made sure everyone was clear and pulled the pins, tossing one after another into the room and ran for the front.

He saw his shadow etched on the wall as the first white phosphorus went off, its brilliance turning everything white. He hoped he was running fast enough when the second exploded.

Out of breath, everyone ran back toward the truck. Sirwan met him halfway. "Is it done?"

"It's done. Get the airplane."

Sirwan turned and ran for his truck. Loading quickly, they drove forward, farther into the base, behind the building that shielded the airplane. Firing commenced again. KB heard two grenades explode and flickers of yellow and orange reflected on the airplane's tail.

"Get out there," he told himself, urging Sirwan to return quickly.

They were lucky. No opposition. The Azeris must have actually thought they were secure here. Sirwan's truck headed back toward them and he sighed in relief. The soldiers from his truck waited for guidance, they hadn't planned for any further action, they needed to load and leave.

"*Şef!*" one of the men yelled. *Boss!* He pointed at the hangar. The huge doors were sliding open. *Great, a chance to put a couple of grenades inside.*

His second thought was: *Crap.*

An armored car, an old Russian BMP, like some dinosaur awakened from a long sleep, came out of the cavernous building. KB saw its 30mm canon before anything else and a couple of orange flashes confirmed it was deadly. A small group of soldiers, no doubt Azeri, ran behind it using the armor for cover. Muzzle flashes showed they intended to fight.

KB didn't need to give an order. His troops spread out on a line and began to fire back, taking up positions in the ditches along the taxiway. The RPG men fired two more rounds, their comrades assisting with reloads. He knew they had to kill it quickly or they were dead. Its frontal armor could withstand an RPG strike. Their machine gun fire slowed the Azeri soldiers, who looked for cover behind the BMP's skirts, but the 30mm was still firing. The canvas of their truck fluttered as several rounds pierced the fabric. It was only a matter of time.

Sirwan must have seen it at the same time. His truck flew across the tarmac directly at the BMP. The canvas top on Sirwan's truck was gone and two grenadiers stood in the rear as it closed the gap, then flames as their rockets streaked toward the target. One flew over the BMP and exploded on the ground beyond, the second hit the suspension breaking a track. The BMP slewed to the right and came to a halt, momentarily throwing off the gunner's aim. The turret rotated back in KB's direction. The gun's sting was still potent.

Sirwan's truck was almost on top of the armor when his crew fired two more RPGs. Both rockets hit the turret, which blew off like a bottle cap under pressure. It flew up in the air to land on the tarmac with a loud bang. The remaining Azeri soldiers, stripped of their protection, ran for the hangar. The troops fired slowly now, picking off the running soldiers one by one; bodies falling to the tarmac. KB ran to the RPG gunners and told them to fire into the hangar. Rockets bounced across the floor of the building and exploded. Fires flared up inside, outlining white drones.

No casualties so far. KB was ecstatic. He waved at Sirwan as his truck pulled up near them. "Let's get out of here. We lead." He jumped in the cab and saw the driver slumped over the wheel, his torso mangled. A 30mm shell had pierced the door. The truck wasn't going anywhere, the instrument panel was destroyed, and smoke curled up from under the hood.

KB jumped out and shouted at Sirwan. One truck and twelve passengers, there was room for all. Sirwan and two others pulled the dead driver out and set him gingerly in the cargo bed of the second truck and the rest of the team scrambled aboard. KB and Sirwan climbed into the cab and they took off.

"We still have plenty of ammunition and RPG rounds," Sirwan said, "in case we meet anyone crossing the dam. The plane—you'll like this, it was a Turkish A-400."

"We're good." KB smiled inside but felt weak and his leg was damp. He pulled out a mini-flashlight. His left trouser leg was shiny black. "I'm hit."

Ten kilometers out, the truck was able pull over and stop. Sirwan had managed to apply a tourniquet while on the road, but now he did a quick assessment. KB appeared to be sleeping, his breathing was shallow and irregular. Sirwan cut the trousers away and saw an entry wound but no exit. Blood seeped out, lots of blood loss. He stuffed a clotting bandage deep into the wound. KB cried out a bit then moaned as his eyes flickered open.

"Can you hear me?" Sirwan asked.

He nodded.

"You'll be fine. The bleeding has stopped."

KB closed his eyes. "Get me home, brother."

JOSHUA SAT AT A TABLE in the hotel restaurant. Soft light filtered by diaphanous drapes settled in on tables, elegantly set awaiting guests to come down from their rooms and maybe one or two tourists who might want to sample the well-reviewed fare but couldn't pay the room rate. Not cheap, but at a higher *niveau* than any other hotel on the Ku'damm. As expected, breakfast that morning was excellent.

He was sipping his first cup of coffee when Gabriel came in and acknowledged him with a nod. He went straight to the buffet and, after heaping his plates with food, came and sat across from Joshua. The waiter came by to pour coffee as soon as Gabriel settled into his chair.

"Forget to have dinner last night?" Joshua asked.

"You know I didn't. I have a fast metabolism."

Jamie joined them, not being a man to pass on a decent breakfast paid for by someone else's expense account. Gabriel's accounting was much more lenient that the USG's standard procedures. Normal per diem would have only permitted Jamie to have a sausage biscuit and a cup of coffee.

At Gabriel's insistence, they had already changed hotels once. He had mentioned something about security, but Joshua thought the crotchety curmudgeon meant his bed wasn't comfortable enough. And comfortable it was. The Hotel Zoo was one of those places that transported its guests out of the mundane and into old world decadence as soon as they crossed the hotel's threshold. A decadence that had been recently upgraded by a large infusion of cash. A very large infusion.

Gabriel decided the restaurant was secure enough to speak. No patrons were within earshot and the staff kept a respectful distance. He also doubted anyone had time to set up an eavesdropping operation.

They all knew timing was everything but Day Zero continued to be a nebulous concept. It had varied from being two weeks away, to four weeks, then maybe six weeks. Mostly due to the information Hammer had given them. Almost five weeks had passed, so that narrowed the window significantly, but there still seemed to be no fixed date.

"I sent our friend a message. Told him the Javelins are underway and then I asked him to arrange for your harbinger—a single drone— to be sent across the border seventy-two hours before kickoff. A recce drone, nothing armed. He said he could handle it. That will give us the date and maybe give the Liths a kick in the pants," said Gabriel.

"Liths? That sounds like a tribe from *Star Wars*. Anyway, we'll need to tell them what it means so they'll be ready," Jamie said between bites of his *Brötchen* and ham.

"You'll need to arrange that. I can't use Matt to pass any more messages. His counterparts are suspicious," Joshua said.

"We'll get it to the DATT and ask him to pass it. That should work." Jamie said.

"As long as he moves the info fast enough. But we still don't have a location for the third leg of Perimeter, do we?" said Joshua.

"The analysts think they've narrowed it down to several promising locations and they're putting high-resolution sensors over them. We might have something soon. Did you ask Hammer if the third module will be replaced?"

"I did and he said they can't get to it. The high command won't allow them to visit the site."

"They're willing to risk a bad launch over compromising the location?"

"Seems so. We may have inadvertently changed things when we quote unquote fixed the other two. Now they must think they're safe," Gabriel said.

"They are safe. Just not in the way they think," said Jamie. "One missile could still launch Armageddon."

"Great, so we still need to find it and then take it out."

"Yeah. But there is good news, sort of. Your Javelin shipment is underway. I sent you the contact regimen for the transfer to give to your friend. And the other news is that the Iranian drones have been held up. Yerevan agreed to impound them for inspection. Unofficially, they are telling the Russians they're upset with the situation in Nagorno. That'll hold things up for a while."

"What did that cost?"

"Unfortunately, too much. Our liaison officer for Honey Bear was badly wounded."

"That's Kipling, isn't it? How bad?" Joshua asked.

"He's gone."

"Damn." Joshua exhaled long and hard, the sound of resignation, of powerlessness. He stared at his hands as if he could change something with them.

"The teams were all airlifted out after the last mission. He was taken to Yerevan, but it was too late. How do you know him?"

"KB and I were on the same team a long time ago," said Joshua.

"A small brotherhood, isn't it?" said Gabriel.

"We few," Joshua said. It was a hoarse whisper. The others saw he was elsewhere and were silent.

So few, and yet so much done. The pain of a comrade's loss was hard to bear. He hoped the sacrifice would be worth it.

IT SOUNDED LIKE AN ANGRY BUZZSAW, although the soldier knew buzzsaws didn't get angry. The noise was eerily similar to recordings he'd heard of the German V-1 rockets falling on London during World War II. A pulse-jet engine announced its presence, buzzing across the sky until the engine cut out, then deadly silence with just a whistle of wind as it fell into the city and exploded.

The whirling propeller buzzed, getting louder and louder, then the drone whizzed over his head through the early morning mists. The engine sputtered once. Bad fuel. The soldier saw its gray V-shaped wing that continued into the countryside and a different sound kicked in. The whoosh of a rocket, and several seconds later, a loud bang. He hoped his comrades got it. The chatter on his radio increased, there was at least one jubilant cry of success before someone told everyone else to shut up. Radio discipline.

The first shot of the war.

Commander Melis placed herself in a defensive position at the doorway, arms crossed tight over her chest, her face set in defiance. "Don't say it."

The team room was empty except for two officers. The troops were still out on a practical exercise.

"I'm sorry, commander," Matt said. "I don't think I understand. Don't say what?"

Melis contemplated saying what she thought the American would say but didn't. The drone incursion had proven that the Americans' information was correct, war was coming sooner than they thought.

"A drone was brought down twenty-five kilometers inside our border near an old army base. It was Russian, a Geran-2 of Iranian-origin.

"Damn! Sorry, ma'am. I mean … whatever. Was it armed?"

"No, Unarmed and unmarked, maybe a test run. No more have been spotted."

"Unmarked? The only place I've seen that was in Syria."

"You saw them in Syria? You were there?"

"In 2017 and '18. The Russians flew drones over us all the time for reconnaissance. We shot a couple down, they were unmarked."

"Shot them down? You weren't fighting the Russians then. Why?"

"Because the Russians, and their allies the Syrian government forces, made a bad decision and attacked our base. We told them to back off but they didn't listen, so we brought everything we had down on them."

"How many were you?"

"Forty-two Americans and around two hundred SDF—Syrian Democratic Forces—against maybe five hundred pro-Bashir government troops and two hundred Russians who turned out to be Wagner mercenaries."

"I think I've heard of this incident."

"The press called it the Battle of Khasham. The Russians and the Syrians lost that one." Matt smiled grimly. "They didn't have the resources. We had the firepower and called it all in on top of them: artillery, air assets, and of course our own small armory."

"How many men did you lose?"

"No Americans, but one of our local SDF counterparts was killed."

"None?"

"None. The bad guys lost maybe two hundred and more wounded. No one is sure exactly and the Russians aren't upfront about such things. Anyway, the two UAVs we shot down were unmarked. I think that could mean this one also belongs to Wagner."

"This isn't coming from one of your mythical agents, is it?" she asked.

"I don't have mythical agents, commander." He was irritated with Melis. She wants information and when he gives it to her, she disparages his sourcing, or his powers of deduction. "And that last tidbit comes from personal experience."

"Take it easy, captain," she said. "I thought your people would want to know. We're looking at the data to see if we can pinpoint where they launched it from, but the initial radar tracking says it came from somewhere inside Belarus."

"If it's alright with you, I'd like to give any info you have to our DATT. Since he gave us the warning, he'd appreciate the gesture."

"I have already cleared it with Colonel Bizauskas. He gave his authorization for that. Our people are passing it through channels, but he thought you might be able to get it there faster. Time seems to be of the essence now."

"Frankly, I'm surprised you've entrusted me with this, ma'am. I thought I'd burned all my bridges with you and the commander."

"Not all of them, captain. Plus, you seem to be more aggressive than the other captains. What do you call it? Forward leaning? That seems appropriate today."

"I think they are just playing it safe with you, commander. After they saw how I got my hands slapped, they don't want to get on your or the colonel's wrong side."

"I don't have a wrong side. Just play by the rules and we'll get along." She allowed herself a tight smile that was accommodating but gave a warning at the same time. Don't mess with me.

"Understood, commander."

"Stop by the front gate. They have a piece of the drone for you."

Matt smiled this time. "Thanks, I'll give it to the DATT, it will make him happy, and he might work harder for us."

Matt started out of the building but stopped short. He turned back to Melis. "I almost forgot. This means we have seventy-two hours to war."

"I haven't forgotten, captain. We plan to go on full alert this evening. So don't forget to come back, we'll need you."

Matt picked up the remnants of the UAV, or the drone as Melis called it, from the guard and studied it for a moment before he carried it to his car. It was a smoking gun in a couple of ways. It was a ragged piece of plastic about ten inches square. He could see Russian words on the interior of the shell that were painted over with what appeared to be Arabic script. A few electronic components were still attached, one of which was marked ABT—Dallas TX. Clearly, a cork had not been put in Iran's supply line. But that wasn't his problem, that was an issue for the export control feds. It would make a nice souvenir piece for someone.

He headed for the capital, stopping by the side of the road to call ahead so the DATT knew he was coming to the Chancery. He sent a quick text as well, the proper key word subtly inserted into the clear text.

Hopefully, dad would see the message in time to meet later.

By the time he turned onto Akmenų street, he heard his phone ping. Assuming it was from his dad, he left it alone as he approached the well-guarded entry to the embassy facility. A police van was parked conspicuously by the side of the road with two cops inside trying to stay warm. Two other policemen with H&K submachine guns strapped across their chests walked the street awaiting whatever terrorist assault might come on their watch. Although they were more likely wondering whether the coffee in their thermos was still warm.

They eyed him carefully as he drove in. His civilian-plated Skoda was an anomaly on a street usually frequented by vehicles with CD plates. Which was why he held up a small placard that displayed the Lithuanian MoD emblem. When they showed no signs of wanting to shoot him, he drove on to the front gate. The entryway was manned by an eclectic mix of civilian security, contractors, Lithuanians, an ex-pat British soldier, and an American manager, the second line of defense for the Americans inside. The first line was the Marine Security Guards— the MSGs—who manned Post One and the rest of the security points inside the Chancery, the big building where the Ambassador and the Foreign Service Officers worked.

The embassy was the beating heart of the American diplomatic effort in any country. In out-of-the-way countries, it might be a sleepy place, like Malta where there wasn't much diplomacy to worry about. In others, it was the center of government and media attention often depending on which rock-star ambassador had been appointed to serve the president's will, like Paris or the Court of St James. In some, it was a beehive, the ambassador constantly working the host government for leverage at the UN, the military assisting, advising, and supplying the local defense forces, and maybe the FBI hunting down terrorist or criminal threats. How effective it could be was another question because so much depended on the focus of the administration in power. *What is the sound of one hand clapping?* Matt didn't have the answer to that, he had no clue how effective this embassy was. What he did know was that it would soon be tested to the maximum.

He looked around at the fences, bollards, armed guards, and blast-proof windows and knew the security precautions necessary, official Americans were targets overseas. But being inside a hardened compound with the isolation that brought meant the embassy personnel were cut off from normal interaction with the locals whose thoughts and opinions often went unheard. Real representation meant meeting with ordinary people, not just the privileged. That's why he would never want to work inside the fence. It was just too hard to break out of the cubicle.

He parked his car in a visitor spot and while the DATT and an assistant walked toward him. *They're excited to get some real evidence.* It would be worth several intelligence reports without them having had to do much fieldwork. He could see the report's text already: *A section of a Russian Geran-2 Unmanned Aerial Vehicle recovered by DAO from a damaged example which was shot down by Lithuanian Air Defense forces and crashed at GEO COORDS (insert appropriate here). The section is apparently constructed of composite plastic … yadda, yadda, et cetera.*

No mention of how or where the office obtained it, because Matt would tell them it was a gift. He didn't want his team's presence advertised in an all-points bulletin that could be read by anyone with a secret clearance around the world. The DATT would pouch the thing back to DIA Headquarters at Joint Base Bolling on the Anacostia River where it would be subjected to even more detailed exploitation. More Brownie points. And then someone will hang it on the wall of the Director's briefing room with a brass plaque describing the hazardous conditions a brave Defense Attaché must have endured to obtain it.

Right.

He got out of the car and opened the trunk, flipping back the army blanket that covered the piece. The Defense Attaché, Lieutenant

Colonel Frank C. Nordheim, looked and prodded, *oohed* and *aahed* as Matt explained the circumstances of acquisition. He didn't need to mention that it was the first drone fired into Lithuania, but he did underline that it had come out of Belarus and provided the crash location.

He didn't dislike Nordheim, he barely knew the man. Matt didn't hang in the same rarified circles that Nordheim frequented, which were usually somewhere close to the Lithuanian General Staff or the DATTs from other diplomatic legations. It could be that he was a great DATT. Could be—some were, some weren't—but Matt was a bit prejudiced based on his previous encounters with them in other countries and the fact that Nordheim had never visited the American teams training here or even asked for a briefing on their mission.

He had his own superiors to worry about, the B-Team commander, Major Mercier, for example. The guy who could ruin his career with one swipe of the pen and Mercier reported to the DATT in country—presently LTC Nordheim. Short of war, the DATT could convince the Ambassador to have him thrown out of country in a heartbeat. Keeping this arcane chain of command happy was what he really had to worry about. It was a mean and vicious cycle. But such was life in the army … at least while he was in Vilnius. And that might change soon. Once hostilities commenced, all bets were off.

Nordheim told his assistant to go back inside and begin to gin up a message template while he scribbled notes. He described how he would send the first as a FLASH Night Action Required to get everyone's attention, even if the message would come into Washington mid-morning Pentagon time. Then he figured he could get two or three more IRs on details.

This was true offensive action. But the DATT was happy—at least until he realized that this meant war was coming.

Once free of the American bastion, Matt headed for the old town. He knew a bookstore where he could hang out for a while before the meet. A quick look at his messages confirmed his father would be at the meet site at 16.30, just as darkness would begin to fall.

The Green Bridge was right where Matt had left it. It was their contingency, initial contact point and then follow the leader to the actual meeting site. His father didn't even approach the bridge proper. Matt saw Joshua on the road leading to it, but then his dad broke right and headed off down the path along the embankment. Matt followed doing a hook under the bridge which gave him an easy look back. Nothing behind or on the opposite bank of the river, he was free of trackers. He made no effort to catch up. Matt left the path and crossed the main road to fall in behind.

After a few more turns, Joshua chose Gediminas Avenue, a street that was new to Matt, and entered a building. Matt got closer and saw the sign over the front, *Jaukios Kačių,* Cozy Cats. At first, he thought it was an erotic bar—he didn't know Dad was into such things. But no, it was a simple speakeasy. There were multiple rooms and he found Joshua in the corner of one, at a table for two.

"Hi, Dad!" He spoke softly, the music wasn't that loud.

Joshua clapped him on the forearm. "Hi." He had a big smile on his face, happy to see his son. "Howzit?" Joshua slipped into Liberian slang as he occasionally did.

"Did you hear about the intruder?" Matt asked.

"No, tell me."

Matt repeated the drone story he'd told Nordheim with the added details that Melis gave him.

He paused when the waitress came. They both ordered tonics and left them. Joshua waited as he watched her walk away.

"Our friend told us it would come, which means he is still in the game and giving us good stuff. I guess it also means that Melis has accepted you?"

"Kinda. Maybe. Not really," said Matt. "She thinks I'm still a wild card."

"She gave you the space junk though. That means something."

"I suppose. What's new with you?"

"A couple of things. Remember what I told you about Perimeter?" Matt nodded. "We may have taken care of two thirds of it. But there's one last piece we need to find. If we can do that, it will take things down a notch. Then maybe we can do some hard negotiations without that sword hanging over our heads."

"If not?"

"I don't really want to think about that, but we're close, the bloodhounds are out in full force." Joshua didn't know what else to tell his son.

Gabriel's and his escapade to the Urals had been only partially successful, if they didn't nail down the location of the last missile, then the Russians still had that one last ace to play, and the time clock was ticking down to Day Zero. At least the Agency agreed to push more information down to the user level, but Hammer hadn't produced anything until the drone flew. Joshua wasn't even sure what would be useful other than an alert before the Russian forces actually began to move. Maybe there wouldn't be a repeat of Pearl Harbor this time. He sighed, the realization that the moment was almost on them. "I guess we were right. They are coming," Joshua said.

With that expectation in mind, they reviewed brevity codes and family vacation plans, not knowing what would happen next. Then Joshua knew it was time to break. Matt would go first, he'd wait. They sat in silence for a moment, each watching the crowd starting to fill the bar. Then Matt tapped the table twice. Their eyes met. "Bye, Dad."

"Stay in touch, son." That meant email, the approved father-to-son network where they could exchange banalities but knew each was out there listening, this time not so far away.

Keep it together. He tried hard as he watched his younger self walk away. Matt moves gracefully, Joshua noted proudly. *A good man with places to go.*

Sitting alone, Joshua switched to Scotch. He called the waitress over and asked for a double. She called it a "Lap Frog" when she brought it, close enough but he thought there was a Scot somewhere who would be offended. He tried figuring out how much time was left before Day Zero, less than seventy-two hours but gave up trying and paid the bill before walking out into the street and heading home to his hotel.

He looked left as he came out, pausing to put on his gloves. The streetlights, inadequate as they were, threw cones of yellow onto the street. He took a step and turned back to his right. A shadow ahead, something, someone, pulled back into the dark, maybe a doorway about fifty meters down the road. Head down to pretend concentration, he walked on. *We shall see.*

He had a straight route back and another for moments like these. Stair-stepping through the neighborhood, he stopped at restaurants to read menus, but nothing obvious. He crossed one street as the light began to turn against him. He walked on a bit and looked at the night sky through the trees. He didn't want to lose anyone. There was an alley he knew, close to his hotel but not a direct line, so he'd give them half a chance. It was dark but security lights provided enough illumination. He heard the footfalls this time, only one person. The alley had a dogleg, he turned the corner and disappeared into a recess to wait.

Soft footfalls came close and slowed down. The shadow came around the corner. A pause. A dark figure passed in front of him, the steps quickened. It was a very short walk to the main street, the tail probably thought he'd turned one way or the other at the sidewalk. Joshua stepped out, checking the empty alley behind him. He followed.

When he got to the street, the shadow hurried away from him. Joshua smiled. *Whoever it is, she's not that well trained.* He walked slowly behind the shadow. Ahead, the woman stopped at an intersection and looked frantically in all directions except the correct one. She hesitated and reached into a pocket. *Her cell.* She spoke into the phone then looked back toward where he stood. He looked back as well. Predictably, there were two heavies about seventy-five meters behind him, one with a cell phone to his ear. The woman stayed put, but the others began to close in on him. Thinking one was better than two, he walked forward. When he got close to the shadow, he said in English, "Are you looking for me, Commander Melis?"

"Who the hell are you?" she said.

He took his hand out of his pocket and returned the CZ into the belt holster he'd pulled it from in the alley.

"A friend," he said. "Let's go somewhere and talk. I'll lead." He turned his back to her hoping she wouldn't stick a knife in it. He also hoped she would be curious enough to follow him.

A café presented itself and Joshua entered. Bare brick walls, abstract art, black-painted ductwork across an open ceiling, a modern Euro-Scania vibe like many others in town. Luckily, it had yet to be overrun by the evening crowd. He ordered from the bar and found a decent spot. He sat down and waited. The waiter was fairly quick and brought his scotch, this time with soda and ice. Under the circumstances, he thought it a good idea to pace himself. A quick text to Matt as he watched the door. Five minutes later Melis followed him inside.

She must be coordinating my arrest.

She had abandoned her coat and the hat she'd been wearing, probably handed them to one of her accomplices. Although her shoes were clunky, he judged she was maybe five foot nine in stocking feet—a tall woman—and nicely dressed. But what caught his attention was her face. She was good looking. Matt had told him that much—tolerable, he'd said—but Joshua had a broader appreciation for women than his son. *Maybe being older also changes the equation.*

He waved when she looked in his direction and, after a last glance behind her, she joined him. He stood and pulled out a chair for her. She could seat herself, but his first assessment would be based on her reaction to his chivalry, and it looked like she wanted to find a different chair. There wasn't one, so she sat. *Resists direction from others,* he decided. He had the spy's seat, watching the front door. He could see the rear door as well … just in case.

She started to speak, but Joshua interrupted, "Would you like a drink?"

When she hesitated, he waved the waiter over. "A glass of wine. Yes?" He turned to Melis who responded. "Yes, Pinot Grigio for me. A big one, thanks."

He looked at her for a moment. "Why were you following me?"

"Who are you?"

"That depends, who are you?"

"You know who I am."

"I do. You are Commander Erin Melis, Lithuanian Naval Intelligence."

"Now you."

"You can call me Thomas. Thomas Steiner, a journalist from Germany."

"I'm supposed to believe you?"

"Why not? I believe you. My papers are very much in order."

"I might need to have them checked out."

"Feel free. Perhaps you need to contact the German Embassy? I have some numbers—"

A glass shattered behind the bar. Knocked off by a bar keep's careless move. The younger crowd applauded. In a place with no band or show, they made their own entertainment. His attention came back to her face. He didn't want to stare but he couldn't look away. Sharp gray-blue eyes, he'd seen that color in arctic ice.

"Why were you meeting Matt Devlin?" she asked.

"We've known each other for a while. I covered Germany's participation in Afghanistan, and we met there. My son is also a soldier, so Matt and I stayed in touch."

The waiter brought her glass of wine, which Melis regarded for a moment and then took a sip. Her eyes searched his for a long while. Something had been triggered.

"What do you talk about?" she asked.

"A lot of things. The potential for war. What the Russians will do. What the Americans will do. What the Lithuanians will do."

"He talks to you about those things?"

"Nothing specific. Just generalities."

"What about drones?" she asked.

He remembered the Wordle word of the day—FEINT. *Cute, commander. I see what you did there.* "I heard your army shot one down today. It was on the local news."

"You heard nothing before today?"

"Not that I can remember."

The trigger must have suddenly tripped in her head, like his suddenly remembering the word of the day…

"Wait. How did you know who I was?"

"He mentioned your name as someone I might want to talk to."

"But how do you know that I am that person?"

"I met him and then immediately after our meeting, you and your people follow me. A simple deduction, commander."

"And how exactly did we know where to find you two?"

"I would assume you tracked his cell."

"You know an awful lot to be just a journalist."

"Would you tell that to my editor? He'd be pleased to hear that."

Melis switched to German. "Tell me this, Mr. Steiner, why do you have a pistol? You know you are required to have a permit in this country."

"I was wondering when you would ask," he said in equally fluent German. "I have been issued a European Firearms Pass. I thought I might hunt a wild boar."

A moment of silence. Joshua took a long pull from his scotch. He was beginning to enjoy talking with Melis.

"A wild boar? With a nine-millimeter pistol?"

"Ten-millimeter, actually. I like to live dangerously. That's why I'm talking to you. Besides, I have nothing to hide." *Well, maybe I do, but that's neither here nor there.*

The bell over the door rang and Joshua looked up to see two big men enter. Young guys, military bearing, nicely dressed but not expensively. They looked around and hesitated when they spotted Melis and Joshua's table. One of them spoke to the bartender, who handed him two drinks. They waited by the door, each with a small beer in hand.

"If I get up and walk out, will your people stop me?"

Melis looked over her shoulder.

"If I say nothing, no. But if you don't tell me who you are and why you're talking with Devlin, I may. Then we'd take you somewhere and have a nice long talk. Without the drinks."

"That's not very hospitable, but, okay, I'll say this much and you should take heed…" he paused long enough for her to blink. "First, I told you who I am. Second, Matt has good instincts and very good sources for his information. If he tells you something, you should believe him. Understand?" He pulled out a business card with his cell number written on the back and dropped it on the table. "And one more thing, I am an old friend of Matt's and for that matter, Lithuania's. I am not a danger to you or your country—we want the same thing."

She inhaled sharply. "You are related to Matt. I see it in your face. Your mannerisms." She was on to something she didn't quite grasp, somewhere between knowledge and confusion, but resolute in conviction. She would figure it out if he gave her more time.

Joshua smiled for the first time. "Some people might mistakenly believe that." He stood up and dropped one hundred Euros on the table and started to leave.

"What if I tell my people to stop you?"

"I'd rather you asked me nicely. Call me and we can talk more, I'd like that. I'm not going anywhere for a while."

A block down the street, Joshua was joined by Gabriel, who walked with a sure-footed bounce to his step.

"What did she want?"

"My meeting with Matt was burnt. She wants to know who I am and why I'm here."

"And?"

"Thomas Steiner, journalist. Damned glad to meet you."

"She didn't believe you."

"She has questions. She may have figured out we're related. I think I'll be hearing from her again."

Gabriel stopped and pulled a box of mints from his pocket and offered them to Joshua. Gabriel dropped one. "Damn." Stooped to pick it up and looked back. The street was empty.

"We're good so far. Anyway, you mean you hope you hear from her again."

"You're reading into things again, Gabriel."

"Why else would you voluntarily give her your business card?"

"To show her that I was being upfront. Wait? You saw that?"

"I was checking out the goons. There was another one outside."

"You saw no need to take them out?"

"Nah, you seemed okay, and nobody moved when you left."

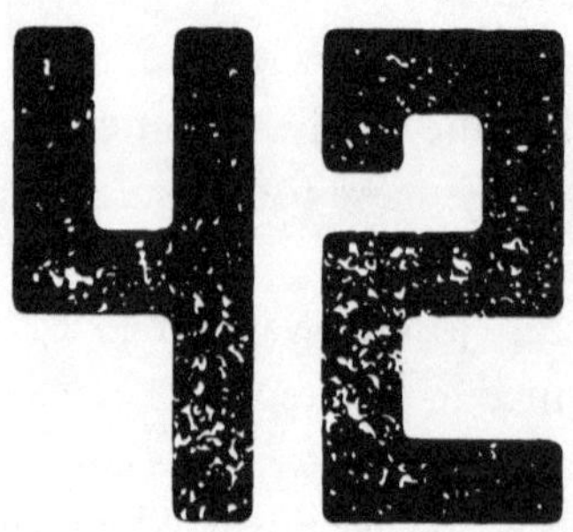

JAMIE STILL COULDN'T GET USED TO THE COLD of the Berlin office. His old bones longed for his home on the big island and his lanai. *Maybe after this.* He waited for the light on the phone to change. "I have you green," he said.

"Bingo," Andra Billings said.

"You found it?" Jamie said. There was a slight pause in the conversation as the secure satellite connection processed the call.

"We did. Gladys is also here. It was a combination of overhead imagery and another bit of luck. A local agent reported seeing a TEL with a missile on board moving through his village at night."

"Shades of Cuba. Have you sent me the location?"

"Yes, you should have it in restricted traffic. Coordinates down to ten meters. Unless they moved it since we tagged it."

"When was that?"

"The last fix was about three hours ago. We're monitoring it with all our available assets. If it changes, I'll ping you."

"Okay, thanks. Now all we have to do is figure out how to neutralize the thing."

"Roger, Jamie. Clairissa said to keep her in the loop. She's talking with the principals to see if anyone has a solution."

"You too. Let me know if anything changes. I'll get back to you," He sat back in the chair after signing off. Next steps needed to happen fast, and another trip seemed to be in order.

One thousand kilometers to the east, Melis seemed to be the one sitting in the catbird seat. "You still insist he is a journalist?"

"Yes," said Matt.

"And he's not some relative of yours?

"No. Shouldn't I have a lawyer or a witness in here if you're going to interrogate me?"

"I'm not interrogating you. I only have questions. It is interesting that you said you met in Afghanistan and then he shows up here. Don't you think that's odd? And he says he's German, but he doesn't look completely German to me."

"I think that's because not all Germans look like Reinhard Heydrich."

"I suppose not, but you look a bit like this Thomas Steiner person."

"I've been told that before and he is a handsome devil, I must admit. But I am not related to him. My mother told me our family has German in our bloodline, but mostly my genes are from Ireland. Maybe there's some Black Irish in there."

"Are you planning to meet him again?"

"I doubt it. I'll be kinda tied up here with my team getting ready for whatever happens next. And since we've received no indication that we are going to pull out, it looks like you're stuck with us."

"For the moment, Captain. But tonight, we are taking a trip to town. Your Defense Attaché has invited us to some kind of briefing at his residence, the Colonel, me, and the team leaders from the joint teams."

"I guess Nordheim finally decided he wants to know what we're doing. It would've been simpler if he'd just come here."

Matt Devlin, along with the unit commander and its intel officer, a quarter of Lithuania's special ops *Aitvaras* team leaders were heading downtown, which would have presented a great target to anyone contemplating a sudden coup de grâce to chop off the head of the firebird. The remainder of the unit were upset and grumbled at having been put on alert while the "big people" partied at some diplomat's social event.

The two unmarked *Aitvaras* vans drove into the residence driveway after most of the guests had already arrived. It was an old-world villa in a leafy suburb of Vilnius. Not too far from the diplomatic quarter, but far enough to be considered remote. There was the usual security to overcome— Police sedans near the end of the cul-de-sac and walking patrols near the gate. At least it seemed usual—none of Aitvaras had been to a reception recently. The neighbors must get used to them or value the extra protection they brought, Matt thought.

When they got into the compound, they discovered it was just a party, the usual drinks and canapés in the grand room off the foyer. The DATT mingled after receiving the guests, most of whom were Americans. Matt saw one or two Lithuanians but no one representing other countries. The event combined host-country appreciation night and farewell. Even the Ambassador was present. It might be the final soirée before the embassy started the evacuation of non-essential personnel. That meant all family members, and anyone deemed superfluous to crisis mode operations, would depart. The DATT would stay, though his wife and kids were already gone. The hope in the diplomatic community was that the Russians would respect their missions.

Commander Melis stayed close to the colonel. It was times like these that she appeared to be as much his aide as his intel officer, unlike the deputy commander who focused solely on becoming the boss. As an intelligence officer, Melis knew that option was not in the cards for her.

The reception was adequate as far as parties went, but the colonel expressed misgivings about being away from his troops at a critical moment. The Russian drone was a shot across the bow and there were preparations that were needed to meet the threat. Perhaps the DATT sensed his unease, because he walked up to him and gestured with a side-long motion of his head, "Colonel Bizauskas, good evening, would you and Commander Melis come with me please?"

Nordheim led the way down a hall lined with portraits of famous American generals that ended in another door. He turned the handle and stood aside to let the two Lithuanians enter first. Inside, another group was waiting, this one all older men in civilian clothing, two of whom she recognized.

Nordheim took his place between the two groups. "I don't think

I need to make introductions, but just in case, Colonel Bizauskas and Commander Melis of *Aitvaras*, I believe you know General Moze Ipolitas—Chief of Defence, and Filip Jaunišys—Director of State Security." He turned to the other three men. "And from the American side, this is Simon Greene, our intelligence chief here in the embassy and Jamie Wheeler, Director of Operations from Langley." He paused for a moment as a third man stepped out from behind the others. "Jamie, you should probably introduce your man."

Melis almost dropped her glass. "Thomas Steiner, the German journalist who has been meeting Captain Devlin," she whispered to Bizauskas.

Jamie smiled and took over, thinking this might be interesting. "Colonel, commander, I'd like to introduce one of my senior officers. I believe you have already met under different circumstances."

Joshua stepped forward and extended his hand to the colonel and then Melis. She appeared unsure if should shake it or not. He smiled broadly at her. "Sorry for the deception, but Mister Wheeler will explain," he said.

"We have decided to declare one of our most important cases to your service and military. Thomas Steiner, as you know him, is our case officer handling an important Russian asset who has provided us with intelligence we believe is vital to your country."

"Why don't you just pass the information to the VSD?" asked Colonel Bizauskas. "Director Jaunišys has a straight line of communication to us."

"A couple of reasons," Jamie said. "The drone your forces shot down was a deliberate signal to us that the Russians are about to begin operations. We gave you that information through our DATT. That drone was launched from a Belarusian base that is extremely important for another reason, which I'll get into in a moment. Most importantly, while we initially believed we could handle this asset without notifying you of his existence, things have changed. Joshua, would you like to continue?"

"If I must. We initially didn't believe our asset's information would be directly pertinent to your country, but once that changed, I decided to share specific information with the one person in-country I could trust not to divulge its source. He passed it to you."

"You shared it with Captain Devlin," Melis said. "That means you are Unicorn!"

"More or less. It was a small subterfuge, but we quickly decided that route wouldn't work well. Unfortunately, Colonel Bizauskas, your intelligence officer is much too perceptive for us," Joshua said.

"That's why I chose her."

Melis was clearly agitated, "Small subterfuge indeed. You're not a German journalist, you're a spy. What's your connection to Devlin?" She was calculating how best to get Joshua out of the diplomatically protected residence so her colleagues could arrest the man.

Joshua looked at Jamie, who nodded almost imperceptibly.

"He's my son."

Melis said something unintelligible in Lithuanian. Jamie looked at Nordheim, who spoke the language. "The most diplomatic translation I can think of is 'Holy Mackerel.'"

Jaunišys, the Director of State Security stepped forward. "We have agreed to share the information gained from this case in return for permitting the Americans to continue to run the case unilaterally. That also means that Mister Steiner, despite his unofficial status, may continue to operate within our borders. Once we've discussed the Belarusian angle, I believe you will understand how that will be to all our benefit."

There was a reason why Jaunišys had been named the most effective public servant in Lithuania.

"Director, if that is the case, then would it be possible for Mister Steiner to be our point of contact for the exchange? I would suggest he work directly with my intelligence chief, Commander Melis," Bizauskas said.

"I don't see why not," Jaunišys said. "Mister Wheeler, what do you think?"

"I understand there has already been some interaction between them, I think that could continue," Jamie said.

Melis and Joshua looked at each other intently. Joshua seemed to be somewhere between bemusement and apprehension. Melis just looked irritated.

Had Joshua been asked how he felt about the arrangement, he would have said Jamie's impression was not far off the mark. He was amused that Melis seemed to be put out by his appearance at the residence and even more so by the fact that she hadn't challenged him further in the bar the previous night. He was also a bit nervous to be working with someone who seemed intelligent but was not pleased to be working with Americans. And effective, he added.

Once glasses had been raised to the new paradigm and refilled, Jamie took the lead. Both he and Joshua had switched to scotch once the obligatory first champagne had been tossed back. Melis stuck with white wine, which pleased Joshua because he thought he'd guessed correctly. Colonel Bizauskas and General Ipolitas had also switched to scotch, which left Nordheim and Jaunišys all the embassy-supplied Taittinger Brut they wanted. The mood was muted, tempered by alcohol and the realization that they were among the few who knew how close to the precipice the world stood.

A map was laid out on a large table, and everyone crowded around. Jamie pointed to a spot southeast of Minsk. "The drone came from this base. It's near Asipovichy and up until 2019, it appeared closed, but it is actually the home base of a missile brigade equipped with short-range Tochka-U and the newer Iskander-M ballistic missiles. Both of those threaten Lithuania, but we are worried about another missile that is located there. Russia has stationed a single RS-28 ICBM missile there, which has a range of around eighteen hundred kilometers. The reason we're concerned is that it's part of Perimeter, the Russian autonomous command launch system."

"I think we're all familiar with Perimeter," said General Ipolitas, "but our tracking of the drone tells us it was launched closer, from only around fifty kilometers from our border."

"Your information is correct," Jamie said. "It was launched close to the border, but our imagery shows it was first transported there from Asipovichy by truck."

"What does that have to do with this RS-28?" Ipolitas had as many misgivings about poking the Russian bear as anyone and the discussion was moving into the national defense realm, no longer about intelligence sharing. His own meager defense force of just over forty thousand, including active soldiers and reservists, was barely enough to fight anything more than a delaying action. Not only that, but he expected he would have to fight in two directions, a main assault from Belarus and another, smaller one from Kaliningrad through the so-called Suwałki Gap, a one-hundred-kilometer-long corridor that some called the most dangerous place on earth. An attack there would probably consist of several hundred thousand Russian and Belarusian troops. He could only hope Poland would be there to help.

Nothing in his professional life prepared Jamie for what he had to say next. Certainly, he had asked people to do things that were illegal or dangerous or both, but never anything at this level, and never a nation-state. And despite having the backing of the director and through her, POTUS, he was still uneasy. "We would like Lithuania's assistance to destroy that missile. The Russian incursion into your territorial space gives your nation the right to self-defense and a retaliatory strike."

"Why can't the United States or NATO do it?" Jaunišys asked.

"We can't act because you haven't asked NATO to invoke Article Five. Even if you did, it would take too long. We would like it taken out of the game soon," said Jamie.

"Why?" Ipolitas said.

"It gives us certain options."

Jamie and Joshua stood at the backdoor of the DATT's residence. The night air was cool and the neighborhood quiet. A dog barked once. No answer. With the door shut, the sounds of the party inside were very faint, which suited Joshua fine. He didn't like big social events even if there was an operational purpose to them. Jamie was about to make one of his usual low-profile exits. One thing about diplomatic residences on cul-de-sacs, there's always another way out that only a few people know about.

"Certain options. That sounds like a bad movie title. But are you really comfortable telling our new friends the drone came from that base? And where did Gabriel go? Shouldn't he share in my pain?" Joshua asked.

"Okay," Jamie said, "so we don't have ironclad proof that the drone came from that base but, according to our analysts, it may have. And I think Gabriel is better off staying the silent partner in this. Just make sure he stays that way—out of sight, out of mind. He's our only contact with Hammer, so he'll pass info to you through your covcom. And you can get it to Melis."

"I'm the official liaison?"

"You're the liaison to the unit. Maybe not official but authorized. Greene, our station chief, will handle everything with Jaunišys."

"Fine. I'll do liaison. When the Russians come across the frontier in about forty-eight hours, what do you want me to do then?"

"Hang on for as long as you can, then run like hell. If you can't make it out, hunker down in the embassy."

"I'll do my best although the embassy isn't the best idea. I do not like living on MREs and bottled water." Joshua glanced behind him. "I should get back to the reception and I think you should get out of Dodge. Clairissa would be really upset if you got caught here."

"I guess I should. Discretion is the better part of valor. And I'm not fond of cabbage water."

Joshua looked around again and Jamie was gone.

Small talk and receptions had never been high on Joshua's list of interesting or fun things to do. He hung about on the fringe as the reception started to taper off. It was a long while before Matt found him. "Melis confronted me," he said. "She told me you were here."

"What did you tell her?"

"I said I knew that. Thanks for the text, otherwise I would have been surprised by your sudden claim of paternity."

"I doubt that, but it was necessary. I guess I'll see you tomorrow at the base. My presence has been declared to our friends and I'm now a liaison."

"This will be very weird, Dad. I don't think Melis is overjoyed at the prospect of both of us being around. Anyway, Colonel Bizauskas told the team leaders to meet him at 0700 hours. There's something being planned."

"You're not part of it." Joshua said, hoping that was true.

"Our orders have always been to just help them prepare. No operational involvement."

"I hope so, both of us don't need to be caught up in this."

Joshua's eyes caught movement coming toward them.

Matt followed his father's look. "Uh-oh, the dragon lady approaches. I better E and E out of here."

"Too late." Melis had already blocked the escape route.

"Well, my two favorite people in Vilnius this evening." There was a hint of derision in her voice.

"Commander Melis," Matt said. "A pleasure. I think I should get with the other team leaders to discuss tomorrow. They might want to leave soon, and I should be with them."

"Sounds like you don't want to talk with me, captain."

"It's not that, ma'am. I just know that you have important things to discuss with my father." Matt's head dipped in a salute as he backed away. Melis didn't try to stop him.

She turned to Joshua when Matt was out of earshot. "You owe me an apology."

"I suppose I do. I'm sorry, I was following orders."

"You know that defense didn't work at Nürnberg."

"I didn't know I was on trial."

"You very well could have been."

"Then I should thank you for letting me walk."

"Yes, you should. I have a question, if you're Captain Devlin's father, what should I call you? Are you also a Devlin? Or is Matt undercover?"

"That was actually three questions, but the answer is Matt's name is really his and I am Thomas Steiner."

"Will that change?"

Was that a leading question? He looked at Melis more carefully than he had before, trying to see what he had missed. Was she flinty—hard-edged—because she, like so many women in a man's world, had to be? Or was she hiding a different side?

"In the future, whatever that may bring, we'll see. But for the time being, I am Thomas. May I call you Erin?"

"For the time being, you may call me Commander Melis."

"Yes, commander." He smiled.

"One last thing, Mister Steiner. Matt told me his mother, your wife I assume, passed away several years ago."

"That's true. My wife died not long after Matt joined the army."

"I'm sorry for your loss." She said the words with the hesitance people have when they're not sure what should be said. "I hope we can work together well. Without any more secrets or deception." Melis reached out to shake his hand.

Joshua took it and shook hers gently. She didn't release her grip when he did, instead she squeezed his hand once more before letting go, her eyes fixed on his. She pulled a business card from her coat pocket and handed it to him. A printed name and rank with the address of her office. No unit designation.

"This will help at the front gate. My direct telephone number is on the back. Call me if you need my assistance." She walked away.

Joshua was confused. For someone trying to keep her distance, she was sending odd signals. Or maybe Sarah had been right, he truly didn't understand women.

BACK IN THE HOTEL, Joshua had his key card at the ready to as the elevator doors opened. He looked down the hallway in both directions from the central lobby and walked to his room. All evening, he'd been wondering if he would see Gabriel again before things kicked off or whether their contact would be limited to secret messaging.

When Gabriel stepped out of the utility room, Joshua reacted like Cato had leapt out of a refrigerator onto an unsuspecting Inspector Clouseau. "Jesus, Batman, you scared the hell out of me."

"You need to work on your situational awareness, Grasshopper. You are too focused on what you see, instead of what you don't."

"Now you're talking like Musashi. What happened to just plain wax on, wax off?"

"You have graduated to the next level."

Joshua quickly opened the door to his room while he was talking and stepped inside while Gabriel followed. "And you're still six steps ahead of me. Okay, so what's up? The boss said we're supposed to do this very low key, like Moscow rules or something."

"Don't worry, I took care of the cameras. Got anything to drink? I brought this." Gabriel proudly produced a bucket of ice he'd retrieved from the machine. Luckily, Joshua had not forgotten Baden Powell's motto to Be Prepared and laid in a supply of Talisker for contingencies such as this.

Gabriel dialed up the TV volume while Joshua poured a couple of glasses. Gabriel could add his ice if he wanted, he was staying neat for his first round.

"Hammer sent a message. Said he hoped we liked his greeting card. It was sent a day early so we still have seventy-two hours to Day Zero. More importantly, the Chef is at the spa."

"The Chef is at the spa. Is that some kind of code?"

"No, think about it. He means Dmitriy Pritzkhin is at the resort."

"That tells me Wagner is there. Which means the shit really is going to hit the fan. What are you going to do?"

"I am leaving tomorrow morning. I'll probably sit in Frankfurt or somewhere until we see where this goes. I was going to give you Hammer's covcom since you're so close."

"Don't. If anything happens to me, we'll lose contact. It's better if you relay messages. You can be the buffer between me and Jamie."

Gabriel appeared to consider the idea for a moment. "Makes sense. Then let's just drink to the future and whatever comes next, brother."

"I thought I was Grasshopper."

"You are, but you can be my brother too." He clinked glasses with Joshua and took a long pull of the eighteen-year-old scotch. He sniffed and twisted the glass back and forth in the light appreciating its deep amber color, took another sip. "Good stuff. When you're finished here, you're welcome to stay at my place anytime. As long as you bring more of this when you come."

Gabriel twisted the glass as the light caught its facets and split into thousands of colored rays that danced across his face. "Baccarat," he said.

"What?" Joshua said watching his comrade.

"The glass. It's Baccarat."

"You like the good stuff, don't you?"

"I might as well. No telling where we'll be tomorrow."

The morning light was muted, the sun not quite over the trees when Joshua pulled up at the gate.

The guard was a bit too serious for Joshua's taste, he seemed to regard visitors with no small amount of disdain almost as if his base was sacrosanct. Even handing over Melis' business card didn't move the guard signal to open the drop bar. Maybe it was the end of his shift, or maybe the German passport Joshua carried, one step above a Russian passport but still poorly regarded since the last big war by most Lithuanians.

Obviously, the compound had gone to a higher alert level, the guard, like the soldiers Joshua glimpsed inside the compound were fully kitted out with protective armor and enough magazines for their H&K submachine guns to sustain a long gunfight. And if that wasn't enough, a semi-automatic VP-9 pistol was strapped to the guard's chest as a back-up. Maybe that was why he was upset. He stood guard instead of prepping for war. He remembered from his own army days long ago that there was one sure way to upset a soldier—put him on some shitty detail while everyone else was preparing for a mission.

"Try calling Commander Melis, please."

The guard looked at him like he was crazy. Joshua wasn't sure if it was because the man regarded him as one of the unclean or because he didn't want to wake the dragon.

"Wait," the guard finally said.

Like he was going to go anywhere. Beyond the gate were bollards that would rip the underside of his car open if he tried to crash through. Behind him was a five-ton cargo truck impatiently waiting to drive over him. He was trapped.

The guard returned five minutes later. "You can go. Drive through and park in front of headquarters over there." He pointed at a building some yards away with a flagpole in front. "Someone will come for you." The drop bar went up, the bollards went down, and the guard waved him on.

"The business card?" Joshua held his hand out the window. "I may need it again."

The guard reluctantly handed the card over. *He must have noticed her cell number on the back and wanted to keep it for himself.*

By the time he was parked, Melis waited on the sidewalk. Joshua wasn't sure what her reception would be, but she extended her hand in greeting. "I got your message. Let's talk to the colonel, he's waiting for us."

The colonel's office was much like the ones he remembered from his own days in the service. Sparse and utilitarian, with furniture made to survive years of soldiers. The colonel had a few souvenirs of his duty hanging on the walls and sitting atop a bookcase. No family photos, just two flags: a national and a unit banner. He stood in front of a regional map of as they entered. He half turned and beckoned them in when Melis knocked at the open door. He didn't stand on ceremony today.

"Show me where this place is exactly," the colonel said.

Joshua had only given approximate coordinates to the spa in his text. He pulled a piece of A4 paper out of his shoulder bag and placed it next to the spot on the map. "This is a sketch of what I remember of the grounds, at least as much as I saw of it."

"This is good. Do you have anything on the interior of the main building?"

"Only a partial floor plan. I assume you're planning to take on Wagner?"

"We are. Your director was only half as persuasive as your president can be. He talked with our Prime Minister last night and we have been given the go ahead to assist you with the missile problem. Before that happens, however, we need to take care of this Wagner issue. I suppose you know that your son is assisting our special forces but for this we will use a different unit, the VPT, our counterterrorism unit. It's a subset of the larger element, just better trained in urban combat and close quarter battle. Commander Melis says your source believes there are around twenty-five to thirty Russians at this location."

"That's the number he gave us, yes. And he's been accurate thus far, but he also said that Dmitriy Pritzkhin is there, the head of Wagner. He may have more close protection folks with him."

"I think we can handle them. We're going in heavy with our armed police as back-up."

"Not your other special forces?" Joshua asked.

"No. The police are well-trained enough. The others are busy getting ready for the big mission over the border. You don't have any updates on that do you?"

"No, the DATT gave you everything we had last night." Jamie had the analysts pull together everything they could find—maps satellite imagery, photos of the missile and its transporter—so the Lithuanians could plan. They even included physical and digital overlays of the Belarusian air defenses with all its locations, radars, and weaponry. Enough to start and, with the addition of a NATO airborne warning and countermeasures platform over Poland, probably enough to get into the target area successfully.

"We will execute a raid on the spa tonight. The strike mission will go tomorrow, everything in sequence. And because Mr. Wheeler says you have experience in this area, you'll be with Commander Melis on the outside."

"I hope you mean outside the spa. I don't have a visa for Belarus."

"No worries, Mister Steiner. That will be an all-Lithuanian project," said the colonel.

"Do you wish to see your son?" Melis asked. They stood at the threshold, ready to go outside.

"No, he doesn't need any distractions. I'm sure he's busy."

"He is, but no worries. As the colonel said, this is an all-Lithuanian affair. Just *Aitvaras* and our aviation element. No outsiders."

"I'm relieved to hear that."

"Listen, I understand what you were doing before. You were protecting Matt. I admire that quality in a man, especially a single father."

"Before you go too far, I wasn't trying to protect him. I was trying to give him what he needed to do his job. Our system of keeping secrets doesn't always make that easy."

Melis searched his eyes again.

Always the best place to look for secrets and weak points.

"Besides, Matt can take care of himself. The only thing I don't like is our being so close to danger at the same time. If I get killed, that's okay. Then he can do whatever the hell he wants with his life as long as its honorable. But I don't want to lose him before I go."

Melis smiled to herself. *This Thomas Steiner person was indeed protecting his son even if it was in his own way. He might not be able to pull his son out of the fire, he'd just give him a way to put it out.*

"Let's get with the mission planners, Thomas. I'm sure they'll have questions about the spa."

"You called me Thomas, commander."

"Sorry, I forgot myself, Mister Steiner. Let's go talk to the VPT."
As she went through the door, her back was turned so he didn't see her
smile.

The VPT headquarters was a modern building on the edge of the
compound. Melis explained that most of the buildings belonged to
VPT. The *Aitvaras* teams the Americans were working with were only
here because it was convenient for the trainers and close to international
and military airports. Otherwise, they were based in Kaunas which
had the dubious distinction of being on the direct rail route between
Kaliningrad and Russia proper. In wartime, one of the first things the
Lithuainian teams would be tasked with would be the destruction of
the rail lines to stop the Russians.

Joshua found himself a step behind as Melis strode along. His
limp more of a hinderance than usual. He didn't complain, it gave him
time to assess the woman in front of him. He had stared at her face so
much that he wasn't exactly sure what the rest looked like. Even in a
loose-fitting, field-green uniform, she looked in shape. Long legs and
an athletic upper body, she hadn't let herself go to seed even if she was
usually a desk-bound senior intel officer.

As soon as Joshua walked in the door, he knew he was in VPT territory.
He had not heard of the VPT before today, but when the colonel
mentioned "CT" Joshua pictured exactly what was in front of him.
Two men wearing blue-gray camouflage, pistol holsters slung low and
strapped to their legs. They weren't wearing their utility vests and armor
yet but would be when they moved out. Their equipment and dress
looked to him as urban door-kicking gear, not the uniform of special
forces troops working in the fields or the forests. They looked up from
the papers on the desk and acknowledged Melis with a salute before
looking at Joshua like he was an intruding alien.

Melis said something in Lithuanian that Joshua took to mean he
was harmless and under her wing. The two men nodded vaguely in his
direction before returning to the duty roster or whatever it was that

had held their attention. Melis continued past their desk and turned down a corridor. "Come on now, Mister Steiner. We must hurry." Her voice more a command than a request. The soldiers chuckled almost, but not quite, to themselves. Joshua made a mental note to tell Melissa the young men were in need of remedial "give proper respect to your elders" training.

Joshua entered the room behind Melis just in time to hear her introduction of him as an American friend. There were around forty soldiers in the room, all dressed in green fatigues, their eyes focused on the stranger in the room, another American but older, in civilian clothing, and something other than a soldier. He smiled as he looked across the room. *Serious dudes here*, he decided.

She spoke in English, so he assumed they did as well or at least understood the language. Once the Russians decided to abandon their occupation of the Baltic countries in 1990, English language classes began to be offered in most schools. The youth of Eastern Europe were eager to pick up anything that distanced them from Moscow.

"He is here to answer your questions about the target and what you may be up against this evening," Melis said.

A man stood up, slightly older than the others but still younger than Joshua. "Welcome, Mister Steiner. I am Major Gudaitis, commander of tonight's operation. I understand you have been inside the compound. Are you familiar with our target requirements?"

"I have been inside, but it's probably best if you ask what you need to know. I will add information where I can."

"Have you been on a military operation before, sir?" another soldier asked.

Joshua thought of a witty comeback but decided it could wait. "I was a soldier once, a long time ago. I am quite familiar with what you do." Joshua held his ego back, but his eyes told the man it was best not to press further.

And so, the questioning began.

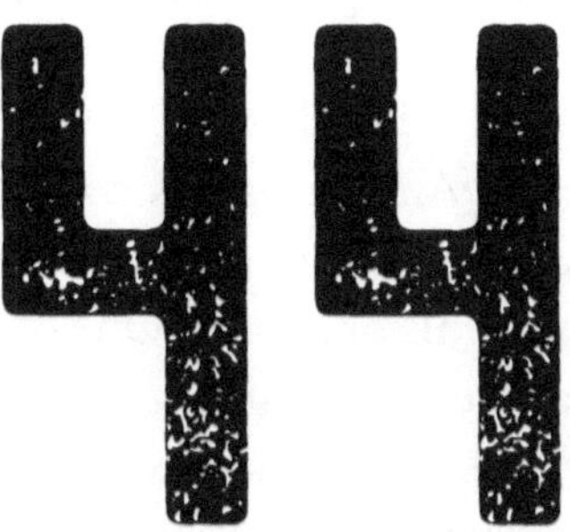

"I WANT YOU AND YOUR TEAM AT OUR BRIEFING," said Lukas.

Matt was standing inside Lukas' team-room. The space had been converted from a team room to a briefing center. The final brief was about to begin.

"Is that an order, captain?" Matt asked. Humor to break the tension.

Captains Lukas Veržbickas and Matt Devlin had grown close over the last six months, their teams had become one fighting unit. But orders were orders, and now they would have to separate before the mission launch.

"It's the best I can do. We wouldn't be as prepared for this if not for your help, but the colonel said it must be up to us alone to do the job."

"At least we're here. I'm surprised the embassy didn't order us out of country."

The equipment was laid out for the colonel's pre-mission inspection, their first operational deployment since Afghanistan. The two teams were still mixing it up in the hangar that had become their home since the alert began. The team's cots were lined up against the walls, tables were set out with everything from their standard HK416 rifles to the two AX50 sniper rifles that they would carry into the target, to the individual compasses each man would carry for escape and evasion should that be necessary.

Unlike some forces, *Aitvaras* did not rely solely on GPS for land navigation. Between dead batteries and Russian electronic interference, the modern ways of doing things weren't always fool-proof. Their back up to find their way home was a paper map, pencil, and a Silva compass.

Matt watched as Colonel Bizauskas led a small entourage into the briefing room. Unlike the Americans, his staff was much smaller. His deputy commander, an operations officer, and an intelligence non-commissioned officer were his only staff. One of the benefits of serving in a tiny army was that there was usually less of a tail to wag the dog. Melis wasn't present. Matt knew she had work to do with his dad and the VPT to prepare for this evening's operation, and other than Matt's team, the only American present was Nordheim, the Defense Attaché. The Agency people were absent. Jamie needed to be in Berlin when things went down, and the local chief was monitoring Russian comms traffic in the embassy for unusual activity. Only two other Lithuanian officers, both colonels from the MOD, were present to witness the briefing.

This mission would be considerably more complex than the spa raid and required three teams to penetrate hostile territory by air. The air mission briefing had already been given by the air crews. What Bizauskas wanted to know was how Captain Veržbickas and his team planned to kill the missile.

A map traced their route, a diagram showed how they would approach, and photos showed their quarry. Lukas Veržbickas didn't need a sixty-four-slide presentation to tell his boss what he would do. He said his piece and then let three of his men describe the operation from insert to exfil. Matt was happy because he was sure some of his briefing techniques had rubbed off on Lukas, his counterpart. Matt's deputy, Ron, was just as sure his own style and motto had made the difference. He called it Hokum's Razor: Don't complicate shit.

There were no questions. Colonel Bizauskas had watched the preparations personally and intermediaries had kept him apprised. His questions indicated that he was more worried about the two critical phases over which he had little control: the helicopter infiltration and exfiltration. A single unjammed radar or a surface to air missile could ruin everyone's day.

When one of the Lithuanian MOD officers—someone obviously

oblivious to weapons technology—asked if they were sure the rifles would do the job, one of the designated snipers held up a very large rifle round.

"Forty-seven grams of copper, steel, and tungsten moving at nine hundred and fifteen meters per second. Norwegian Raufoss .50 BMG caliber ammo can pierce half an inch of hardened steel plate and is explosive and incendiary as well. The Russian missiles are no match for it."

Towards mid-afternoon, Veržbickas' team loaded up a truck while the other two *Aitvaras* teams loaded their own. Lukas motioned Matt over. "We can take two of you with us to the airfield for the load rehearsal, your other team leaders are going, so pick someone and come with me."

Matt grabbed his deputy, Ron Schaffer, and climbed in the back of the truck with the Lithuanian team. They submitted themselves to the ribbing they got because Veržbickas rode up front while they had to travel with the enlisted troops. Matt didn't tell them it was standard procedure in SF for team leaders to suffer indignities with their men. If they didn't, their team probably wouldn't follow them anywhere.

The troops bantered among themselves, while Matt and Ron sat back and were mostly silent. This trip was much like many they had made previously in their careers. They would be the guys whose job was to assist the deploying team which included taking them to the airfield for their mission launch. They would wait back in the operations center as the liaison between the guys in the field and headquarters, making sure they weren't forgotten. It was a tradition in SF that went back to the Second World War, its value being that if the wheel doesn't squeak, it won't get greased. From here on out, it would be watch, listen, and wait. Matt hated the idea of staying behind but had little choice in the decision.

Protesting brakes and the sound of doors opening and slamming signaled their arrival at the airfield. The driver came to the rear and opened the tail gate, which fell with a crash, the chains jangling. Matt and Ron followed the nearly fifty soldiers as they filed into a camouflage-painted hangar. Matt looked around at the unfamiliar terrain, he'd never been on this field.

Lukas joined him. "This is an auxiliary airfield. We use it for deployments, usually at night because we like to believe the Russians think it's closed. That's why we park old trucks on the runway during the day and keep our aircraft inside."

When they entered the brightly lit hangar, Matt paused. In front of him were three helicopters, their main rotors folded and stowed along the very angular fuselages—the rear rotors enclosed like some of the French airframes. They were painted a mottled, dark grayish green. "What are those?"

"You've never seen them before? They're part American, part Swedish."

"Part Swedish? Not Ikea, I hope."

"Nope. We call them *Valkirija.*"

"Valkyrie," Matt repeated.

"Officially, they are JSS-92s. A joint Sikorsky-Saab collaboration. Stealthy. I think there are twenty in the world. We have five and we'll use three tomorrow. Two will be in reserve."

"I want one."

"I don't think you can afford the upkeep."

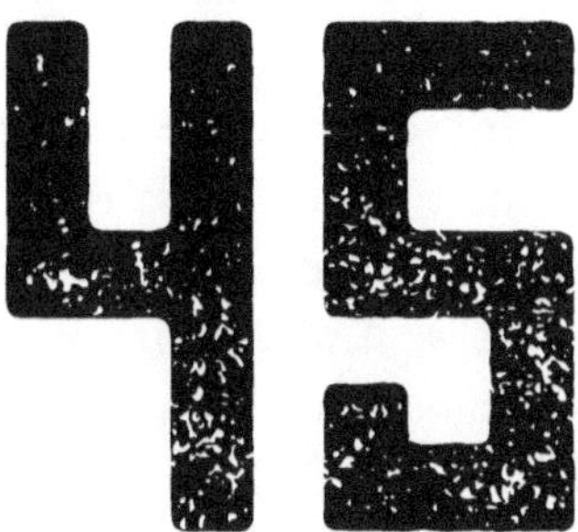

A LINE OF TRUCKS WAS PARKED outside VPT headquarters, all brand-new Oshkosh armored patrol vehicles followed by five Land Cruiser HiLux arctic terrain pickups. Melis tugged at Joshua's sleeve. "You're staring."

Joshua was. Much like his son Matt, he was fascinated with cool technology and gear and his hosts were catering to that addiction. He could tell it was going to be a fun evening.

"We've put several unmarked police sedans in the area watching for activity," Major Gudaitis said. "Ground teams have also moved into the wood line around the facilities. We encountered one outpost, but it was neutralized. We'll have to move soon before the Russians miss their man. You two get the first HiLux. You will be the last ones onto the property. Just remember the trucks are not armored."

Joshua assumed that neutralized was meant in the passive form, like arrested, drugged, maimed, or critically injured, probably not killed. But then the Russians, especially Wagner mercenaries, were not looked on kindly by most western Europeans.

The convoy began to move and Melis and Joshua dashed to their designated vehicle and hopped in the back of the crew-cab. The truck's bed was filled with all manner of equipment, from ladders to fire extinguishers, useful items for an urban assault.

"You have that toy pistol with you?" Melis asked.

"Yeah, not that I intend on using it. It's not very effective against a bunch of crazed mercenaries."

Melis pulled a larger pistol from her satchel and handed it to Joshua. "A VP-9 just like the big boys." Joshua unwound the belt that wrapped the holster and gingerly pulled the pistol out. "It's loaded," she said.

Joshua checked it. "Indeed, it is." Two additional magazines were in a pouch. "This is the best gift ever. I'm ready for bear. Thank you, Erin." He smiled at his new partner.

"It's Commander Melis. And you are authorized to shoot only Russian bears. Try not to shoot any real ones. We protect them here."

Joshua stood on the road inside what the VPT planner had called the exclusion zone. He remembered the route and forest from his previous visits. The police had blocked the main road and the known tracks through the forest. The spa resort enclave had been effectively cut off. No one in, no one out. Civilian vehicles would be stopped on a pretext and the occupants isolated, along with their phones. None had appeared on the road as of yet.

Additional teams were moving into the area on foot, not just observers but snipers and small hunter teams. This was where the value of special forces made itself known, unlike most police, they were well-versed in moving in the field without being observed. They would ensure no one escaped the main force when it rolled in.

Melis came back to the truck. "We move in five minutes. We will enter the main house once it's secured and do the target exploitation. I have two soldiers to assist. You can help."

"I just hope we're not being trolled," Joshua said, wistfully and half to himself.

Melis whirled around. "What do you mean?"

"It's a trout fishing thing. You bait a hook and cast it into the water hoping someone will swallow it. I hope this isn't a ploy to catch us off guard."

"Maybe you should have thought about that earlier. It's kind of late to call this off."

Engines started up down the road. He thought about Matt.

"You're not really thinking about that are you, Thomas?"

"I always question plans just before they are implemented. And then I go ahead with them anyway. Most of the time, I prove myself wrong."

"Hopefully we're about to find out how wrong you are. But we wouldn't have found a guard in the woods otherwise."

Unless…

The trucks rolled. The ones in front without lights. The second wave slowed at the gate. They would follow up and maneuver as necessary to the main house, the main barn, and the other barn in the woods. Joshua hadn't seen any other buildings but there were probably others to be found and searched.

His window was down, he wanted to hear things happen, not just imagine them in the dark. Everyone but him and Melis had been given night optics.

They were through the gate and rolling up the road when lights came on to the front. The entire convoy went to full illumination. The main villa came into sight—its light blazing brightly—as troops jumped from their armored cars and ran up the stairs. They were about one hundred meters back when he heard the first crack of gun shots. The barn was illuminated with spotlights, he could see soldiers running around and the occasional muzzle flash. Doors were pried open and slammed shut again after flash bangs were thrown inside. Larger flashes were followed by the sharp report of explosives that illuminated the landscape. The fir trees appearing then disappearing like an old movie scene, all viewed from the ringside seat of the Toyota.

A voice crackled over the radio. The code words were in Lithuanian.

"Let's go," said Melis. "The house is secure."

Joshua led this time. He knew the layout. A flash and then a bang as a grenade detonated bright and loud not fifty meters away. Melis ducked, glancing over at the smoke.

"New at this?" he asked.

She almost said something, but drove on. They ran through the doors and into the big foyer. The lights were still on—no one had killed the power yet—two bad guys in civvies lay sprawled on the staircase leaking fluids. The doors into the grand hall stood open. One trooper guarded the room. There were two more Russians down on the ruined carpet. A lot of rooms to search and exploit, but at least they weren't in hostile territory.

"Where is everyone?" Joshua asked the guard.

"Some are still upstairs. The others have gone on to other buildings," the soldier said.

Joshua did a quick scan of the room. It was as he remembered it. Nothing had changed.

"There'll be an office somewhere, probably upstairs, with papers or files," he said.

Melis's two assistants ran for the staircase to the upper level, but she raised her hand for Joshua to signal *Hold*, her other hand over her earphone. There was still a lot of noise. She dropped her hand. "There is no sign of Pritzkhin yet. Ideas?"

Joshua's eyes went to the bookcase. The latch was undisturbed. "I thought someone was going to search the tunnel?"

"They should have."

"The door hasn't been touched. They missed it." Joshua manipulated the wood as he'd seen Andriy do, and the door clicked open.

He looked back at Melis as he pulled his pistol from the holster. "Someone may escape. We don't have time to wait." He plunged into the darkness.

The air was cooler than he remembered and there was an updraft, a breeze played against his face. *The doors must be open down there.* He shuffled downward, the only light coming from the glowing strips on the wall. Melis walked behind him and when he paused, her arm brushed his back. He was glad he didn't feel the metal of her pistol. Then her hand touched his shoulder as if to tell him she was there.

He pushed on, the light becoming brighter on the stairs—the lights were on in the cellar. He took each corner slowly, moving quicker between corners, doing a quick check and pushing on until the final short set of stairs led straight to the source of the light. He walked at a half-crouch, his pistol held at the ready, chest high. He moved along the wall slower now, using its angle to partially obscure his presence. He came to the opening to the room and found two men moving a long case onto a small ATV. The case was similar to ones he'd seen before that held a surface-to-air missile.

Melis looked over his shoulder. Two more men watched the process unaware of anything else. Joshua stepped into the room, searching quickly from side to side then back to the men in front of him. A quick glance behind him motioned Melis to move away from him and off to the side.

There was a metallic clank as her foot connected with something, loud and unwelcome. She gasped. He looked down. By the time Joshua turned back to the men, two had dropped the case and brought their rifles to bear. The other two sprinted for a pile of boxes and cover. A burst came from a Kalashnikov, wild, unaimed.

The concrete over Joshua's head detonated and shards fell, a cloud of dust obscured his vision. Joshua aimed as best he could, fired two rounds, and dove for cover. "Get down." He hoped she'd already taken the cue.

Another burst of fire hit the wall. He heard a command, it sounded like "Get them," in Russian. He risked a look after shifting to the side. Two men moved rapidly toward him, barrels held too low.

Inexperienced.

His pistol was already up on target. He fired two quick rounds, shifted again, double-tapped two more. One went down, the other threw himself to the side amongst the boxes.

Advantage me.

He raised up again and fired twice into the box in front of his target. He checked for the other two, gone. Joshua moved forward and found a boot sticking out into the open. He carefully aimed and fired a single round into the ankle. A howl went up and the man rolled. Now Joshua had a torso to aim at. He double tapped and the body went limp.

Joshua looked at his pistol, the slide was back.

Where did all my rounds go?

He dropped the empty magazine and reloaded. Something slammed him in the back. He went down among the boxes.

The roar of pistol fire drowned everything out. Through the ringing of his ears, he heard gun shots and muffled voices. It took a minute to shake off the shock and pick himself up.

The armor plate saved my butt.

Melis was deeper inside the cavernous room. He couldn't see anyone else. The lights flickered and went out.

Shit.

No sooner had he thought that, the flashes began. The bullets sang around him.

They can't see either.

But he could see Melis' outline in front of him in the pitch black. Every flash silhouetted her figure, erect, vulnerable. He wanted to yell at her to get down. Couldn't. His words wouldn't come.

Then he saw them. Through the flashes, through the smoke and the darkness. He knew where they were. He burst forward, only a second had passed, and knocked Melis down with his shoulder. A step to the left, fired two rounds, pivot, and two more rounds, and two more.

A swirling silence enveloped Joshua. His ears rang despite the defenders he wore. The light blossomed as his eyes quickly adjusted to the dark. The acrid smell of burnt nitrocellulose burned his nostrils. He exhaled and moved forward. With a small flashlight he found the switch and the lights flashed on brightly.

"Where are you?" Joshua said. He saw a swish of hair among some boxes as Melis sat up and tossed her head.

"You hit me. Hard."

"Sorry, I thought you'd get shot standing there."

"Thank you. I probably would have. Couldn't see a thing."

Joshua put out his hand, which Melis took as she stood up. "Everyone gone?"

"Think so." Joshua walked back towards where he'd seen the shooters and stopped. Two bodies were sprawled out, blood leaking onto the concrete floor. He turned a head with the tip of his boot. The face, eyes staring at the ceiling, was one he'd seen before.

"Mademoiselle, it seems we have killed the Chef."

THE HANGAR WAS A HIVE OF ACTIVITY with the kind of last-minute, frantic efforts to figure what has been forgotten or what major aspect of the operation has not been considered and planned for. The helicopter crews had rolled their birds out onto the tarmac, the fuel tanks having been topped off the night before. The pilots were going over their last minute checklists.

"Let's go, boss," Ron said. "They're loading out and need our help."

"Always a bridesmaid, never a bride," said Matt.

"You're jealous."

"Of course, I'm jealous, you twit. I want to be involved."

"Give it a breather, boss. I expect we'll have lots of chances to die for our country soon enough."

"I hate it when you're so damn optimistic." Matt grabbed his utility vest and threw it on over his jumpsuit. He didn't need anything else.

This was, after all, an operation that had been planned and rehearsed for over thirty-six hours. Matt remembered that the Son Tay Raid into North Vietnam had taken over six months to plan, prepare, and execute. But then, like Patton said, a good plan executed quickly and with violence of action is better than a perfect plan executed too late. Tomorrow would be too late.

All that remained was one last check of imagery, a recheck of the coordinates programmed into the flight computers, and a count of personnel and equipment. Matt and his team assisted the Lithuanians where they could, but a well-oiled machine doesn't need much help. They just made sure nothing was left behind and no accidents happened.

One hour to launch. The teams were milling about in nervous anticipation of the load signal. Matt and Ron stood nearby, watching the activity, looking for a place to help but everything seemed to be well in hand.

Lukas broke off from his team and walked up to Matt. "You're ready?" Matt asked.

"Almost. I don't know if you counted but I only have thirteen men."

Matt hadn't noticed the absent soldier in the swirl of activity. "I didn't. Who are you missing?"

"Darius. My executive officer. He hurt his ankle this morning."

"So, you're going in short-handed."

"Would you fill in?" Lukas said.

Matt wasn't prepared for the question. A sharp inhale. "Your colonel would never permit that."

"I told him I was short one man and that I wanted you because you know the mission as well as anyone."

"What did he say?"

"He said he couldn't authorize you—an American—to go along."

"Well, that's that then."

"You're not listening. He didn't say you couldn't go. He just said he can't say it."

Matt looked at Lukas for a long, hard second then yelled, "Mister Schaffer, would you come here, please!"

The Valkyries weren't silent, but they were quieter than a standard Blackhawk. Their angular fuselage was designed to reduce their radar signature, which helped when the enemy's air defense system was described as porcupine-like. And the reason why an AWACS was up and about to turn on its best electronics to smoke the enemy. It would be later described as a joint NATO exercise over the Baltic Sea, but Belarus would experience a mysterious jamming of most everything associated with early warning.

The three helicopters skimmed the tops of the trees in V-formation. They flew southwest, then went low into the Suwałki Gap and turned east. The border would come quickly and all they could hope for was no warning light indicating a missile launch. Matt glimpsed an iridescent blur outside the port hole—the rotors of the helicopter flying next to them on the starboard side. Only tiny infrared lights let the pilots of each helo know the location of the other aircraft. Matt hadn't put on his night vision goggles yet. He would do that when they were on final approach. He did recheck the gear he'd already checked at least twelve times, patting himself down until he was satisfied that everything was in its place and ready for action.

Two helos would set down one kilometer on either side of the target to drop their teams. Those teams would secure a single road that crossed the site from north to south. Lukas's team would then be dropped close to the edge of the compound to find and disable the RS-28. Hopefully, it would be in its usual hiding spot between the trees. It had been camouflaged with net screening that did not make things invisible to the radar, infrared, and thermal imagery of a satellite high overhead. Or the woodcutter who happened to hate Russians and was a friendly purveyor of intelligence to the West.

On the port side of the helo, a yellow-orange glow lit up the clouds fifty kilometers to the north. Minsk, the capital city, was not yet on a wartime footing. They had another one hundred kilometers to go. Everyone around him was quiet. Gone was the kidding and joking of several hours before.

A while later, a red cabin light flashed twice. It was the signal to stand by. Lukas spoke with the crew chief. Their heads close together in conference. Lukas's head came up and he flashed his fingers one time, making sure everyone saw there were five minutes to go. Seat belts came off those who wore them. Vests and assault packs were shifted into position. Rifles were held muzzles to the deck. All eyes were on Lukas, who'd moved to the aft of the helo. He'd be first off. Matt would be in Darius' position in the middle with the team sergeant out last.

The helo's tempo changed, a momentary weightlessness as it slowed and began to drop, slowly at first then quicker as the pilot chose his touchdown point and flared at the last second. Matt felt his legs almost buckle as gravity reversed and the helo hit the ground, the wheel gear taking most of the shock. The rear ramp was opened, and the troops tumbled out, half to the right, half to the left. He was out and face down in the damp grass, flattened by the rotor wash as the helo picked up and disappeared as fast as it came in.

The three helos would head to their pre-planned loiter point and wait while the teams did their thing. Matt spun around. The storage site was as he'd seen it in the imagery and renderings, a fence surrounding several bunkers, and a small building, its lights ablaze as guards tumbled out the door.

From above, a loud buzz and a cylinder of hot yellow light and steel touched the building. Matt looked up from his kneeling position. One of the Valkyries hovered overhead, it's mini-gun and a one thousand round burst making short work of the Russians and the wood shack. Then their angel was gone, and the night turned quiet.

It was silent except for the crackling of small fires the incendiary rounds started. Lukas's men spread out along the fence line. The men split up. Two groups with a sniper and a spotter each. Then the rest strung out individually. The spotters peered into the compound with thermal imagery to locate the missile. Matt could see a row of ten TELs, their deadly burdens strapped to their backs. They were smaller shorter-range missiles—but still dangerous.

The hard clank of a round being chambered and then the flash and blast of a half-inch round being thrown down range. Lukas ordered them to take out all the missiles, not just the main target. A second rifle began to fire, there was another row of missiles behind the bunkers. One by one, each missile was perforated by a single round. They'd never fly. Half the Belarusian missile inventory was about to be made useless. Matt was surprised by the lack of opposition, but then the Russians had probably thought they would be safe here.

Matt got up and ran to Lukas. "Can you see it?"

"I'm not sure. Wait." He spoke into the radio. "Cease fire. Where's Demon?" The codeword for the RS-28. No answer.

"It's not in its parking spot," a soldier finally said.

Matt felt his stomach sink.

"We have to go inside," Lukas said. The breachers were already at work cutting open the fence. "Snipers, resume fire. Destroy all the missiles you can."

The heavy rhythmic fire, the metallic ring of ejecting cartridges, and chambering of rounds continued.

"Breaching team, on me." Lukas took his six men in hand. "Bunker one." He pointed three men in towards their target, "Bunker two, with me. Matt, go with the other team."

Lukas ran.

Matt was unclear as to his role other than keeping up with the sprinting men. Theirs was the closest bunker. The breacher took a small explosive charge from his bag and placed it on the door lock, a heavy but simple Russian padlock on a hasp. "Back off," he said as he lay out the wire. Once safe around the corner of the bunker wall, he fired the charge. A loud bang and the hiss of metal flying past. Another man with a pry bar forced the door the rest of the way open. An empty space greeted their flashlights. Matt felt his stomach drop even further.

Where is it?

Lukas ran up to their position. "Dry hole."

"Same here."

"Where then?"

"No idea. Where would they have moved it?".

"Regroup!" Lukas called. If they couldn't find it, the mission was over.

The team reassembled near the gate, then spread out in a defensive position to await the helo as Lukas called for extraction. Matt looked around frantically with the thermal scope he'd appropriated from one of the spotters. Still nothing as the Valkyrie appeared overhead and settled in on them.

"Load!" Lukas ordered. Everyone climbed on. Matt stood at the tailgate's base, still searching. "No use, Matt. We must go now."

"Tell the pilot to do one circle around the area, low and slow as possible," Matt said as he climbed aboard.

"I'll try."

They lifted off and did a slight turn. Lukas spoke into his microphone and the pilot skidded the helo to the right and then slowly forward. Matt sat on the floor with the crew chief and stared at the ground with the scope, swinging it back and forth covering as much as he could. Still nothing in sight.

The pilot flew a slow circle, hewing left and right to cover as much ground as he could. Only so much time remained before AWACs would turn its systems off and the evening sky became very dangerous.

Matt sat back and stared up into the fuselage. "Nothing. Not a damn thing."

Lukas kneeled next to him. "We did the best we could, Matt."

Twenty some missiles knocked out inside the lair deep inside Belarus. *Just not the most important one.* Matt sat up and hooked into the safety harness the crew chief offered him. Falling out of a helicopter in enemy territory was not a good outcome.

The helo began to pick up speed, the others would head back on parallel but separate tracks along routes believed to be free of air defense systems.

Matt scanned the ground behind them as the helo followed a road just above the treetops. Panning from side to side.

"I see something, just behind us off the road," Matt said.

The helo slowed and turned sideways, crabbing at the sky, barely moving.

Matt braced himself against the fuselage and looked again. *Oh, hell yes…* There it was, the missile stood fully erect in a small clearing, its bulbous nose above the treetops, the TEL below partially camouflaged by netting. *Of course, they moved it out of the parking bay because they're on alert. It's ready to launch.*

"We found it," he said to the pilot. "Go around and set up about one hundred meters down the road. Tailgate to the target. Give us a stable platform."

He raised himself to a kneel, signaled to Lukas, and pointed. "It's Demon. Get your snipers."

One sniper flopped down and took his position at the tailgate, his AX50 loaded and ready.

"We're in position," the pilot said. "I'll hold her steady for as long as you need but make it fast."

Matt nodded to Lukas who had kneeled next to the sniper. Then he motioned to the second sniper who also knelt. Lukas spoke with the man for a moment who passed his heavy rifle to Matt.

"It's yours, Matt. You found it," Lukas said over the intercom.

Matt took the rifle and got into position.

"Quickly people. We're a sitting duck right now," the pilot urged.

Matt chambered a round. *At this range even I can't miss.*

The dark green silhouette of the missile filled his reticle. He aimed just below the nose cone.

"You have it?" Lukas asked.

Matt gave a thumbs up with his off hand.

A tap on his shoulder.

Two rounds. The second rifle barked. Two more. Four rounds pierced the missile's skin. Lukas confirmed the hits. A white glow flared as fire took hold. The burning chemicals would finish the job.

Lukas gave a thumbs up. "Demon is dead," he said into his mike.

The helo turned and ran for home.

THE PILOT OF LUKAS' HELO ignored the usual pattern and rolled past the other two Valkyries, then turned onto a taxiway past the hangars. The crew chief took Matt's rifle and said something to him that he could barely hear over the engines. Something that ended with "Hasta la vista, Baby." Lithuanians apparently loved Arnold.

It would have been a moment to savor had the American Defense Attaché not been there to greet them when they touched down. The DATT said he was looking for Captain Devlin. One of the Lithuanian staffers was trying to restrain Nordheim but he was out of control, accosting the men as they came off the other aircraft.

Matt got the idea and jumped off the still rolling helicopter and ran into the brush. He moved into the tree line and entered the hangar from the back door just as his comrades entered through the front.

Ron reached him first and helped him dump his tactical gear and return to his role of a despondent stay behind. The second person Matt saw was an angry Naval Commander Melis accompanied by an older version of himself. Melis lit into him like an angry cat, while his father watched with a serene smile on his face.

After a full minute of dressing down, Melis stood with her hands on her hips and a look of satisfaction that changed to puzzlement at Matt's expression.

"You know you're cursing at me in Lithuanian, right?" Matt understood what she was saying of course, "But I don't mind. I feel like one of you now."

His father was a different story. Joshua grabbed Matt by the shoulders and hugged him. "My stupid son. Thank God, you're okay."

Things calmed when Colonel Bizauskas arrived on the scene. He shook Matt's hand, "Thank you for all you've done here and don't mind your Attaché. He gives us things so we tolerate him." Dropping Matt's hand with a wink, he went back to his troops.

Melis looked at Matt then Joshua and shook her head. "You two are a quite the pair."

Nordheim, on the other hand, was irreconcilable. Matt saw him across the hangar barking at Lukas, with his arms moving like an autogyro propellor. Lukas stood calmly in front of him, arms folded over his chest, reluctantly listening. Lukas pointed to where Matt stood and said something that looked like a dismissal before he walked away with his hands in the air, the universal sign for I give up. Ron and the two other team leaders picked Nordheim off like a trio of NFL front line guards and attested to the fact that Matt never left the hangar, Nordheim looked like an angry bear deprived of his food.

When things had calmed somewhat, Joshua sent a text. Gabriel called the next morning. "I sent Hammer the news by covcom last night after you confirmed the missile's destruction," Gabriel said over the secure comms. "He came back this morning and said things have been delayed indefinitely. Apparently Vukashenko got cold feet and won't let the Russians move through Belarus. He also mentioned something about an accidental fire at a military base."

"Then we've accomplished something," Joshua said.

"For the time being, Grasshopper. Hammer says Volodya is still hungry and will never be satisfied until he gets his empire."

"What's next then?"

"I for one am going home for a while."

"Oregon or Valletta?"

"Valletta. You, for one, should talk to Jamie.

"I will. I'd like to have some quality time with Matt but he's going back to Germany with his team. Everyone seems to want to evaluate what just happened here."

"Well, keep me in mind. My offer still stands." With that Gabriel disconnected.

"What's this?" Melis said.

Standing in her office, Joshua had a stray thought about Greeks bearing gifts.

"A going away present," he said. He placed an olive-drab bag, the kind pilots keep their flight helmets in between missions, with a box inside on her desk.

She pulled out the box and opened the top flaps. "It won't go off, will it?"

Joshua smiled. "No, I decided you're okay as far as squids go."

"Squids?"

"Navy people."

"That's almost sweet of you." She opened the box and tugged on the cloth wrapping.

"Be careful. It's kind of delicate."

She carefully pulled the present from the box and set it on her desk. She looked at Joshua.

"It's from me and Matt together, kinda. He said he appreciated your leadership style."

"Ha. Now I know it's a bomb."

"No, really. He likes you too, maybe in a different sort of way than I do, but he does."

Melis looked at Joshua again and shook her head. "I don't think I will ever understand you," she said as she flipped off the wrapping carefully.

She gasped. "Where did this come from?"

"The spa. I picked it up while you were doing the document exploitation. Since the owners forfeited everything, I thought I'd take it as a keepsake."

Melis gingerly cupped the decorated egg and picked it up, inspecting it closely. "It's beautiful."

"I must admit that it looks like a Fabergé. Even the hallmarks look authentic, but it's probably just a forgery."

"Are you trying to bribe me?"

"Why would I want to do that? I just wanted to say I'm sorry for the trouble I've caused and to thank you for everything you did for Matt and me."

"Nothing more?"

"For your trouble," Joshua said.

Her eyes were considerably brighter than the last time he looked into them. The ice-blue had become a more brilliant hue that danced as she smiled.

"That's all?"

"I can't think of anything."

"Maybe you should think about that a bit. I owe you something too you know," she said.

"What for?" He said but it came out a bit strangled. His skin was turning goosebumpy.

"For saving my life down in the cave."

"I would have done that for anyone."

"Anyone?"

"Maybe not anyone…"

"I would hope not. I think you have higher standards than that."

"Maybe," Joshua was beginning to feel not like himself. He was feeling warm as if someone pulled the control rods without telling him.

He blurted out, "Maybe we could have dinner together sometime?"

Melis stepped closer to Joshua.

Joshua almost stepped back but he held his ground. He wanted to be inside her space.

"That would be nice. When?"

His brain was burning. He usually had his pitch ready before a meeting, every point covered, every answer scripted. This time he wasn't prepared. He stumbled.

"Ahhh—, I need to go to Berlin to meet with the boss. How about after that? When I return?"

"Promise?"

Joshua nodded yes, his tongue tied, his heart skipping.

JOSHUA STIRRED HIS COFFEE looking out at all the people on Unter den Linden. They weren't far from the American Embassy. It was just down the street, close to the Brandenburg Gate and the Reichstag. All the things he'd seen them many times over the years but really had no desire to see again at the moment. Especially by himself.

"I guess Andriy got what he wanted," said Jamie. He shook out the newspaper and watched the front door of the café at the same time.

"I suppose," said Joshua. "Although the route he chose was pretty extreme."

Jamie laid the *Berliner Morgenpost* on the table, its frontpage headline in bold type:

Pynya Tot
Pynya dead

"Gabriel did think he was altruistic. He was probably right. Listen to the names, Pynya, Aleksandr Petrakov from the security council, Boris Belyaev of the FSB, and, of course, our very own, Andriy Kuznetsov. The plane went down somewhere over the Black Sea near Pynya's estate. No indications of foul play."

"I imagine there won't be any indications. He probably had the black boxes taken out of the airplane. Speaking of boxes—what happened with Perimeter?"

"Dead air, we didn't pick up any change in the rocket forces status.

Maybe the system didn't work, or someone decided it was an error. We just don't know, and we probably won't with Kuznetsov gone," Jamie said.

"Too bad. It would have been nice to find out what he did."

"You sound sad that he's gone."

"I'm always sad when one of our assets gets killed. Never gets any easier."

"Like KB?" Jamie asked.

"No, KB wasn't an asset. You know that. KB was my friend and a good comrade, almost family."

"There are different degrees of sorrow, I believe."

"You should know. You've lost plenty of comrades over the years," Joshua said.

"I still find myself wondering if it has all been worth it."

"Time will tell."

"But you've lost a few too."

"Not as many as you. A solo operator doesn't make as many friends."

"Indeed." Jamie raised his coffee cup. "To family, comrades, and friends."

Joshua clinked with Jamie and drank. "We need something better than this to toast them."

"You're right, maybe later. What's up for you now?"

"I'm going to fly down and visit Gabriel tomorrow. Might stay a while to decompress. It's nice down there this time of year."

"What about Matt?"

"I'll come back in a week or so and visit before they pack out. He said there still is some work to be done."

"And Melis?"

"What about her?" said Joshua.

"You mean you don't wanna see where that might lead?"

"There's nothing there, Jamie."

Jamie sat back and eyed Joshua a moment. "Some apex predator you are."

EPILOGUE

WATER FELL MUSICALLY INTO THE BASIN below the fountain. Joshua smelled the scent of orange blossoms. They filled the tree branches early this year and a lone dragonfly flitted between the flowers and the floating lily leaves atop the water. Joshua took a sip of Eva Maria's cold lemon-aide and reveled in the calmness of the courtyard as she scurried about with a smile on her face. Ice cubes tinkled as he set down the glass. During the Raj in India, there hadn't been ice for the gin and tonics. *Now that would be a hard life.*

"What's next? How you going to keep busy?" Gabriel asked, flipping a page in the book he was reading.

"I'm not sure. I may go home and find a nice place to kick back where it's never too cold. Read a lot, play with my car, maybe write. Maybe I should go back to Vilnius before that. I owe Melis dinner out." He'd been thinking about what Jamie said, but he just wasn't sure if he was there yet.

"You should go see her. You'll regret it if you don't. Then come back here and stay here a while."

"Maybe, I need a break." Maybe he could tolerate the Mediterranean diet a while longer.

"You're not going to work for Jamie anymore?"

"Not if I can help it. My contract is finished. I returned my covcom and all the toys. Now I can settle back and live off my princely civil service retirement and disability pay."

"Still, we did good. You have to admit that, Grasshopper."

"I certainly hope so."

After all these years, he was stuck in the same swamp, half-way in and not sure if he wanted to go back or continue on into the unknown. He was happy in the afterglow of a mission well done. Not too many problems or much hassle—it's always that way after the fact. Maybe we did end up saving the world for all the moms and apple pie. *I could do just one more. Or I could just look forward to an easy life.*

"We'll see how your easy life goes. My place in Oregon is open and free if you want. It's far from all the craziness of Portland and Seattle and there's a nice general store nearby. There's even a three-car garage. I know you need that."

"I might take you up on that. Do have any plans?"

"I have another year or so on my contract. I'll hang here until they need something again. Speaking of Jamie, he sent me a note on my covcom this morning. Interesting news from Moscow. It looks like Alexi Murakhovsky is being positioned to take over. He's a reformist, you know. And Minister of Defense Shoygin was arrested by Viktor Solovyov no less."

"Solovyov, the SVR Deputy?"

"Former Deputy. He's in charge now. But here's the kicker, Murakhovsky's number two is a new guy on the block, Dmytri Andriyovich Kuznetsov."

"Andriyovich Kuznetsov? Does that mean he's Hammer's son?" Joshua said.

"I believe so. Jamie has all the analysts trying to figure that out."

"So that's what this was all about. Hammer gave up his life so his son could take power!"

"I'm not so sure. There's a bit of a wrinkle in the story."

"What do you mean?"

"The giving up his life part. That's what I'm not sure about. I got a text from Hammer's covcom a couple of days after the missile was destroyed. I still have it. Look." Gabriel took out a mobile telephone and punched in a code and waited, his head bobbing in anticipation.

"Here it is." He turned the phone around and held it out to Joshua to read.

> TELL THOMAS I AM SORRY FOR BERLIN. I WAS TOO SLOW TO STOP IT. KORLOV WAS STUPID, DESERVED WORSE. EVERYTHING ELSE NECESSARY FOR RUSSIA. THANK YOU FOR TAKING CARE OF ME. GOODBYE.

"This is his last testament?" Joshua asked.

"I thought so until I checked Hammer's bank account. Before this op, it held about ten million Euro for a life's work, but it was emptied the day after the plane crash. And not by us."

Joshua laughed. "Then he pulled a fast one. He's alive?"

"A fast one? No, this operation must have taken Andriy years to put together. Is he alive? Who knows? Who was he anyway? Who was the Kuznetsov on the airplane? I'm not sure we ever knew who he was or is. Maybe he's alive, but if he is, perhaps we shouldn't mention it."

"To Jamie?"

"To anyone."

Joshua saw the wisdom in that. It was only the two of them who could expose Andriy.

"What if the Agency checks his bank account?"

"I took care of that. By the way, speaking of accounts. I quoted the Javelins to Andriy at black market rates. The USG's invoice was at the official rate, which was somewhat less than what he paid, so after I reimbursed Hammer's account there is some money left over. I'm on contract and am paid by my proprietary, but it's way too much for me alone. Do you want a job?"

"What's the job and how much are we talking about?"

"Call it 'able assistant' and the money would include a signing bonus of five mil."

"Dollars?"

"Euro, a bit more than dollars."

"I don't know. Something bothers me about that money arming the Russians."

"Don't worry about the Javelins, Jamie fixed them. Just don't be on the dock in Kaliningrad when they arrive."

Eva Maria came quietly into the courtyard behind Gabriel, almost floating, and put her hand on his shoulder. He must have known she was there because he didn't flinch. She looked at Joshua. "There's someone here to see Mister Joshua."

"Would you bring them in please?" Eva Maria smiled at Gabriel a moment and then headed for the front door.

"Your maid seems happy that you've come back," Joshua said.

Gabriel smiled, "She's not my maid. We just don't advertise the fact. She prefers to play things low key."

Gabriel stood up when Eva Maria returned, leading someone down the hallway. Joshua stood as well.

"Welcome, mademoiselle," Gabriel said, as the woman stepped into the courtyard.

Melis came to a stop. "Thank you. You must be Gabriel." She shook his hand. "And you must be…" Her eyes sparkled, the cold arctic gray-blue ice Matt described had melted, and something else he hadn't seen before, laughter maybe.

"Joshua Devlin. Pleased to meet you."

"My name is Erin Melis, you may call me Erin."

"How did you find us?" Joshua asked.

"How else would I find you? Mister Wheeler told me."

"He would. He's always watching out for me. Where's Matt?" Joshua asked.

"How would I know? It's not Matt I came to see."

In one hand Erin had a carry-on bag, in the other the helmet bag he'd given her.

"You brought the egg?"

"I did. I have questions. It might be the last time I'll be able to use my diplomatic passport to travel."

"What questions?"

"First, you promised me dinner, but I couldn't wait. So where are we going?"

"I know a place,' Joshua said, "but what other questions?'

"This thing," she held up the bag. "It's beautiful and all, but it came from the Russians. I can't keep it. There would be questions. I'm an officer in the Lithuanian Navy, after all."

"No one knows where it came from."

"I do. I can't just put it over my fireplace or anything. So, you need to help me figure out what to do with it. Maybe you should take it back."

"It was my gift to you."

"It's not like it was expensive for you.

"No, but it might be if I have to take it back."

"Why?"

"Because then I'll have to get you something else."

"We'll talk about that later. For now, we need to decide what to do with it."

"Do with what?" asked Gabriel after having watched the conversation with a puzzled look on his face.

"The egg."

"What egg?" Gabriel asked.

"The one from the villa," said Erin.

"Oh, that. The Fabergé."

"It's not a Fabergé. Joshua said it was a forgery," Erin said.

Joshua held up his hands in mock surrender. Gabriel looked at his protégé and Erin as if deciding whether to intervene in a marital squabble.

"I saw it when Joshua and I were at the villa." Gabriel said. "It is a Fabergé. You'll never be able to sell it, it's one of the Czar's missing eggs and too well known,"

"Then what do we do with it? I can't keep a Fabergé," Erin said.

"I said, you can't sell it. I didn't say I couldn't," said Gabriel. "Just give me the names of your favorite charities."

"Deal, Gabriel. Now, if you'll show me where I can unpack, I can get ready for the evening." Then she turned back to Joshua. "And don't you run off again. We need to discuss that son of yours." She touched her hand to his cheek, holding it a moment, the blue in her eyes much warmer than before, and went up the stairs to her room, Eva Maria showing the way.

Joshua was looking up, watching Erin as she turned onto the balcony toward her room.

"She's quite a woman," Gabriel said.

"Yes," said Jamie. All he could manage.

"Thinking about Sarah?"

"Who told you about Sarah?" Surprised, Joshua glanced at his comrade.

"Jamie."

"He would."

"You never mention her."

"I used to. All the time. It's painful to think about her now."

"It's good to speak her name, otherwise she will be forgotten."

"I miss her very much."

"You should. But it's time to move on, Joshua. It's time."

ACKNOWLEDGEMENTS

MY THANKS GO OUT TO THE MANY PEOPLE who have encouraged me along the way or at least didn't say anything to stop me. My wife who tolerates my repeated requests to read and re-read my words, the friends and neighbors who keep my spirits up by asking when is the next one coming out. The principals at Double Dagger Books—Phil and Vincent—who are standing behind this book and hopefully more to come. I also want to thank my mentors in active service and those I read — most especially Charles McCarry whose advice on "occupational hazards" I have included herein. Not to forget all the "beta" readers who read, critiqued, and gave good counsel—DM, SE, and MFB among them. Above all, I thank my family for being there despite whatever craziness I got into all these many years.

Dedicated to KBR,
a great soldier, intelligence officer, teacher, and friend.

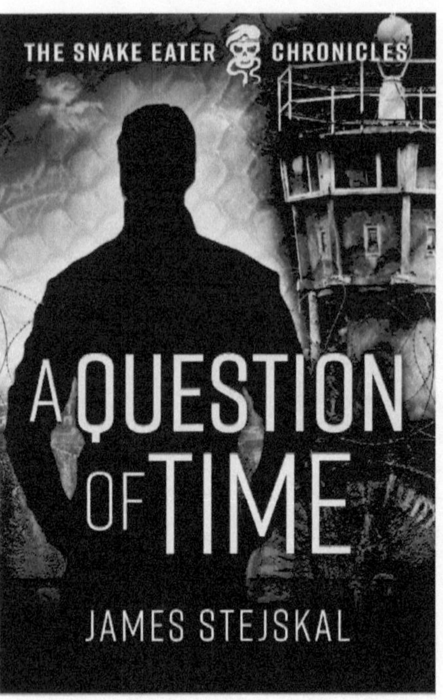

THE SNAKE EATER CHRONICLES
A QUESTION OF TIME
JAMES STEJSKAL

THE SNAKE EATER CHRONICLES
APPOINTMENT IN TEHRAN
JAMES STEJSKAL

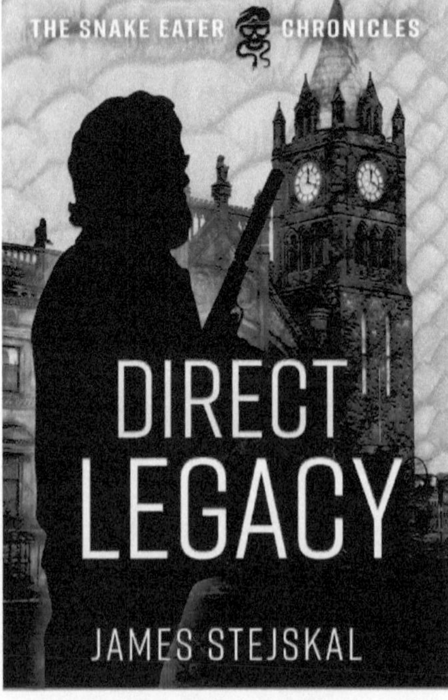

THE SNAKE EATER CHRONICLES
DIRECT LEGACY
JAMES STEJSKAL

THE SNAKE EATER CHRONICLES
DEAD HAND
JAMES STEJSKAL

AbØUT THE AUTHØR

JAMES STEJSKAL spent thirty-five years as a "Green Beret" and CIA case officer living and conducting operations around the world during the Cold War and after 9/11. He has written five military history books, along with numerous articles, and received accolades for his book Masters of Mayhem: Lawrence of Arabia and the British Military Mission to the Hejaz. His fiction centers on intelligence and special operations and Dead Hand is the fourth book in his The Snake Eater Chronicles. He lives in northern Virginia with his wife, Wanda.

DOUBLE‡DAGGER

— www.doubledagger.ca —

Double Dagger Books is Canada's only military-focused publisher. Conflict and warfare have shaped human history since before we began to record it. The earliest stories that we know of, passed on as oral tradition, speak of war, and more importantly, the essential elements of the human condition that are revealed under its pressure.

We are dedicated to publishing material that, while rooted in conflict, transcend the idea of "war" as merely a genre. Fiction, non-fiction, and stuff that defies categorization, we want to read it all.

Because if you want peace, study war.

www.ingramcontent.com/pod-product-compliance
Lightning Source LLC
Chambersburg PA
CBHW021122190726
48288CB00008B/2451